THE MOUNTAIN MEN

To Todd from Mother
1973

THE MOUNTAIN MEN

The Song of Three Friends
The Song of Hugh Glass
The Song of Jed Smith

Volume I of *A Cycle of the West*

BY

JOHN G. NEIHARDT

UNIVERSITY OF NEBRASKA PRESS · LINCOLN

First Bison Book printing: June 1971
Second Bison Book printing: August 1971
Third Bison Book printing: May 1972

The Song of Three Friends, The Song of Hugh Glass, and
The Song of Jed Smith are reproduced from the second
(1961) printing of *A Cycle of the West,* published by the
Macmillan Company, by arrangement with the author.

INTRODUCTION

In 1912, at the age of 31, I began work on the following cycle of heroic *Songs*, designed to celebrate the great mood of courage that was developed west of the Missouri River in the nineteenth century. The series was dreamed out, much of it in detail, before I began; and for years it was my hope that it might be completed at the age of 60—as it was. During the interval, more than five thousand days were devoted to the work, along with the fundamentally important business of being first a man and a father. It was planned from the beginning that the five *Songs*, which appeared at long intervals during a period of twenty-nine years, should constitute a single work. They are now offered as such.

The period with which the *Cycle* deals was one of discovery, exploration and settlement—a genuine epic period, differing in no essential from the other great epic periods that marked the advance of the Indo-European peoples out of Asia and across Europe. It was a time of intense individualism, a time when society was cut loose from its

[v]

roots, a time when an old culture was being overcome by that of a powerful people driven by the ancient needs and greeds. For this reason only, the word "epic" has been used in connection with the *Cycle*; it is properly descriptive of the mood and meaning of the time and of the material with which I have worked. There has been no thought of synthetic *Iliads* and *Odysseys*, but only of the richly human saga-stuff of a country that I knew and loved, and of a time in the very fringe of which I was a boy.

This period began in 1822 and ended in 1890. The dates are not arbitrary. In 1822 General Ashley and Major Henry led a band of a hundred trappers from St. Louis, "the Mother of the West," to the beaver country of the upper Missouri River. During the following year a hundred more Ashley-Henry men ascended the Missouri. Out of these trapper bands came all the great continental explorers after Lewis and Clark. It was they who discovered and explored the great central route by way of South Pass, from the Missouri River to the Pacific Ocean, over which the tide of migration swept westward from the 40's onward.

The Song of Three Friends and *The Song of Hugh Glass* deal with the ascent of the river and with characteristic adventures of Ashley-Henry men in the country of the upper Missouri and the Yellowstone.

The Song of Jed Smith follows the first band of Americans through South Pass to the Great Salt Lake, the first band of Americans to reach Spanish California by an overland trail, the first white men to cross the great central desert from the Sierras to Salt Lake.

The Song of the Indian Wars deals with the period of migration and the last great fight for the bison pastures between the invading white race and the Plains Indians—the Sioux, the Cheyenne and the Arapahoe.

The Song of the Messiah is concerned wholly with the conquered people and the worldly end of their last great dream. The period closes with the Battle of Wounded Knee in 1890, which marked the end of Indian resistance on the Plains.

It will have been noted from the foregoing that the five *Songs* are linked in chronological order; but in addition to their progress in time and across the vast land, those who may feel as I have felt while the tales were growing may note a spiritual progression also—from the level of indomitable physical prowess to that of spiritual triumph in apparent worldly defeat. If any vital question be suggested in *The Song of Jed Smith*, for instance, there may be those who will find its age-old answer once again in the final *Song* of an alien people who also were men, and troubled.

But, after all, "the play's the thing"; and while

[vii]

it is true that a knowledge of Western history and the topography of the country would be very helpful to a reader of the *Cycle,* such knowledge is not indispensable. For here are tales of men in struggle, triumph and defeat.

Those readers who have not followed the development of the *Cycle* may wish to know, and are entitled to know, something of my fitness for the task assumed a generation ago and now completed. To those I may say that I did not experience the necessity of seeking material about which to write. The feel and mood of it were in the blood of my family, and my early experiences aroused a passionate awareness of it. My family came to Pennsylvania more than a generation before the Revolutionary War, in which fourteen of us fought; and, crossing the Alleghenies after the war, we did not cease pioneering until some of us reached Oregon. Any one of my heroes, from point of time, could have been my paternal grandfather, who was born in 1801.

My maternal grandparents were covered-wagon people, and at the age of five I was living with them in a sod house on the upper Solomon in western Kansas. The buffalo had vanished from that country only a few years before, and the signs of them were everywhere. I have helped, as a little boy could, in "picking cow-chips" for winter fuel. If I write of hot-winds and grasshoppers, of prairie fires and blizzards, of dawns and noons and sunsets and nights, of brooding heat and thunderstorms in vast lands, I knew them early. They were the vital facts of my world, along with the talk of the old-timers who knew such fascinating things to talk about.

I was a very little boy when my father introduced me to the Missouri River at Kansas City. It was flood time. The impression was tremendous, and a steadily growing desire to know what had happened on such a river led me directly to my heroes. Twenty years later, when I had come to know them well, I built a boat at Fort Benton, Montana, descended the Missouri in low water and against head winds, dreamed back the stories men had lived along the river, bend by bend. This experience is set forth in *The River and I.*

In northern Nebraska I grew up at the edge of the retreating frontier, and became intimately associated with the Omaha Indians, a Siouan people, when many of the old "long-hairs" among them still remembered vividly the time that meant so much to me. We were good friends. Later, I became equally well acquainted among the Oglala Sioux, as my volume, *Black Elk Speaks*, reveals; and I have never been happier than while living with my friends among them, mostly unreconstructed "long-hairs," sharing, as one of them, their thoughts, their feelings, their rich memories that often reached far back into the world of my *Cycle*.

When I have described battles, I have depended far less on written accounts than upon the reminiscences of men who fought in them—not only Indians, but whites as well. For, through many years, I was privileged to know many old white men, officers and privates, who had fought in the Plains Wars. Much of the material for the last two *Songs* of the series came directly from those who were themselves a part of the stories.

For the first three *Songs*, I was compelled to depend chiefly upon early journals of travel and upon an intimate knowledge of Western history generally. But while I could not have known my earlier heroes, I have known old men who had missed them, but had known men who knew some of them well; and such memories at second hand can be most illuminating to one who knows the facts already. For instance, I once almost touched even Jedediah Smith himself, the greatest and most mysterious of them all, through an old plainsman who was an intimate friend of Bridger, who had been a comrade of Jed!

Such intimate contacts with soldiers, plainsmen, Indians and river men were an integral part of my life for many years, and I cannot catalog them here. As for knowledge of the wide land with which the *Cycle* deals, those who know any

[x]

part of it well will know that I have been there too.

Those who are not acquainted with early Western history will find a good introduction to the *Cycle* in Harrison Dale's *The Ashley-Henry Men* —or perhaps my own book, *The Splendid Wayfaring*.

I can see now that I grew up on the farther slope of a veritable "watershed of history," the summit of which is already crossed, and in a land where the old world lingered longest. It is gone, and, with it, all but two or three of the old-timers, white and brown, whom I have known. My mind and most of my heart are with the young, and with the strange new world that is being born in agony. But something of my heart stays yonder, for in the years of my singing about a time and a country that I loved, I note, without regret, that I have become an old-timer myself!

The foregoing was set down in anticipation of some questions that readers of good will, potential friends, might ask.

JOHN NEIHARDT

Columbia, Mo., 1948.

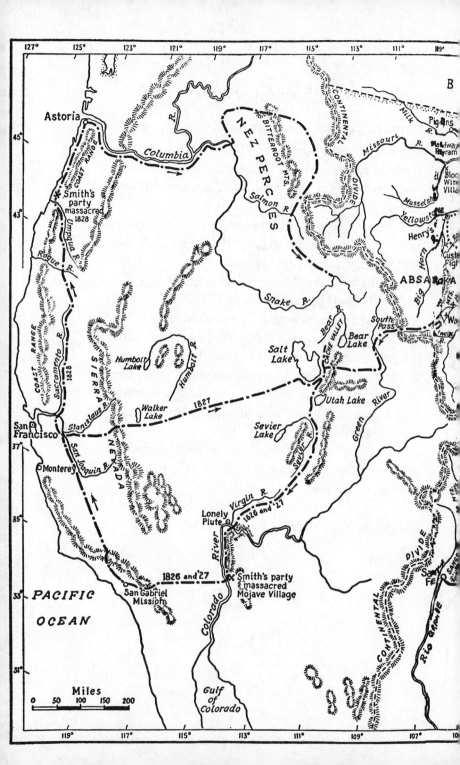

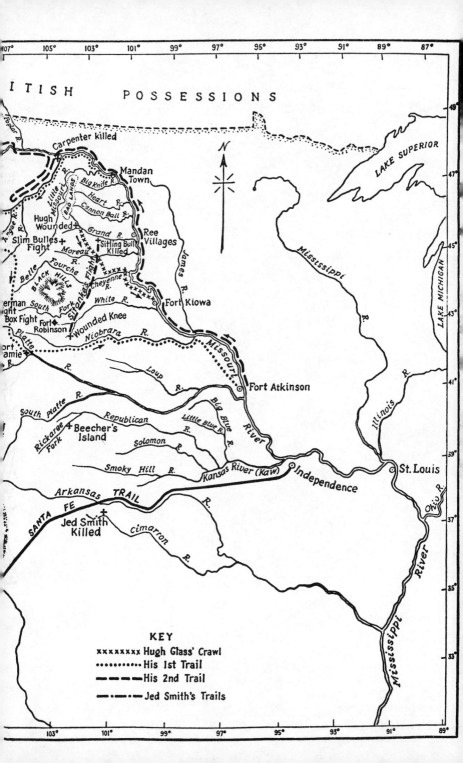

THE SONG OF THREE FRIENDS

TO HILDA

Οἶον τὸ γλυκύμαλον ἐρεύθεται ἄκρῳ ἐπ᾽ ὔσδῳ
ἄκρον ἐπ᾽ ἀκροτάτῳ · λελάθοντο δὲ μαλοδρόπηες·
οὐ μὰν ἐκλελαθοντ᾽, αλλ᾽ οὐκ εδύναντ᾽ ἐπίκεσθαι.

THE SONG OF THREE FRIENDS

I

ASHLEY'S HUNDRED

Who now reads clear the roster of that band?
Alas, Time scribbles with a careless hand
And often pinchbeck doings from that pen
Bite deep, where deeds and dooms of mighty men
Are blotted out beneath a sordid scrawl!

One hundred strong they flocked to Ashley's call
That spring of eighteen hundred twenty-two;
For tales of wealth, out-legending Peru,
Came wind-blown from Missouri's distant springs,
And that old sireny of unknown things
Bewitched them, and they could not linger more.
They heard the song the sea winds sang the shore
When earth was flat, and black ships dared the
    steep
Where bloomed the purple perils of the deep
In dragon-haunted gardens. They were young.

Albeit some might feel the winter flung
Upon their heads, 'twas less like autumn's drift
Than backward April's unregarded sift
On stout oaks thrilling with the sap again.
And some had scarce attained the height of men,
Their lips unroughed, and gleaming in their eyes
The light of immemorial surprise
That life still kept the spaciousness of old
And, like the hoarded tales their grandsires told,
Might still run bravely.

                    For a little span
Their life-fires flared like torches in the van
Of westward progress, ere the great wind 'woke
To snuff them.   Many vanished like a smoke
The blue air drinks; and e'en of those who burned
Down to the socket, scarce a tithe returned
To share at last the ways of quiet men,
Or see the hearth-reek drifting once again
Across the roofs of old St. Louis town.

And now no more the mackinaws come down,
Their gunwales low with costly packs and bales,
A wind of wonder in their shabby sails,
Their homing oars flung rhythmic to the tide;
And nevermore the masted keelboats ride
Missouri's stubborn waters on the lone
Long zigzag journey to the Yellowstone.

Their hulks have found the harbor ways that know
The ships of all the Sagas, long ago —
A moony haven where no loud gale stirs.
The trappers and the singing *voyageurs*
Are comrades now of Jason and his crew,
Foregathered in that timeless rendezvous
Where come at last all seekers of the Fleece.

Not now of those who, dying, dropped in peace
A brimming cup of years the song shall be:
From Mississippi to the Western Sea,
From Britain's country to the Rio Grande
Their names are written deep across the land
In pass and trail and river, like a rune.

Pore long upon that roster by the moon
Of things remembered dimly.   Tangled, blear
The writing runs; yet presently appear
Three names of men that, spoken, somehow seem
Incantatory trumpets of a dream
Obscurely blowing from the hinter-gloom.
Of these and that inexorable doom
That followed like a hound upon the scent,
Here runs the tale.

II

THE UP–STREAM MEN

When Major Henry went
Up river at the head of Ashley's band,
Already there were robins in the land.
Home-keeping men were following the plows
And through the smoke-thin greenery of boughs
The scattering wild-fire of the fruit bloom ran.

Behold them starting northward, if you can.
Dawn flares across the Mississippi's tide;
A tumult runs along the waterside
Where, scenting an event, St. Louis throngs.
Above the buzzling voices soar the songs
Of waiting boatmen — lilting *chansonettes*
Whereof the meaning laughs, the music frets,
Nigh weeping that such gladness can not stay.
In turn, the herded horses snort and neigh
Like panic bugles.   Up the gangplanks poured,
Go streams of trappers, rushing goods aboard
The snub-built keelboats, squat with seeming
    sloth —
Baled three-point blankets, blue and scarlet
    cloth,

4

Rum, powder, flour, guns, gauderies and lead.
And all about, goodbyes are being said.
Gauche girls with rainy April in their gaze
Cling to their beardless heroes, count the days
Between this parting and the wedding morn,
Unwitting how unhuman Fate may scorn
The youngling dream.   For O how many a lad
Would see the face of Danger, and go mad
With her weird vixen beauty; aye, forget
This girl's face, yearning upward now and wet,
Half woman's with the first vague guess at woe!

And now commands are bellowed, boat horns
      blow
Haughtily in the dawn; the tumult swells.
The tow-crews, shouldering the long cordelles
Slack from the mastheads, lean upon the sag.
The keelboats answer lazily and drag
Their blunt prows slowly in the gilded tide.
A steersman sings, and up the riverside
The gay contagious ditty spreads and runs
Above the shouts, the uproar of the guns,
The nickering of horses.

                              So, they say,
Went forth a hundred singing men that day;
And girlish April went ahead of them.
The music of her trailing garment's hem

Seemed scarce a league ahead. A little speed
Might yet almost surprise her in the deed
Of sorcery; for, ever as they strove,
A gray-green smudge in every poplar grove
Proclaimed the recent kindling. Aye, it seemed
That bird and bush and tree had only dreamed
Of song and leaf and blossom, till they heard
The young men's feet; when tree and bush and
        bird
Unleashed the whole conspiracy of awe!
Pale green was every slough about the Kaw;
About the Platte, pale green was every slough;
And still the pale green lingered at the Sioux,
So close they trailed the marching of the South.
But when they reached the Niobrara's mouth
The witchery of spring had taken flight
And, like a girl grown woman over night,
Young summer glowed.

                    And now the river rose,
Gigantic from a feast of northern snows,
And mightily the snub prows felt the tide;
But with the loud, sail-filling South allied,
The tow-crews battled gaily day by day;
And seldom lulled the struggle on the way
But some light jest availed to fling along
The panting lines the laughter of the strong,

For joy sleeps lightly in the hero's mood.
And when the sky-wide prairie solitude
Was darkened round them, and the camp was set
Secure for well-earned sleep that came not yet,
What stories shaped for marvel or for mirth! —
Tales fit to strain the supper-tightened girth,
Looped yarns, wherein the veteran spinners vied
To color with a lie more glorified
Some thread that had veracity enough,
Spun straightway out of life's own precious
          stuff
That each had scutched and heckled in the raw.
Then thinner grew each subsequent guffaw
While drowsily the story went the rounds
And o'er the velvet dark the summer sounds
Prevailed in weird crescendo more and more,
Until the story-teller with a snore
Gave over to a dream a tale half told.

And now the horse-guards, while the night grows
          old,
With intermittent singing buffet sleep
That surges subtly down the starry deep
On waves of odor from the manless miles
Of summer-haunted prairie.   Now, at whiles,
The kiote's mordant clamor cleaves the drowse.
The horses stamp and blow; about the prows

Dark waters chug and gurgle; as with looms
Bugs weave a drone; a beaver's diving booms,
Whereat bluffs grumble in their sable cowls.
The devil laughter of the prairie owls
Mocks mirth anon, like unrepentant sin.
Perceptibly at last slow hours wear thin
The east, until the prairie stares with morn,
And horses nicker to the boatman's horn
That blares the music of a day begun.

So through the days of thunder and of sun
They pressed to northward. Now the river
    shrank,
The grass turned yellow and the men were lank
And gnarled with labor. Smooth-lipped lads
    matured
'Twixt moon and moon with all that they
    endured,
Their faces leathered by the wind and glare,
Their eyes grown ageless with the calm far
    stare
Of men who know the prairies or the seas.
And when they reached the village of the
    Rees,
One scarce might say, This man is young, this
    old,
Save for the beard.

Here loitered days of gold
And days of leisure, welcome to the crews;
For recently had come the wondrous news
Of beaver-haunts beyond the Great Divide —
So rich a tale 'twould seem the tellers lied,
Had they not much fine peltry to attest.
So now the far off River of the West
Became the goal of venture for the band;
And since the farther trail lay overland
From where the Great Falls thundered to no
    ear,
They paused awhile to buy more ponies here
With powder, liquor, gauds and wily words.
A horse-fond people, opulent in herds,
The Rees were; and the trade was very good.

Now camped along the river-fringing wood,
Three sullen, thunder-brewing, rainless days,
Those weathered men made merry in their
    ways
With tipple, euchre, story, jest and song.
The marksmen matched their cleverness; the
    strong
Wrestled the strong; and brawling pugilists
Displayed the boasted power of their fists
In stubborn yet half amicable fights.
And whisky went hell-roaring through the nights

Among the lodges of the fuddled Rees.
Thus merrily the trappers took their ease,
Rejoicing in the thread that Clotho spun;
For it was good to feel the bright thread run,
However eager for the snipping shears.

O joy long stifled in the ruck of years!
How many came to strange and bitter ends!
And who was merrier than those three friends
Whom here a song remembers for their woe?

Will Carpenter, Mike Fink and Frank Talbeau
Were they — each gotten of a doughty breed;
For in the blood of them the ancient seed
Of Saxon, Celt and Norman grew again.
The Mississippi reared no finer men,
And rarely the Ohio knew their peers
For pluck and prowess — even in those years
When stern life yielded suck but to the strong.
Nor in the hundred Henry took along
Was found their match — and each man knew it
    well.
For instance, when it suited Mike to tell
A tale that called for laughter, as he thought,
The hearer laughed right heartily, or fought
And took a drubbing.   Then, if more complained,
Those three lacked not for logic that explained

The situation in no doubtful way.
"Me jokes are always funny" Mike would say;
And most men freely granted that they were.

A lanky, rangy man was Carpenter,
Quite six feet two from naked heel to crown;
And, though crow-lean, he brought the steelyard
    down
With twice a hundred notched upon the bar.
Nor was he stooped, as tall men often are;
A cedar of a man, he towered straight.
One might have judged him lumbering of gait,
When he was still; but when he walked or ran,
He stepped it lightly like a little man —
And such a one is very good to see.
Not his the tongue for quip or repartee;
His wit seemed slow; and something of the child
Came o'er his rough-hewn features, when he
    smiled,
To mock the porching brow and eagle nose.
'Twas when he fought the true import of those
Grew clear, though even then his mien deceived;
For less in wrath, he seemed, than mildly
    grieved —
Which made his blows no whit less true or hard.
His hair was flax fresh gleaming from the card;
His eyes, the flax in bloom.

A match in might,
Fink lacked five inches of his comrade's height,
And of his weight scarce twenty pounds, they
    say.
His hair was black, his small eyes greenish gray
And restless as though feeling out of place
In such a jocund plenilunar face
That seemed made just for laughter.   Then one
    saw
The pert pugnacious nose, the forward jaw,
The breadth of stubborn cheekbones, and one
    knew
That jest and fight to him were scarcely two,
But rather shifting phases of the joy
He felt in living.   Careless as a boy,
Free handed with a gift or with a blow,
And giving either unto friend or foe
With frank good will, no man disliked him long.
They say his voice could glorify a song,
However loutish might the burden be;
And all the way from Pittsburg to the sea
The Rabelaisian stories of the rogue
Ran wedded to the richness of his brogue.
And wheresoever boatmen came to drink,
There someone broached some escapade of Fink
That well might fill the goat-hoofed with delight;
For Mike, the pantagruelizing wight,

Was happy in the health of bone and brawn
And had the code and conscience of the faun
To guide him blithely down the easy way.
A questionable hero, one might say:
And so indeed, by any civil law.
Moreover, at first glimpse of him one saw
A bull-necked fellow, seeming over stout;
Tremendous at a heavy lift, no doubt,
But wanting action.   By the very span
Of chest and shoulders, one misjudged the man
When he was clothed.   But when he stripped to
    swim,
Men flocked about to have a look at him,
Moved vaguely by that body's wonder-scheme
Wherein the shape of God's Adamic dream
Was victor over stubborn dust again!

O very lovely is a maiden, when
The old creative thrill is set astir
Along her blood, and all the flesh of her
Is shapen as to music!   Fair indeed
A tall horse, lean of flank, clean-limbed **for**
    speed,
Deep-chested for endurance!   Very fair
A soaring tree, aloof in violet air
Upon a hill!   And 'tis a glorious thing
To see a bankfull river in the spring

Fight homeward! Children wonderful to see —
The Girl, the Horse, the River and the Tree —
As any suckled at the breast of sod;
Dissolving symbols leading back to God
Through vista after vista of the Plan!
But surely none is fairer than a man
In whom the lines of might and grace are one.

Bronzed with exposure to the wind and sun,
Behold the splendid creature that was Fink!
You see him strolling to the river's brink,
All ease, and yet tremendously alive.
He pauses, poised on tiptoe for the dive,
And momently it seems the mother mud,
Quick with a mystic seed whose sap is blood,
Mysteriously rears a human flower.
Clean as a windless flame the lines of power
Run rhythmic up the stout limbs, muscle-
    laced,
Athwart the ropy gauntness of the waist,
The huge round girth of chest, whereover spread
Enormous shoulders. Now above his head
He lifts his arms where big thews merge and
    flow
As in some dream of Michelangelo;
And up along the dimpling back there run,
Like lazy serpents stirring in the sun,

Slow waves that break and pile upon the slope
Of that great neck in swelling rolls, a-grope
Beneath the velvet softness of the skin.
Now suddenly the lean waist grows more thin,
The deep chest on a sudden grows more deep;
And with the swiftness of a tiger's leap,
The easy grace of hawks in swooping flight,
That terrible economy of might
And beauty plunges outward from the brink.

Thus God had made experiment with Fink,
As proving how 'twere best that men might
        grow.

One turned from Mike to look upon Talbeau —
A little man, scarce five feet six and slim —
And wondered what his comrades saw in him
To justify their being thus allied.
Was it a sort of planetary pride
In lunar adoration? Hark to Mike:
"Shure I declare I niver saw his like —
A skinny whiffet of a man! And yit —
Well, do ye moind the plisint way we mit
And how he interjooced hisself that day?
'Twas up at Pittsburg, liquor flowin' fray
And ivrybody happy as a fool.
I cracked me joke and thin, as is me rule,

Looked round to view the havoc of me wit;
And ivrywan was doubled up wid it,
Save only wan, and him a scrubby mite.
Says I, and shure me language was polite,
'And did ye hear me little joke?' says I.
'I did' says he. 'And can't ye laugh, me
      b'y?'
'I can't' says he, the sassy little chap.
Nor did I git me hand back from the slap
I give him till he landed on me glim,
And I was countin' siventeen of him
And ivry dancin' wan of him was air!
Faith, whin I hit him he was niver there;
And shure it seemed that ivry wind that blew
Was peltin' knuckles in me face.   Hurroo!
That toime, fer wance, I got me fill of fun!
God bless the little whiffet!   It begun
Along about the shank of afthernoon;
And whin I washed me face, I saw the moon
A-shakin' wid its laughther in the shtrame.
And whin, betoimes, he wakened from his
      drame,
I says to him, 'Ye needn't laugh, me b'y:
A cliver little man ye are,' says I.
And Och, the face of me!   I'm tellin' fac's —
Ye'd wonder did he do it wid an ax!
'Twas foine!   'Twas art!"

Thus, eloquent with pride,
Mike Fink, an expert witness, testified
To Talbeau's fistic prowess.

Now they say
There lived no better boatmen in their day
Than those three comrades; and the larger
  twain
In that wide land three mighty rivers drain
Found not their peers for skill in marksmanship.
Writes one, who made the long Ohio trip
With those boon cronies in their palmy days,
How once Mike Fink beheld a sow at graze
Upon the bank amid her squealing brood;
And how Mike, being in a merry mood,
Shot off each wiggling piglet's corkscrew tail
At twenty yards, while under easy sail
The boat moved on.   And Carpenter could bore
A squirrel's eye clean at thirty steps and more —
So many say.   But 'twas their dual test
Of mutual love and skill they liked the best
Of all their shooting tricks — when one stood up
At sixty paces with a whisky cup
Set brimming for a target on his head,
And felt the gusty passing of the lead,
Hot from the other's rifle, lift his hair.
And ever was the tin cup smitten fair
  c

By each, to prove the faith of each anew:
For 'twas a rite of love between the two,
And not a mere capricious feat of skill.
"Och, shure, and can ye shoot the whisky, Bill?"
So Mike would end a wrangle. "Damn it,
    Fink!
Let's bore a pair of cups and have a drink!"
So Carpenter would stop a row grown stale.
And neither feared that either love might fail
Or either skill might falter.

               Thus appear
The doughty three who held each other dear
For qualities they best could comprehend.

Now came the days of leisure to an end —
The days so gaily squandered, that would
    seem
To men at length made laughterless, a dream
Unthinkably remote; for Ilion held
Beneath her sixfold winding sheet of Eld
Seems not so hoar as bygone joy we prize
In evil days.   Now vaguely pale the skies,
The glimmer neither starlight's nor the morn's.
A rude ironic merriment of horns
Startles the men yet heavy with carouse,
And sets a Ree dog mourning in the drowse,

Snout skyward from a lodge top. Sleepy birds
Chirp in the brush. A drone of sullen words
Awakes and runs increasing through the camp.
Thin smoke plumes, rising in the valley damp,
Flatten among the leathern tents and make
The whole encampment like a ghostly lake
Where bobbing heads of swimmers come and go,
As with the whimsy of an undertow
That sucks and spews them. Raising dust and
    din,
The horse-guards drive their shaggy rabble in
From nightlong grazing. *Voyageurs*, with packs
Of folded tents and camp gear on their backs,
Slouch boatward through the reek. But when
    prevails
The smell of frying pans and coffee pails,
They cease to sulk and, greatly heartened,
    sing
Till ponies swell the chorus, nickering,
And race-old comrades jubilate as one.

Out of a roseless dawn the heat-pale sun
Beheld them toiling northward once again —
A hundred horses and a hundred men
Hushed in a windless swelter. Day on day
The same white dawn o'ertook them on their
    way;

And daylong in the white glare sang no bird,
But only shrill grasshoppers clicked and whirred,
As though the heat were vocal.   All the while
The dwindling current lengthened, mile on
    mile,
Meandrous in a labyrinth of sand.

Now e'er they left the Ree town by the Grand
The revellers had seen the spent moon roam
The morning, like a tipsy hag bound home.
A bubble-laden boat, they saw it sail
The sunset river of a fairy tale
When they were camped beside the Cannon-
    ball.
A spectral sun, it held the dusk in thrall
Nightlong about the Heart.   The stars alone
Upon the cluttered Mandan lodges shone
The night they slept below the Knife.   And
    when
Their course, long westward, shifted once again
To lead them north, the August moon was new.

The rainless Southwest wakened now and blew.
A wilting, worrying, breath-sucking gale
That roared one moment in the bellied sail,
Next moment slackened to a lazy croon.
Now came the first misfortune.   All forenoon

With line and pole the sweating boatmen strove
Along the east bank, while the horseguards
    drove
The drooping herd a little to the fore.
And then the current took the other shore.
Straight on, a maze of bar and shallow lay,
The main stream running half a mile away
To westward of a long low willow isle.
An hour they fought that stubborn half a mile
Of tumbled water. Down the running planks
The polesmen toiled in endless slanting ranks.
Now swimming, now a-flounder in the ooze
Of some blind bar, the naked cordelle crews
Sought any kind of footing for a pull;
While gust-bedevilled sails, now booming full,
Now flapping slack, gave questionable aid.

The west bank gained, along a ragged shade
Of straggling cottonwoods the boatmen sprawled
And panted. Out across the heat-enthralled,
Wind-fretted waste of shoal and bar they saw
The string of ponies ravelled up a draw
That mounted steeply eastward from the vale
Where, like a rampart flung across the trail,
A bluff rose sheer. Heads low, yet loath to
    graze,
They waxed and withered in the oily haze,

Now ponies, now a crawling flock of sheep.
Behind them three slack horseguards, half
      asleep,
Swayed limply, leaning on their saddle-bows.

The boat crews, lolling in a semi-doze,
Still watch the herd; nor do the gazers dream
What drama nears a climax over stream,
What others yonder may be watching too.
Now looming large upon the lucent blue,
The foremost ponies top the rim, and stare
High-headed down the vacancies of air
Beneath them; while the herders dawdle still
And gather wool scarce halfway up the hill —
A slumbrous sight beheld by heavy eyes.

But hark! What murmuring of far-flung cries
From yonder pocket in the folded rise
That flanks the draw? The herders also hear
And with a start glance upward to the rear.
Their spurred mounts plunge! What do they
      see but dust
Whipped skyward yonder in a freakish gust?
What panic overtakes them? Look again!
The rolling dust cloud vomits mounted men,
A ruck of tossing heads and gaudy gears
Beneath a bristling thicket of lean spears
Slant in a gust of onset!

Over stream
The boatmen stare dumfounded. Like a dream
In some vague region out of space and time
Evolves the swiftly moving pantomime
Before those loungers with ungirded loins;
Till one among them shouts *"Assiniboines!"*
And swelling to a roar, the wild word runs
Above a pellmell scramble for the guns,
Perceived as futile soon. Yet here and there
A few young hotheads fusillade the air,
And rage the more to know the deed absurd.
Some only grind their teeth without a word;
Some stand aghast, some grinningly inane,
While some, like watch-dogs rabid at the chain,
Growl curses, pacing at the river's rim.

So might unhappy spirits haunt the dim
Far shore of Styx, beholding outrage done
To loved ones in the region of the sun —
Rage goaded by its own futility!

For one vast moment strayed from time, they see
The war band flung obliquely down the slope,
The flying herdsmen, seemingly a-grope
In sudden darkness for their saddle guns.
A murmuring shock! And now the whole scene
    runs

Into a dusty blur of horse and man;
And now the herd's rear surges on the van
That takes the cue of panic fear and flies
Stampeding to the margin of the skies,
Till all have vanished in the deeps of air.
Now outlined sharply on the sky-rim there
The victors pause and taunt their helpless
  foes
With buttocks patted and with thumbs at nose
And jeers scarce hearkened for the wind's guffaw.
They also vanish.   In the sunwashed draw
Remains no sign of what has come to pass,
Save three dark splotches on the yellow grass,
Where now the drowsy horseguards have their
  will.

At sundown on the summit of the hill
The huddled boatmen saw the burial squad
Tuck close their comrades' coverlet of sod —
Weird silhouettes on melancholy gray.
And very few found anything to say
That night; though some spoke gently of the
  dead,
Remembering what that one did or said
At such and such a time. And some, more
  stirred
With lust of vengeance for the stolen herd,

Swore vaguely now and then beneath their breath.
Some, brooding on the imminence of death,
Grew wistful of their unreturning years;
And some who found their praying in arrears
Made shift to liquidate the debt that night.

But when once more the cheerful morning light
Came on them toiling, also came the mood
Of young adventure, and the solitude
Sang with them. For 'tis glorious to spend
One's golden days large-handed to the end —
The good broadpieces that can buy so much!
And what may hoarders purchase but a crutch
Wherewith to hobble graveward?

                                 On they pressed
To where once more the river led them west;
And every day the hot wind, puff on puff,
Assailed them; every night they heard it sough
In thickets prematurely turning sere.

Then came the sudden breaking of the year.

Abruptly in a waning afternoon
The hot wind ceased, as fallen in a swoon
With its own heat. For hours the swinking
    crews
Had bandied scarcely credible good news

Of clouds across the dim northwestward plain;
And they who offered wagers on the rain
Found ready takers, though the gloomy rack,
With intermittent rumbling at its back,
Had mounted slowly.   Now it towered high,
A blue-black wall of night across the sky
Shot through with glacial green.

                                        A mystic change!
The   sun   was   hooded   and   the   world   went
        strange —
A picture world!   The hollow hush that fell
Made loud the creaking of the taut cordelle,
The   bent   spar's   groan,   the   plunk   of   steering
        poles.
A bodeful calm lay glassy on the shoals;
The current had the look of flowing oil.
They saw the cloud's lip billow now and boil —
Black breakers gnawing at a coast of light;
They saw the stealthy wraith-arms of the night
Grope for the day to strangle it;   they saw
The up-stream reaches vanish in a flaw
Of driving sand: and scarcely were the craft
Made fast to clumps of willow fore and aft,
When with a roar the blinding fury rolled
Upon them;   and the breath of it was cold.
There fell no rain.

That night was calm and clear:
Just such a night as when the waning year
Has set aflare the old Missouri wood;
When Greenings are beginning to be good;
And when, so hollow is the frosty hush,
One hears the ripe persimmons falling — *plush!* —
Upon the littered leaves. The kindly time!
With cider in the vigor of its prime,
Just strong enough to edge the dullest wit
Should neighbor folk drop in awhile to sit
And gossip. O the dear flame-painted gloam,
The backlog's sputter on the hearth at home —
How far away that night! Thus many a
     lad,
Grown strangely old, remembered and was sad.
Wolves mourned among the bluffs. Like hanks
     of wool
Fog flecked the river. And the moon was full.

A week sufficed to end the trail. They came
To where the lesser river gives its name
And meed of waters to the greater stream.
Here, lacking horses, they must nurse the
     dream
Of beaver haunts beyond the Great Divide,
Build quarters for the winter trade, and bide
The coming up of Ashley and his band.

So up and down the wooded tongue of land
That thins to where the rivers wed, awoke
The sound of many axes, stroke on stroke;
And lustily the hewers sang at whiles —
The better to forget the homeward miles
In this, the homing time.   And when the geese
With cacophonic councils broke the peace
Of frosty nights before they took to wing;
When cranes went over daily, southering,
And blackbirds chattered in the painted wood,
A mile above the river junction stood
The fort, adjoining the Missouri's tide.
Foursquare and thirty paces on a side,
A wall of sharpened pickets bristled round
A group of sod-roofed cabins.   Bastions frowned
From two opposing corners, set to brave
A foe on either flank; and stout gates gave
Upon the stream, where now already came
The Indian craft, lured thither by the fame
Of traders building by the mating floods.

III

TO THE MUSSELSHELL

Now came at dawn a party of the Bloods,
Who told of having paddled seven nights
To parley for their people with the Whites,
The long way lying 'twixt a foe and foe;
For ever on their right hand lurked the Crow,
And on their left hand, the Assiniboine.
The crane-winged news, that where the waters
    join
The Long Knives built a village, made them sad ·
Because the pastures thereabouts were bad,
Sustaining few and very scrawny herds.
So they had hastened hither, bringing words
Of kindness from their mighty men, to tell
What welcome waited on the Musselshell
Where stood the winter lodges of their band.

They rhapsodized the fatness of that land:
Lush valleys where all summer bison ran
To grass grown higher than a mounted man!
Aye, winter long on many a favored slope
The bison grazed with goat and antelope,

Nor were they ever leaner in the spring!
One heard the diving beaver's thundering
In all the streams at night; and one might hear
Uncounted bull elks whistle, when the year
Was painted for its death. Their squaws were
      good,
Strong bearers of the water and the wood,
With quiet tongues and never weary hands;
Tall as the fighting men of other lands,
And good to look upon. These things were so!
Why else then should Assiniboine and Crow
Assail the Bloods?

                    Now flaring up, they spoke
Of battles and their haters blown as smoke
Before the blizzard of their people's ire,
Devoured as grass before a prairie fire
That licks the heavens when the Northwind
      runs!
But, none the less, their warriors needed guns
And powder. Wherefor, let the Great White
      Chief
Return with them, ere yet the painted leaf
Had fallen.   If so be he might not leave
This land of peoples skillful to deceive,
Who, needing much, had scarce a hide to sell —
Then send a party to the Musselshell

To trade and trap until the grass was young
And calves were yellow. With no forkéd tongue
The Bloods had spoken. Had the White Chief
     ears?

So Major Henry called for volunteers;
And Fink was ready on the word to go
"And chance the bloody naygurs"; then Tal-
     beau,
Then Carpenter; and after these were nine,
In whom young blood was like a beading wine,
Who lusted for the venture.

                              Late that night
The Bloods set out for home. With day's first
     light
The dozen trappers followed, paddling west
In six canoes. And whatso suited best
The whimsies of the savage or his needs,
The slim craft carried — scarlet cloth and beads,
Some antiquated muskets, powder, ball,
Traps, knives, and little casks of alcohol
To lubricate the rusty wheels of trade!

So, singing as they went, the blithe brigade
Departed, with their galloping canoes
Heeding the tune. They had no time to lose;

For long and stubborn was the upstream way,
And when they launched their boats at break of
   day
They heard a thin ice tinkle at the prows.

A bodeful silence and a golden drowse
Possessed the land.   The Four Winds held their
   breath
Before a vast serenity of death,
Wherein it seemed the reminiscent Year —
A yearning ghost now — wrought about its bier
Some pale hallucination of its May.
Bleak stretched the prairie to the walls of day,
So dry, that where a loping kiote broke
Its loneliness, it smouldered into smoke:
And when a herd of bison rumbled past,
'Twas like a great fire booming in a blast,
The rolling smudge whereof concealed the flame.

Proceeding in the truce of winds, they came
In five days to the vale the Poplar drains.
A trailing flight of southbound whooping cranes,
Across the fading West, was like a scrawl
Of cabalistic warning on a wall,
And counselled haste.   In seven days they
   reached
The point where Wolf Creek empties in, and
   beached

Their keels along its dusty bed. In nine,
Elk Prairie and the Little Porcupine,
Now waterless, had fallen to the rear.
The tenth sun failed them on the lone frontier
Where flows the turbid Milk by countless bends
And where Assiniboian country ends
And Blackfoot Land begins. The hollow gloom
All night resounded with the beaver's boom;
A wolf pack yammered from a distant hill;
Anon a rutting elk cried, like a shrill
Arpeggio blown upon a flageolet.
A half day more their lifting prows were set
To westward; then the flowing trail led south
Two days by many a bend to Hell Creek's mouth
Amid the Badlands. Gazing from a height,
The lookout saw the marching of the Night
Across a vast black waste of peaks and deeps
That could have been infernal cinder-heaps,
The relics of an ancient hell gone cold.

That night they saw a wild aurora rolled
Above the lifeless wilderness. It formed
Northeastwardly in upright waves that stormed
To westward, sequent combers of the bow
That gulfed Polaris in their undertow
And hurtled high upon the Ursine Isles
A surf of ghostly fire. Again, at whiles,

A shimmering silken veil, it puffed and swirled
As 'twere the painted curtain of the world
That fluttered in a rising gale of doom.
And when it vanished in the starry gloom
One said "'Twill blow to-morrow."

                                        So it did.
Ere noon they raised the Half Way Pyramid
Southwestward;   saw its wraith-like summit
     lift
And seem to float northwest against a drift
Of wind-whipped dust.   The lunar hills about —
Where late a bird's note startled like a shout
The hush that seemed the body of old Time —
Now bellowed where the hoofs of Yotunheim
Foreran the grizzled legions of the Snow.
'Twas peep of day when it began to blow,
A zephyr growing stronger with the light,
And now by fits it churned the river white
And whipped the *voyageurs* with freezing spray.
The windward reaches took their breath away.
Ghost-white and numb with cold, from bend to
     bend,
Where transiently the wind became a friend
To drive them south, they battled; till at
     last
Around a jutting bluff they met a blast

That choked as with a hand upon their throats
The song they sang for courage; hurled their
    boats
Against the farther shore and held them pinned.

A sting of spitting snow was in the wind.
Southwest by west across the waste, where fell
A murky twilight, lay the Musselshell —
Two days of travel with the crow for guide.
Here must they find them shelter, and abide
The passing of the blizzard as they could.
The banks bore neither plum nor cottonwood
And all the hills were naked as a hand.
But where, debouching from the broken land,
A river in the spring was wont to flow,
A northward moving herd of buffalo
Had crossed the river, evidently bound
From failing pastures to the grazing ground
Along the Milk: and where the herd had
    passed
Was scattered *bois de vache* enough to last
Until the storm abated.   So they packed
Great blanketfuls of sun-dried chips, and stacked
The precious fuel where the wind was stilled —
A pocket hemmed by lofty bluffs and filled
With mingled dusk and thunder; bore therein
Canoes and cargo, pitched their tents of skin

About a central heap of glowing chips,
And dined on brittle bull-meat dried in strips,
With rum to wash it down.

                              It snowed all night.
The earth and heavens, in the morning light,
Were one white fury; and the stream ran slush.
Two days and nights the gale boomed; then a
    hush
Fell with the sun; and when the next dawn
    came —
A pale flare flanked by mockeries of flame —
The river lay as solid as the land.

Now caching half their goods, the little band
Resumed the journey, toiling under packs;
And twice they felt the morning at their backs,
A laggard traveller; and twice they saw
The sunset dwindle to a starry awe
Beyond the frozen vast, while still they pressed
The journey — bearded faces yearning west,
White as the waste they trod. Then one day
    more,
Southwestward, brought them to the jutting shore
That faced the goal.

                              A strip of poplars stretched
Along a winding stream, their bare boughs etched

Black line by line upon a flat of snow
Blue tinted in the failing afterglow.
Humped ponies 'mid the drifts and clumps of sage
Went nosing after grudging pasturage
Where'er it chanced the blizzard's whimsic flaws
Had swept the slough grass bare. A flock of
    squaws
Chopped wood and chattered in the underbrush,
Their ax strokes thudding dully in the hush,
Their nasal voices rising shrill and clear:
And, circled 'neath a bluff that towered sheer
Beside the stream, snug lodges wrought of hide,
Smoke-plumed and glowing with the fires inside,
Made glad the gazers.   Even as they stood,
Content to stare a moment, from the wood
The clamor deepened, and a running shout
Among the lodges brought the dwellers out,
Braves, squaws, papooses;   and the wolf dogs
    bayed;
And up the flat the startled ponies neighed,
Pricking their ears to question what befell.

So came Fink's party to the Musselshell,
Gaunt, bearded, yet — how gloriously young
And then, what feasts of bison fleece and tongue
Of browned *boudin* and steaming humprib stew!
What roaring nights of wassailing they knew —

Gargantuan regales — when through the town
The fiery liquor ravined, melting down
The tribal hoard of beaver!   How they made
Their merest gewgaws mighty in the trade!
Aye, merry men they were! Nor could they
          know
How even then there came that wraith of woe
Amongst them;   some swift-fingered Fate that
          span
The stuff of sorrow, wove 'twixt man and man
The tangling mesh, that friend might ruin friend
And each go stumbling to a bitter end —
A threefold doom that now the Song recalls.

IV

THE NET IS CAST

There was a woman.

                   What enchantment falls
Upon that far off revel! How the din
Of jangling voices, chaffering to win
The lesser values, hushes at the words,
As dies the dissonance of brawling birds
Upon a calm before the storm is hurled!
Lo, down the age-long reaches of the world
What rose-breatht wind of ghostly music creeps!

And was she fair — this woman? Legend keeps
No answer; yet we know that she was young,
If truly comes the tale by many a tongue
That one of Red Hair's party fathered her.
What need to know her features as they were?
Was she not lovely as her lover's thought,
And beautiful as that wild love she wrought
Was fatal? Vessel of the world's desire,
Did she not glow with that mysterious fire
That lights the hearth or burns the rooftree down?
What face was hers who made the timeless town

A baleful torch forever? Hers who wailed
Upon the altar when the four winds failed
At Aulis? What the image that looked up
On Iseult from the contemplated cup
Of everlasting thirst? What wondrous face
Above the countless cradles of the race
Makes sudden heaven for the blinking eyes?
One face in truth! And once in Paradise
Each man shall stray unwittingly, and see —
In some unearthly valley where the Tree
With golden fruitage perilously fraught
Still stands — that image of God's afterthought.
Then shall the world turn wonderful and strange!

Who knows how came that miracle of change
To Fink at last? For he was not of such
As tend to prize one woman overmuch;
And legend has it that, from Pittsburg down
To Baton Rouge, in many a river town
Some blowsy Ariadne pined for Mike.
"It is me rule to love 'em all alike."
He often said, with slow, omniscient wink,
When just the proper quantity of drink
Had made him philosophic; "Glass or gourd,
Shure, now, they're all wan liquor whin they're
      poured!
Aye, rum is rum, me b'y!"

Alas, the tongue!
How glibly are its easy guesses flung
Against the knowing reticence of years,
To echo laughter in the time of tears,
Raw gusts of mocking merriment that stings!
Some logic in the seeming ruck of things
Inscrutably confutes us!

Now had come
The time when rum no longer should be rum,
But witchwine sweet with peril.   It befell
In this wise, insofar as tongue may tell
And tongues repeat the little eyes may guess
Of what may happen in that wilderness,
The human heart.   There dwelt a mighty man
Among the Bloods, a leader of his clan,
Around whose life were centered many lives,
For many sons had he of many wives;
And also he was rich in pony herds.
Wherefore, they say, men searched his lightest
        words
For hidden things, since anyone might see
That none had stronger medicine than he
To shape aright the stubborn stuff of life.
Among the women that he had to wife
Was she who knew the white man when the band
Of Red Hair made such marvel in the land,

She being younger then and little wise.
But in that she was pleasing to the eyes
And kept her fingers busy for her child
And bore a silent tongue, the great man smiled
Upon the woman, called her to his fire
And gave the Long Knife's girl a foster sire,
So that her maidenhood was never lean,
But like a pasture that is ever green
Because it feels a mountain's sunny flank.

Now in the season when the pale sun shrank
Far southward, like another kind of moon,
And dawns were laggard and the dark came soon,
It pleased the great man's whim to give a feast.
'Twas five days after Carpenter went east
With eight stout ponies and a band of three
To lift the cache; a fact that well might be
Sly father to the great man's festive mood —
A wistfully prospective gratitude,
Anticipating charity!

               It chanced
That while the women sang and young men
    danced
About the drummers, and the pipe went round,
And ever 'twixt the songs arose the sound
Of fat dog stewing, Fink, with mournful eyes
And pious mien, lamented the demise

Of "pore owld Fido," till his comrades choked
With stifled laughter; soberly invoked
The plopping stew ("Down, Rover! Down, me
    lad!");
Discussed the many wives the old man had
In language more expressive than polite.
So, last of all his merry nights, that night
Fink clowned it, little dreaming he was doomed
To wear that mask of sorrow he assumed
In comic mood, thenceforward to the last.
For even as he joked, the net was cast
About him, and the mystic change had come,
And he had looked on rum that was not rum —
The Long Knife's daughter!

                    Stooped beneath a pack
Of bundled twigs, she pushed the lodge-flap
    back
And entered lightly; placed her load of wood
Beside the fire; then straightened up and stood
One moment there, a shapely girl and tall.
There wasn't any drama: that was all.
But when she left, the wit had died in Fink.
He seemed a man who takes the one more drink
That spoils the fun, relaxes jaw and jowl
And makes the jester, like a sunstruck owl,
Stare solemnly at nothing.

All next day
He moped about with scarce a word to say,
And no one dared investigate his whim.
But when the twilight came, there fell on him
A sentimental, reminiscent mood,
As though upon some frozen solitude
Within him, breathed a softening chinook,
Far strayed across the alplike years that look
On what one used to be and what one is.
And when he raised that mellow voice of his
In songs of lovers wedded to regret,
'Tis said that, unashamed, men's eyes grew
        wet,
So poignantly old memories were stirred.
And much his comrades marvelled as they
        heard
That ribald jester singing thus of love.
Nor could they solve the mystery thereof,
Until at dawn they saw him rise and take
A rifle of the latest Hawkin make,
Ball, powder, and a bolt of scarlet goods,
And hasten to the fringe of cottonwoods
Where rose the great man's lodge smoke.   Then
        they knew;
For thus with gifts the Bloods were wont *to*
        woo
The daughter through the sire.

The white sun burned
Midmost the morning steep when he returned
Without his load and humming as he went.
And hour by hour he squatted in his tent
And stared upon the fire; save now and then
He stirred himself to lift the flap again
And cast an anxious gaze across the snows
Where stood the chieftain's lodge.   And well did
    those
Who saw him know what sight he hoped to see;
For 'twas the custom that the bride-to-be
Should carry food to him she chose to wed.
Meanwhile, with seemly caution, be it said,
Fink's men enjoyed a comedy, and laid
Sly wagers on the coming of the maid —
She would! She wouldn't! So the brief day
    waned.

Now when the sun, a frosty specter maned
With corruscating vapors, lingered low
And shadows lay like steel upon the snow,
An old squaw, picking faggots in the brush,
Saw that which set her shrieking in the hush.
"They come!   They come!" Then someone
    shouted "Crows!"
The town spewed tumult, men with guns and
    bows,

Half clad and roaring; shrill hysteric wives
With sticks of smoking firewood, axes, knives;
Dogs,   bristle-necked   and   snarling.   So   they
    pressed
To meet a foe, as from a stricken nest
The hornet swarm boils over.

                              Blinking, dazed
With sudden light and panic fear, they gazed
About the frozen waste; and then they saw
Eight laden ponies filing up the draw,
Their nostrils steaming, slack of neck and slow.
Behind them, stumbling in the broken snow,
Three   weary   trappers   trudged,   while   in   the
    lead
Strode Carpenter.   A goodly sight, indeed!
Upstanding, eagle-faced and eagle-eyed,
The ease of latent power in his stride,
He dwarfed the panting pony that he led;
And when the level sunlight 'round his head
Made glories in the frosted beard and hair,
Some Gothic fighting god seemed walking there,
Strayed from the dim Hercynian woods of old.

How little of a story can be told!
Let him who knows what happens in the seed
Before the sprout breaks sunward, make the deed

A plummet for the dreaming deeps that surged
Beneath the surface ere the deed emerged
For neat appraisal by the rule of thumb!
The best of Clio is forever dumb,
To human ears at least.   Nor shall the Song
Presume to guess and tell how all night long,
While roared the drunken orgy and the trade,
Doom quickened in the fancy of a maid,
The daughter of the Long Knife; how she saw,
Serenely moving through a spacious awe
Behind shut lids where never came the brawl,
That shining one, magnificently tall,
A day-crowned mortal brother of the sun.
Suffice it here that, when the night was done
And morning, like an uproar in the east,
Aroused the town still heavy with the feast,
All men might see what whimsic, fatal bloom
A soil, dream-plowed and seeded in the gloom,
Had nourished unto blowing in the day.

'Twas then the girl appeared and took her way
Across the snow with hesitating feet.
She bore a little pot of steaming meat;
And when midmost the open space, she turned
And held it up to where the morning burned,
As one who begs a blessing of the skies.
Unconscious of the many peeping eyes,

Erect, with wrapt uplifted face she stood —
A miracle of shapely maidenhood —
Before the flaming god.   And many heard,
Or seemed to hear by piecing word to word,
The prayer she muttered to the wintry sky:
"O Sun, behold a maiden!   Pure am I!
Look kindly on the little gift I give;
For, save you smile upon it, what can live?
Bright Father, hear a maiden!"   Then, as one
Who finds new courage for a task begun,
She turned and hastened to the deed.

                                          They say
There was no dearth of gossiping that day
Among the lodges.   Shrewish tongues there were
That clacked no happy prophecies of her.
And many wondered at the chieftain's whim.
The Long Knife's girl had wrought a spell on
      him;
Why else then was he silent?   See her shrink
A moment there before the tent of Fink,
As one who feels a sudden sleety blast!
But look again!   She starts, and hurries past!
All round the circled village, lodges yawn
To see how brazen in the stare of dawn
A petted girl may be.   For now, behold!
Was ever maiden of the Bloods so bold?

She stops before another tent and stoops,
Her fingers feeling for the buckskin loops
That bind the rawhide flap.   'Tis opened wide.
The slant white light of morning falls inside,
And half the town may witness at whose feet
She sets the little pot of steaming meat —
'Tis Carpenter!

V

THE QUARREL

            Perceptibly, at length,
The days grew longer, and the winter's strength
Increased to fury. Down across the flat
The blizzards bellowed; and the people sat
Fur-robed about the smoky fires that stung
Their eyes to streaming, when a freak gust flung
The sharp reek back with flaws of powdered snow.
And much the old men talked of long ago,
Invoking ghostly Winters from the Past,
Till cold snap after cold snap followed fast,
And none might pile his verbal snow so deep
But some athletic memory could heap
The drifts a trifle higher; give the cold
A greater rigor in the story told;
Put bellows to a wind already high.
And ever greater reverence thereby
The old men won from gaping youths, who heard,
Like marginalia to the living word,
The howling of the poplars tempest-bent,
The smoke-flap cracking sharply at the vent,

The lodge poles creaking eerily.   And O!
The happy chance of living long ago,
Of having wrinkles now and being sires
With many tales to tell around the fires
Of days when things were bigger!   All night
    long
White hands came plucking at the buckskin thong
That bound the door-flap, and the writhing dark
Was shrill with spirits.   By the snuffling bark
Of dogs men knew that homesick ghosts were
    there.
And often in a whirl of chilling air
The weird ones entered, though the flap still held;
Built up in smoke the shapes they knew of eld,
Grew thin and long to vanish as they came.

Now had the scandal, like a sudden flame
Fed fat with grasses, perished in the storm.
The fundamental need of keeping warm
Sufficed the keenest gossip for a theme;
And whimsies faded like a warrior's dream
When early in the dawn the foemen cry.

The time when calves are black had blustered
    by —
A weary season — since the village saw
The chief's wife pitching for her son-in-law

The nuptial lodge she fashioned.   Like a bow
That feels the arrow's head, the moon hung
    low
That evening when they gave the wedding
    gifts;
And men had seen it glaring through the rifts
Of wintry war as up the east it reeled,
A giant warrior's battle-bitten shield —
But now it braved no more the charging air.
Meanwhile the lodge of Carpenter stood there
Beside the chieftain's, huddled in the snows,
And, like a story everybody knows,
Was little heeded now.

                    But there was one
Who seldom noted what was said or done
Among his comrades; he would sit and look
Upon the fire, as one who reads a book
Of woeful doings, ever on the brink
Of ultimate disaster.   It was Fink:
And seeing this, Talbeau was sick at heart
With dreading that his friends might drift apart
And he be lost, because he loved them both.
But, knowing well Mike's temper, he was loath
To broach the matter.   Also, knowing well
That silence broods upon the hottest hell,
He prayed that Fink might curse.

                       So worried past
The days of that estrangement.   Then at last
One night when round their tent the blizzard
    roared
And, nestled in their robes, the others snored,
Talbeau could bear the strain no more and spoke.
He opened with a random little joke,
Like some starved hunter trying out the range
Of precious game where all the land is strange;
And, as the hunter, missing, hears the grim
And spiteful echo-rifles mocking him,
His own unmirthful laughter mocked Talbeau.
He could have touched across the ember-glow
Mike's brooding face — yet Mike was far away.
And O that nothing more than distance lay
Between them — any distance with an end!
How tireless then in running to his friend
A man might be! For suddenly he knew
That Mike would have him choose between the
    two.
How could he choose 'twixt Carpenter and Fink?
How idle were a choice 'twixt food and drink
When, choosing neither, one were sooner dead!

Thus torn within, and hoarse with tears unshed,
He strove again to find his comrade's heart:
"O damn it, Mike, don't make us drift apart!

Don't do it, Mike!   This ain't a killin' fuss,
And hadn't ought to faze the three of us
That's weathered many a rough-and-tumble fight!
W'y don't you mind that hell-a-poppin' night
At Baton Rouge three years ago last fall —
The time we fit the whole damned dancin' hall
And waded out nigh belly-deep in men?
O who'd have said a girl could part us, then?
And, Mike, that fracas in the Vide Poche dive!
Can you forget it long as you're alive? —
A merry time!   Us strollin' arm-in-arm
From drink to drink, not calculatin' harm,
But curious, because St. Louis town
Fair boiled with greasy mountain men, come
    down
All brag and beaver, howlin' for a spree!
And then — you mind? — a feller jostled me —
'Twas at the bar — a chap all bones and big.
Says he in French: 'You eater of a pig,
Make room for mountain men!'   And then says
    you
In Irish, aimin' where the whiskers grew,
And landin' fair: 'You eater of a dog,
Make room for boatmen!'   Like a punky log
That's water-soaked, he dropped.   What hap-
    pened then?
A cyclone in a woods of mountain men —

That's what!   O Mike, you can't forget it
    now!
And what in hell's a woman, anyhow,
To memories like that?"

                So spoke Talbeau,
And, pausing, heard the hissing of the snow,
The snoring of the sleepers, and the cries
Of blizzard-beaten poplars.   Still Fink's eyes
Upon the crumbling embers pored intent.
Then momently, or so it seemed, there went
Across that alien gaze a softer light,
As when bleak windows in a moony night
Flush briefly with a candle borne along.
And suddenly the weary hope grew strong
In him who saw the glimmer, and he said:
"O Mike, I see the good old times ain't dead!
Why don't you fellers shoot the whisky cup
The way you used to do?"

                Then Fink looked up.
'Twas bad the way the muscles twitched and
    worked
About his mouth, and in his eyes there lurked
Some crouchant thing.   "To hell wid you!" he
    cried.
So love and hate that night slept side by side;

And hate slept well, but love lay broad awake
And, like a woman, for the other's sake
Eked out the lonely hours with worrying.

Now came a heartsick yearning for the spring
Upon Talbeau; for surely this bad dream
Would vanish with the ice upon the stream,
Old times be resurrected with the grass!
But would the winter ever, ever pass,
The howling of the blizzard ever cease?
So often now he dreamed of hearing geese
Remotely honking in the rain-washed blue;
And ever when the blur of dawn broke through
The scudding rack, he raised the flap to see,
By sighting through a certain forkéd tree,
How much the sun made northward.

                                    Then, one day,
The curtain of the storm began to fray;
The poplars' howling softened to a croon;
The sun set clear, and dusk revealed the moon —
A thin-blown bubble in a crystal bowl.
All night, as 'twere the frozen prairie's soul
That voiced a hopeless longing for the spring,
The wolves assailed with mournful question-
    ing
The starry deeps of that tremendous hush.

Dawn wore the mask of May — a rosy flush.
It seemed the magic of a single bird
Might prove the seeing of the eye absurd
And make the heaped-up winter billow green.
On second thought, one knew the air was keen —
A whetted edge in gauze. The village fires
Serenely builded tenuous gray spires
That vanished in the still blue deeps of awe.
All prophets were agreed upon a thaw.
And when the morning stood a spearlength high,
There grew along the western rim of sky
A bank of cloud that had a rainy look.
It mounted slowly. Then the warm chinook
Began to breathe a melancholy drowse
And sob among the naked poplar boughs,
As though the prairie dreamed a dream of June
And knew it for a dream. All afternoon
The gale increased. The sun went down blood-
     red;
The young moon, perilously fragile, fled
To early setting. And the long night roared.

Tempestuously broke the day and poured
An intermittent glory through the rifts
Amid the driven fog. The sodden drifts
Already grooved and withered in the blast;
And when the flying noon stared down aghast,

The bluffs behind the village boomed with
      flood.
What magic in that sound to stir the blood
Of winter-weary men! For now the spring
No longer seemed a visionary thing,
But that which any morning might bestow.
And most of all that magic moved Talbeau;
For, scrutinizing Fink, he thought he saw
Some reflex of that February thaw —
A whit less curling of the upper lip.
O could it be returning comradeship,
That April not beholden to the moon
Nor chatteled to the sun?

                              That afternoon
They played at euchre.   Even Fink sat in;
And though he showed no eagerness to win,
Forgot the trumps and played his bowers wild,
There were not lacking moments when he smiled,
A hesitating smile 'twixt wan and grim.
It seemed his stubborn mood embarrassed him
Because regret now troubled it with shame.

The great wind died at midnight. Morning
      came,
Serene and almost indolently warm —
As when an early April thunder storm

Has cleansed the night and vanished with the
    gloom;
When one can feel the imminence of bloom
As 'twere a spirit in the orchard trees;
When, credulous of blossom, come the bees
To grumble 'round the seepages of sap.
So mused Talbeau while, pushing back the flap,
Instinctively he listened for a bird
To fill the hush. Then presently he heard —
And 'twas the only sound in all the world —
The trickle of the melting snow that purled
And tinkled in the bluffs above the town.
The sight of ragged Winter patched with brown,
The golden peace and, palpitant therein,
That water note, spun silverly and thin,
Begot a wild conviction in the man:
The wounded Winter weakened; now began
The reconciliation! Hate would go
And, even as the water from the snow,
Old comradeship come laughing back again!

All morning long he pondered, while the men
Played seven-up. And scarce a trick was
    played
But someone sang a snatch of song or made
A merry jest. And when the game was balked
By one who quite forgot his hand, and talked

Of things in old St. Louis, none demurred.
And thus, by noon, it seemed the lightest word
Of careless salutation would avail
To give a happy ending to the tale
Of clouded friendship.   So he 'rose and went,
By studied indirection, to the tent
Of Carpenter, as one who takes the air.
And, as he raised the flap and entered there,
A sudden gale of laughter from the men
Blew after him.   What music in it then!
What mockery, when memory should raise
So often in the coming nights and days
The ruthless echo of it!

               Click on click
Amid the whirlwind finish of a trick
The cards fell fast, while King and Queen and Ace,
With meaner trumps for hounds, pursued the chase
Of wily Knave and lurking Deuce and Ten;
When suddenly the game-enchanted men
Were conscious of a shadow in the place,
And glancing up they saw the smiling face
Of Carpenter, thrust in above Talbeau's.
"How goes it, Boys?" said he; and gaily those
Returned the greeting.   "Howdy, Mike!"   he
     said;
And with a sullen hanging of the head

Fink mumbled "Howdy!"   Gruff — but what
    of that?
One can not doff displeasure like a hat —
'Twould dwindle snow-like.

                          Nothing else would do
But Carpenter should play.   Now Fink played
    too;
And, having brought his cherished ones together,
Talbeau surrendered to the languid weather
And, dreamily contented, watched the sport.
All afternoon the pictured royal court
Pursued its quarry in the mimic hunt;
And Carpenter, now gayer than his wont,
Lost much; while Fink, with scarce a word to say,
His whole attention fixed upon the play,
Won often.   So it happened, when the sun
Was near to setting, that the day seemed won
For friendliness, however stood the game.
But even then that Unseen Player came
Who stacks the shuffled deck of circumstance
And, playing wild the Joker men call Chance,
Defeats the Aces of our certainty.

The cards were dealt and Carpenter bid three.
The next man passed the bid, and so the next.
Then Fink, a trifle hesitant and vexed,

Bid four on spades.   And there was one who said
In laughing banter: "Mike, I'll bet my head
As how them spades of your'n 'll dig a hole!"
And in some subtle meaning of the soul
The wag was more a prophet than he knew.

Fink held the Ace and Deuce, and that made two:
His black King scored another point with
　　Knave.
But Carpenter, to whom that Weird One gave
A band of lesser trumps to guard his Ten,
Lay low until the Queen had passed, and then
Swept in a last fat trick for Game, and scored.
And now the players slapped their knees and
　　roared:
"You're set!   You're in the hole!   He set you,
　　Mike!"

Then suddenly they saw Fink crouch to strike;
And ere they comprehended what they saw,
There came a thud of knuckles on a jaw
And Carpenter rolled over on the ground.
One moment in a breathless lapse of sound
The stricken man strove groggily to 'rise,
The emptiness of wonder in his eyes
Turned dreamily with seeming unconcern
Upon Mike's face, where now began to burn

The livid murder-lust.   'Twixt breath and breath
The hush and immobility of death
Made there a timeless picture.   Then a yell,
As of a wild beast charging, broke the spell.
Fink sprang to crush, but midway met Talbeau
Who threw him as a collie dog may throw
A raging bull.   But Mike was up again,
And wielding thrice the might of common men,
He gripped the little man by nape and thigh
And lightly lifted him and swung him high
And flung him; and the smitten tent went down.
Then 'rose a roar that roused the teeming town,
And presently a shouting rabble surged
About the wreck, whence tumblingly emerged
A knot of men who grappled Fink and clung.
Prodigiously he rose beneath them, flung
His smashing arms, man-laden, forth and back;
But stubbornly they gripped him, like a pack
That takes uncowed the maulings of a bear.
"Let Carpenter get up!"   they cried.   "Fight
     fair!
Fight fair!   Fight fair!"

                              Quite leisurely the while
The stricken man arose, a sleepy smile
About his quiet eyes.   Indeed, he seemed
As one but lately wakened, who has dreamed

A pleasing dream.   But when he stroked his
    beard
And gazed upon his fingers, warmly smeared
With crimson from the trickle at his jaw,
His eyes went eagle-keen with what they saw.
The stupor passed.   He hastily untied
His buckskin shirt and, casting it aside,
Stood naked to the hips.   The tumult ceased
As, panting hard, the *voyageurs* released
Their struggling charge and, ducking to a swing
Of those freed arms, sought safety, scamper-
    ing.

Fink also stripped his shirt; and as the man
Stood thus revealed, a buzz of wonder ran
Amid the jostling rabble.   Few there were
Who in that moment envied Carpenter,
Serenely poised and waiting placid browed:
For shall a lonely cedar brave a cloud
Bulged big and shapen to the cyclone's whirl?
Lo, even as the body of a girl,
The body of the blond was smooth and white;
But vaguely, as one guesses at the might
Of silent waters running swift and deep,
One guessed what stores of power lay asleep
Beneath the long fleet lines of trunk and limb.
Thus God had made experiment with him;

And, groping for the old Adamic dream,
Had found his patterns in the tree and stream,
As Fink's in whirling air and hungry flame.

Now momently the picture there became
A blur of speed.   Mike rushed.   The tiptoe town
Craned eagerly to see a man go down
Before that human thunder gust.   But lo!
As bends a sapling when the great winds blow,
The other squatted, deftly swayed aside,
And over him the slashing blows went wide.
Fink sprawled.   But hardly had a spreading
     roar
O'errun the town, when silence as before
Possessed the scene; for Mike flashed back again
With flame-like speed, and suddenly the men
Clenched, leaning neck to neck.

                         Without a word,
Like horn-locked bulls that strive before the herd,
They balanced might with might; till Mike's
     hands whipped
Beneath the other's arm-pits, met and gripped
Across the broad white shoulders.   Then began
The whole prodigious engine of the man
To bulge and roll and darken with the strain.
Like rivulets fed suddenly with rain,

The tall one's thews rose ropily and flowed
Converging might against the growing load
Of those tremendous arms that strove to crush.

Their labored breathing whistled in the hush.
One saw the blond man's face go bluish red,
As deeper, deeper sank Fink's shaggy head
Amid his heaped-up shoulder brawn.   One knew
That very soon the taller of the two
Must yield and take that terrible embrace.

A tense hypnotic quiet filled the place.
The men were like two wrestlers in a dream
That holds an endless moment; till a scream
Fell stab-like on the hush.   One saw Talbeau,
Jaws set, hands clenched, eyes wild, and bending
    low,
As though he too were struggling, slowly bowed
Beneath Fink's might.   And then —

                              What ailed the crowd?
Swept over by a flurry of surprise,
They swayed and jostled, shouting battle-cries
And quips and jeers of savage merriment.
One moment they had seen the tall man bent,
About to break: then, falling back a-haunch,
His feet had plunged against the other's paunch
And sent Fink somersaulting.

                                    Once again
A silence fell as, leaping up, the men
Were mingled briefly in a storm of blows.
Now, tripping like a dancer on his toes,
The blond man sparred; while, like a baited bear,
Half blinded with the lust to crush and tear,
Fink strove to clutch that something lithe and
       sleek
That stung and fled and stung. Upon his cheek
A flying shadow laid a vivid bruise;
Another — and his brow began to ooze
Slow drops that spattered on his bearded jaw.
Again that shadow passed — his mouth went raw,
And like a gunshot wound it gaped and bled.

Fink roared with rage and plunged with lowered
       head
Upon this thing that tortured, hurled it back
Amid the crowd. One heard a thud and smack
Of rapid blows on bone and flesh — and then
One saw the tall man stagger clear again
With gushing nostrils and a bloody grin,
And down his front the whiteness of the skin
Was striped with flowing crimson to the waist.
Unsteadily he wheeled about and faced
The headlong hate of his antagonist.
Now toe to toe and fist to flying fist,

They played at give and take; and all the while
The blond man smiled that riddle of a smile,
As one who meditates upon a jest.

Yet surely he was losing! Backward pressed,
He strove in vain to check his raging foe.
Fink lunged and straightened to a shoulder
    blow
With force enough to knock a bison down.
The other dodged it, squatting. Then the
    town
Discovered what a smile might signify.
For, even as the futile blow went by,
One saw the lithe white form shoot up close in,
A hooked white arm jab upward to the chin —
Once — twice — and yet again. With eyes a-
    stare,
His hands aloft and clutching at the air,
Fink tottered backward, limply lurched and fell.

Then came to pass what stilled the rabble's
    yell,
So strange it was. And 'round the fires that
    night
The wisest warriors, talking of the fight,
Could not explain what happened at the end.
No friend, they said, makes war upon a friend;

Nor does a foe have pity on a foe:
And yet the tall white chief had bathed with
    snow
The bloody mouth and battered cheek and brow
Of him who fell!

                Queer people, anyhow,
The Long Knives were — and hard to under-
    stand!

VI

THE SHOOTING OF THE CUP

Bull-roaring March had swept across the land,
And now the evangelic goose and crane,
Forerunners of the messianic Rain,
Went crying through the wilderness aloft.
Fog hid the sun, and yet the snow grew soft.
The monochrome of sky and poplar bough,
Drab tracery on drab, was stippled now
With swelling buds; and slushy water ran
Upon the ice-bound river that began
To stir and groan as one about to wake.

Now, while they waited for the ice to break,
The   trappers   fashioned   bull-boats — willow
    wrought
To bowl-like frames, and over these drawn taut
Green bison hides with bison sinew sewn.
And much they talked about the Yellowstone:
How fared their comrades yonder since the fall?
And would they marvel at the goodly haul
Of beaver pelts these crazy craft should bring?
And what of Ashley starting north that spring

With yet another hundred? Did his prows
Already nose the flood? — Ah, cherry boughs
About St. Louis now were loud with bees
And white with bloom; and wading to the knees,
The cattle browsed along the fresh green sloughs!
Yes, even now the leaning cordelle crews
With word from home (so far away, alas!)
Led north the marching armies of the grass,
As 'twere the heart of Summertime they towed!

So while they shaped the willow frames and sewed
The bison hides, the trappers' hearts were light.
They talked no longer now about the fight.
That story, shaped and fitted part by part,
Unwittingly was rounded into art,
And, being art, already it was old.
When this bleak time should seem the age of gold,
These men, grown gray and garrulous, might tell
Of wondrous doings on the Musselshell —
How Carpenter, the mighty, fought, and how
Great Fink went down. But spring was coming
        now,
And who's for backward looking in the spring?

Yet one might see that Mike still felt the sting
Of that defeat; for often he would brood,
Himself the center of a solitude

Wherein the friendly chatter of the band
Was like a wind that makes a lonely land
Seem lonelier.   And much it grieved Talbeau
To see a haughty comrade humbled so;
And, even more, he feared what wounded pride
Might bring to pass, before their boats could
    ride
The dawnward reaches of the April floods
And leave behind the village of the Bloods;
For now it seemed a curse was on the place.
Talbeau was like a man who views a race
With all to lose: so slowly crept the spring,
So surely crawled some formless fatal thing,
He knew not what it was.   But should it win,
Life could not be again as it had been
And spring would scarcely matter any more.
The daybreak often found him at the shore,
A ghostly figure in the muggy light,
Intent to see what progress over night
The shackled river made against the chain.

And then at last, one night, a dream of rain
Came vividly upon him.   How it poured!
A witch's garden was the murk that roared
With bursting purple bloom. 'Twas April
    weather,
And he and Mike and Bill were boys together

Beneath the sounding shingle roof at home.
He smelled the odor of the drinking loam
Still rolling mellow from the recent share;
And he could feel the meadow greening there
Beyond the apple orchard.   Then he 'woke
And raised the flap.   A wraith of thunder-smoke
Was trailing off along the prairie's rim.
Half dreaming yet, the landscape puzzled him.
What made the orchard seem so tall and lean?
And surely yonder meadow had been green
A moment since!   What made it tawny now?
And yonder where the billows of the plow
Should glisten fat and sleek — ?

                    The drowsy spell
Dropped off and left him on the Musselshell
Beneath the old familiar load of care.
He looked aloft.   The stars had faded there.
The sky was cloudless.   No, one lonely fleece
Serenely floated in the spacious peace
And from the distance caught prophetic light.
In truth he had heard thunder in the night
And dashing rain; for all the land was soaked,
And where the withered drifts had lingered, smoked
The naked soil.   But since the storm was gone,
How strange that still low thunder mumbled on —

An unresolving cadence marred at whiles
By dull explosions! Now for miles and miles
Along the vale he saw a trail of steam
That marked the many windings of the stream,
As though the river simmered. Then he knew.
It was the sound of April breaking through!
The resurrection thunder had begun!
The ice was going out, and spring had won
The creeping race with dread!

                    His ringing cheers
Brought out the blinking village by the ears
To share the news; and though they could not
    know
What ecstasy of triumph moved Talbeau,
Yet lodge on lodge took up the joyous cry
That set the dogs intoning to the sky,
The drenched cayuses shrilly nickering.
So man and beast proclaimed the risen Spring
Upon the Musselshell.

                  And all day long
The warring River sang its ocean song.
And all that night the spirits of the rain
Made battle music with a shattered chain
And raged upon the foe. And did one gaze
Upon that struggle through the starry haze,

One saw enormous bodies heaved and tossed,
Where stubbornly the Yotuns of the Frost
With shoulder set to shoulder strove to stem
The wild invasion rolling over them.
Nor in the morning was the struggle done.
Serenely all that day the doughty Sun,
A banished king returning to his right,
Beheld his legions pouring to the fight,
Exhaustless; and his cavalries that rode —
With hoofs that rumbled and with manes that
    flowed
White in the war gust — crashing on the foe.
And all that night the din of overthrow
Arose to heaven from the stricken field;
A sound as of the shock of spear and shield,
Of wheels that trundled and the feet of hordes,
Of shrieking horses mad among the swords,
Hurrahing of attackers and attacked,
And sounds as of a city that is sacked
When lust for loot runs roaring through the night.
Dawn looked upon no battle, but a flight.
And when the next day broke, the spring flood
    flowed
Like some great host that takes the homeward
    road
With many spoils — a glad triumphal march,
Of which the turquoise heaven was the arch.

Now comes a morning when the tents are down
And packed for travel; and the whole Blood town
Is out along the waterfront to see
The trappers going.   Dancing as with glee,
Six laden bull-boats feel the April tide
And sweep away.   Along the riverside
The straggling, shouting rabble keeps abreast
A little while; but, longer than the rest,
A weeping runner races with the swirl
And loses slowly.   'Tis the Long Knife's girl,
Whom love perhaps already makes aware
How flows unseen a greater river there —
The never-to-be-overtaken days.
And now she pauses at the bend to gaze
Upon the black boats dwindling down the long
Dawn-gilded reach.   A merry trapper's song
Comes liltingly to mock her, and a hand
Waves back farewell.   Now 'round a point of land
The bull-boats disappear; and that is all —
Save only that long waiting for the fall
When he would come again.

                    All day they swirled
Northeastwardly.   The undulating world
Flowed by them — wooded headland, greening
    vale
And naked hill — as in a fairy tale

Remembered in a dream.   And when the flare
Of sunset died behind them, and the air
Went weird and deepened to a purple gloom,
They saw the white Enchanted Castles loom
Above them, slowly pass and drift a-rear,
Dissolving in the starry crystal sphere
'Mid which they seemed suspended.

                        Late to camp,
They launched while yet the crawling valley damp
Made islands of the distant hills and hid
The moaning flood.   The Half Way Pyramid
That noon stared in upon them from the south.
'Twas starlight when they camped at Hell Creek's
    mouth,
Among those hills where evermore in vain
The Spring comes wooing, and the April rain
Is tears upon a tomb.   And once again
The dead land echoed to the songs of men
Bound dayward when the dawn was but a streak.
Halfway to noon they sighted Big Dry Creek,
Not choked with grave dust now, but carolling
The universal music of the spring.
Then when the day was midway down the sky,
They reached the Milk.   And howsoe'er the
    eye
Might sweep that valley with a far-flung gaze,
It found no spot uncovered with a maze

Of bison moving lazily at browse —
Scarce wilder than a herd of dairy cows
That know their herdsman.

                        Now the whole band willed
To tarry.   So they beached their boats and killed
Three fatling heifers; sliced the juicy rumps
For broiling over embers; set the humps
And loins to roast on willow spits, and threw
The hearts and livers in a pot to stew
Against the time of dulling appetites.
And when the stream ran opalescent lights
And in a scarlet glow the new moon set,
The feast began.   And some were eating yet,
And some again in intervals of sleep,
When upside down above the polar steep
The Dipper hung.   And many tales were told
And there was hearty laughter as of old,
With Fink's guffaw to swell it now and then.
It seemed old times were coming back again;
That truly they had launched upon a trip
Whereof the shining goal was comradeship:
And tears were in the laughter of Talbeau,
So glad was he.   For how may mortals know
Their gladness, save they sense it by the fear
That whispers how the very thing held dear
May pass away?

             The smoky dawn was lit,
And, suddenly become aware of it,
A flock of blue cranes, dozing on the sand,
With startled cries awoke the sprawling band
And took the misty air with moaning wings.
Disgruntled with the chill drab scheme of things,
Still half asleep and heavy with the feast,
The trappers launched their boats. But when
      the east
Burned rosily, therefrom a raw wind blew,
And ever with the growing day it grew
Until the stream rose choppily and drove
The fleet ashore. Camped snugly in a grove
Of cottonwoods, they slept. And when the gale,
Together with the light, began to fail,
They 'rose and ate and set a-drift again.

It seemed the solid world that mothers men
With twilight and the falling moon had passed,
And there was nothing but a hollow vast,
By time-outlasting stars remotely lit,
And they who at the central point of it
Hung motionless; while, rather sensed than seen,
The phantoms of a world that had been green
Stole by in silence — shapes that once were
      trees,
Black wraiths of bushes, airy traceries

Remembering the hills.   Then sleep made swift
The swinging of the Dipper and the lift
Of stars that dwell upon the day's frontier;
Until at length the wheeling hollow sphere
Began to fill.   And just at morningshine
They landed at the Little Porcupine.

Again they slept and, putting off at night,
They passed the Elk Horn Prairie on the right
Halfway to dawn and Wolf Creek.   One night
     more
Had vanished when they slept upon the shore
Beside the Poplar's mouth.   And three had
     fled
When, black against the early morning red,
The Fort that Henry builded heard their calls,
And sentries' rifles spurting from the walls
Spilled drawling echoes.   Then the gates swung
     wide
And shouting trappers thronged the riverside
To welcome back the homing *voyageurs*.

That day was spent in sorting out the furs,
With eager talk of how the winter went;
And with the growing night grew merriment.
The hump and haunches of a bison cow
Hung roasting at the heaped-up embers now

On Henry's hearth. The backlog whined and
    popped
And, sitting squat or lounging elbow-propped,
Shrewd traders in the merchandise of tales
Held traffic, grandly careless how the scales
Tiptilted with a slight excessive weight.
And when the roast was finished, how they ate!
And there was that which set them singing too
Against the deep bass music of the flue,
While catgut screamed ecstatic in the lead,
Encouraging the voices used and keyed
To vast and windy spaces.

                                    Later came
A gentler mood when, staring at the flame,
Men ventured reminiscences and spoke
About Kentucky people or the folk
Back yonder in Virginia or the ways
They knew in old St. Louis; till the blaze
Fell blue upon the hearth, and in the gloom
And melancholy stillness of the room
They heard the wind of midnight wail outside.
Then there was one who poked the logs and cried:
"Is this a weeping drunk? I swear I'm like
To tear my hair! Sing something lively, Mike!"
And Fink said nought; but after poring long
Upon the logs, began an Irish song —

A gently grieving thing like April rain,
That while it wakes old memories of pain,
Wakes also odors of the violet.
A broken heart, it seemed, could ne'er forget
The eyes of Nora, dead upon the hill.
And when he ceased the men sat very still,
As hearing yet the low caressing note
Of some lost angel mourning in his throat.
And afterwhile Mike spoke: "Shure, now," said
    he,
"'Tis in a woman's eyes shtrong liquors be;
And if ye drink av thim — and if ye drink —"
For just a moment in the face of Fink
Talbeau beheld that angel yearning through;
And wondering if Carpenter saw too,
He looked, and lo! the guileless fellow — grinned!

As dreaming water, stricken by a wind,
Gives up the imaged heaven that it knows,
So Fink's face lost the angel.   He arose
And left the place without a word to say.

The morrow was a perfect April day;
Nor might one guess — so friendly was the sun,
So kind the air — what thread at length was
    spun,
What shears were opened now to sever it.
No sullen mood was Mike's.   His biting wit

Made gay the trappers busy with the fur;
Though more and ever more on Carpenter
His sallies fell, with ever keener whet.
And Carpenter, unskilled in banter, met
The sharper sally with the broader grin.
But, by and by, Mike made a jest, wherein
Some wanton innuendo lurked and leered,
About the Long Knife's girl.   The place went
    weird
With sudden silence as the tall man strode
Across the room, nor lacked an open road
Among the men.   A glitter in his stare
Belied the smile he bore; and, pausing there
With stiffened index finger raised and held
Before the jester's eyes, as though he spelled
The slow words out, he said: "We'll have no
    jokes
In just that way about our women folks!"
And Fink guffawed.

              They would have fought again,
Had not the Major stepped between the men
And talked the crisis by.   And when 'twas past,
Talbeau, intent to end the strife at last,
Somehow persuaded Fink to make amends,
And, as a proof that henceforth they were
    friends,

Proposed the shooting of the whisky cup.
"Shure, b'y," said Mike, "we'll toss a copper up
And if 'tis heads I'll thry me cunning first.
As fer me joke, the tongue of me is cursed
Wid double j'ints — so let it be forgot!"
And so it was agreed.

                  They cleared a spot
And flipped a coin that tinkled as it fell.
A tiny sound — yet, like a midnight bell
That sets wild faces pressing at the pane,
Talbeau would often hear that coin again,
In vivid dreams, to waken terrified.
'Twas heads.

                And now the tall man stepped aside
And, beckoning Talbeau, he whispered: "Son,
If anything should happen, keep my gun
For old time's sake.   And when the Major
    pays
In old St. Louis, drink to better days
When friends were friends, with what he's owing
    me."
Whereat the little man laughed merrily
And said: "Old Horse, you're off your feed
    to-day;
But if you've sworn an oath to blow your pay,

I guess the three of us can make it good!
Mike couldn't miss a target if he would."
"Well, maybe so," said Carpenter, and smiled.

A windless noon was brooding on the wild
And in the clearing, eager for the show,
The waiting trappers chatted.   Now Talbeau
Stepped off the range.   The tall man took his
    place,
The grin of some droll humor on his face;
And when his friend was reaching for his head
To set the brimming cup thereon, he said:
"You won't forget I gave my gun to you
And all my blankets and my fixin's too?"
The small man laughed and, turning round, he
    cried:
"We're ready, Mike!"

                   A murmur ran and died
Along the double line of eager men.
Fink raised his gun, but set it down again
And blew a breath and said: "I'm gittin' dhry!
So howld yer noddle shtiddy, Bill, me b'y,
And don't ye shpill me whisky!"   Cedar-straight
The tall man stood, the calm of brooding Fate
About him.   Aye, and often to the end
Talbeau would see that vision of his friend —

A man-flower springing from the fresh green sod,
While, round about, the bushes burned with God
And mating peewees fluted in the brush.

They heard a gun lock clicking in the hush.
They saw Fink sighting — heard the rifle crack,
And saw beneath the spreading powder rack
The tall man pitching forward.

                    Echoes fled
Like voices in a panic.   Then Mike said:
"Bejasus, and ye've shpilled me whisky, Bill!"

A catbird screamed.   The crowd stood very still
As though bewitched.

           "And can't ye hear?" bawled Fink;
"I say, I'm dhry — and now ye've shpilled me
    drink!"
He stooped to blow the gasses from his gun.

And now men saw Talbeau.   They saw him run
And stoop to peer upon the prostrate man
Where now the mingling blood and whisky ran
From oozing forehead and the tilted cup.
And in the hush a sobbing cry grew up:
"My God!   You've killed him, Mike!"

                        Then growing loud,
A wind of horror blew among the crowd
And set it swirling round about the dead.
And over all there roared a voice that said:
"I niver mint to do it, b'ys, I swear!
The divil's in me gun!"   Men turned to stare
Wild-eyed upon the center of that sound,
And saw Fink dash his rifle to the ground,
As 'twere the hated body of his wrong.

Once more arose that wailing, like a song,
Of one who called and called upon his friend.

VII

THE THIRD RIDER

It seemed the end, and yet 'twas not the end.
A day that wind of horror and surprise
Blew high; and then, as when the tempest dies
And only aspens prattle, as they will,
Though pines win silence and the oaks are still,
By furtive twos and threes the talk survived.
To some it seemed that men were longer lived
Who quarreled not over women.   Others guessed
That love was bad for marksmanship at best —
The nerves, you know! Still others pointed
  out
Why Mike should have the benefit of doubt;
For every man, who knew a rifle, knew
That there were days you'd split a reed in two,
Off-hand at fifty paces; then, one day,
Why, somehow, damn your eyes, you'd blaze
  away
And miss a bull!   No doubt regarding that!
"But," one replied, "'tis what you're aiming at,
Not what you hit, determines skill, you know!"—
An abstract observation, apropos

Of nothing in particular, but made
As just a contribution to the trade
Of gunnery!   And others would recall
The center of that silence in the hall
The night one lay there waiting, splendid, still,
And nothing left to wait for.   Poor old Bill!
There went a man, by God! Who knew his
          like —
So meek in might? And some remembered
          Mike —
The hearth-lit room — the way he came to look
Upon that face — and how his shoulders shook
With sobbing as he moaned: "My friend!   My
          friend!"

It seemed the end, and yet 'twas not the end,
Though men cared less to know what cunning
          gnome
Or eyeless thing of doom had ridden home
The deadly slug.   And then there came a day
When Major Henry had a word to say
That seemed, at last, to lay the ghost to rest.
He meant to seek the River of the West
Beyond the range, immensely rich in furs,
And for the wiving prows of *voyageurs*
A virgin yearning.   Yonder one might glide
A thousand miles to sunset, where the tide

Is tempered with an endless dream of May!
So much and more the Major had to say —
Words big with magic for the young men's
      ears.
And finally he called for volunteers —
Two men to hasten to the Moreau's mouth,
Meet Ashley's party coming from the south
And bid them buy more horses at the Grand
Among the Rees. Then, pushing through the
      band,
Mike Fink stood forth, and after him, Talbeau.

Now Henry thought 'twere wiser they should
      go
By land, although the river trail, he knew,
Were better. But a wind of rumor blew
Up stream. About the region of the Knife,
It seemed, the Grovans tarried, nursing strife
Because the Whites were favoring their foes
With trade for guns; and, looking on their
      bows,
The Grovans hated. So the rumor said.
And thus it came to pass the new trail led
About six days by pony to the south;
Thence eastward, five should find the Moreau's
      mouth
And Ashley toiling up among the bars.

The still white wind was blowing out the stars
When yawning trappers saw the two men row
Across the river with their mounts in tow —
A red roan stallion and a buckskin mare.
And now the ponies gain the far bank there
And flounder up and shake themselves like dogs.
And now the riders mount and breast the
        fogs
Flung down as wool upon the flat. They dip
And rise and float, submerging to the hip,
Turn slowly into shadow men, and fade.
And some have said that when the ponies neighed,
'Twas like a strangled shriek; and far ahead
Some ghostly pony, ridden by the dead,
Called onward like a bugle singing doom.
And when the valley floor, as with a broom,
Was swept by dawn, men saw the empty land.

Not now the Song shall tell of Henry's band
Ascending to the Falls, nor how they crossed
The Blackfoot trail, nor how they fought and
        lost,
Thrown back upon the Yellowstone to wait
In vain for Ashley's hundred. Yonder, Fate
Led southward through the fog, and thither
        goes
The prescient Song.

                                The April sun arose
And fell; and all day long the riders faced
A rolling, treeless, melancholy waste
Of yellow grass; for 'twas a rainless time,
Nor had the baby green begun to climb
The steep-kneed hills, but kept the nursing
      draws.
And knee to knee they rode with scarce a pause,
Save when the ponies drank; and scarce a word,
As though the haunting silence of a third,
Who rode between them, shackled either tongue.
And when along the sloughs the twilight flung
Blue haze, and made the hills seem doubly bleak,
They camped beside a songless little creek
That crawled among the clumps of stunted plum
Just coming into bud.   And both sat dumb
Beside a mewing fire, until the west
Was darkened and the shadows leaped and pressed
About their little ring of feeble light.
Then, moved by some vague menace in the
      night,
Fink forced a laugh that wasn't glad at all,
And joked about a certain saddle gall
That troubled him — a Rabelaisian quip
That in the good old days had served to strip
The drooping humor from the dourest jowl.
He heard the laughter of the prairie owl,

A goblin jeering.   Gazing at the flame,
Talbeau seemed not to hear.   But when there
    came
A cry of kiotes, peering all about
He said : "You don't suppose they'll dig him
    out ?
I carried heavy stones till break of day.
You don't suppose they'll come and paw away
The heavy stones I packed, and pester Bill ?"
"Huh uh," Fink grunted ; but the evening chill
Seemed doubled on a sudden ; so he sought
His blanket, wrapped it closely, thought and
    thought
Till drowsy nonsense tumbled through his skull.

Now at that time of night when comes a lull
On stormy life ; when even sorrow sleeps,
And sentinels upon the stellar steeps
Sight morning, though the world is blind and
    dumb,
Fink wakened at a whisper : "Mike ! He's come !
Look ! Look !"   And Mike sat up and blinked
    and saw.
It didn't walk — it burned along the draw —
Tall, radiantly white ! It wasn't dead —
It smiled — it had a tin cup on its head —
Eh ? — Gone !

Fink stirred the embers to a flare.
What dream was this? The world seemed
  unaware
That anything at all had come to pass.
Contentedly the ponies nipped the grass
There in the darkness; and the night was still.
They slept no more, but nursed the fire until
The morning broke; then ate and rode away.

They weren't any merrier that day.
And each spoke little, save when Fink would swear
And smirch the virtue of the buckskin mare
For picking quarrels with the roan he rode.
(Did not the Northwind nag her like a goad,
And was there any other horse to blame?)

The worried day dragged on and twilight came —
A dusty gray. They climbed a hill to seek
Some purple fringe of brush that marked a creek.
The prairie seemed an endless yellow blur:
Nor might they choose but tarry where they were
And pass the cheerless night as best they could,
For they had seen no water-hole or wood
Since when the sun was halfway down the sky;
And there would be no stars to travel by,
So thick a veil of dust the great wind wove.
They staked their ponies in a leeward cove,
And, rolling in their blankets, swooned away.

Talbeau awoke and stared. 'Twas breaking
    day!
So soon? It seemed he scarce had slept a wink!
He'd have another snooze, for surely Fink
Seemed far from waking, sprawled upon the
    ground,
His loose mouth gaping skyward with a sound
As of a bucksaw grumbling through a knot.
Talbeau dropped back and dreamed the sun was
    hot
Upon his face. He tried but failed to stir;
Whereat he knew that he was Carpenter
And hot-breatht wolves were sniffing round his
    head!
He wasn't dead! He really wasn't dead!
Would no one come, would no one drive them off?
His cry for help was nothing but a cough,
For something choked him. Then a shrill long
    scream
Cut knife-like through the shackles of his dream,
And once again he saw the lurid flare
Of morning on the hills.

                      What ailed the mare?
She strained her tether, neighing. And the
    roan?
He squatted, trembling, with his head upthrown,

And lashed his tail and snorted at the blast.
Perhaps some prowling grizzly wandered past.
Talbeau sat up.   What stifling air! How warm!
What sound was that? Perhaps a thunder
    storm
Was working up.   He coughed; and then it
    broke
Upon him how the air was sharp with smoke;
And, leaping up, he turned and looked and knew
What birdless dawn, unhallowed by the dew,
Came raging from the northwest!   Half the
    earth
And half the heavens were a burning hearth
Fed fat with grass inflammable as tow!
He shook Fink, yelling: "Mike, we've got to go!
All hell's broke loose!"

                    They cinched the saddles on
With hands that fumbled; mounted and were
    gone,
Like rabbits fleeing from a kiote pack.
They crossed the valley, topped a rise, looked
    back,
Nor dared to gaze.   The firm, familiar world,
It seemed, was melting down, and Chaos swirled
Once more across the transient realms of form
To scatter in the primal atom-storm

The earth's rich dust and potency of dreams.
Infernal geysers gushed, and sudden streams
Of rainbow flux went roaring up the skies
Through ghastly travesties of Paradise,
Where, drowsy in a tropic summertide,
Strange gaudy flowers bloomed and aged and
    died —
Whole seasons in a moment.   Bloody rain,
Blown slant like April silver, spewed the plain
To mock the fallow sod; and where it fell
Anemones and violets of hell
Foreran the fatal summer.

                         Spurs bit deep.
Now down the hill where shadow-haunted sleep
Fell from the broken wind's narcotic breath,
The ponies plunged.   A sheltered draw, where
    death
Seemed brooding in the silence, heard them
    pass.
A hollow, deep with tangled jointed grass,
Snatched at the frantic hoofs.   Now up a slope
They clambered, blowing, at a stumbling lope
And, reined upon the summit, wheeled to stare.
The stallion snorted, and the rearing mare
Screamed at the sight and bolted down the wind.
The writhing Terror, scarce a mile behind,

Appeared to gain; while far to left and right
Its flanks seemed bending in upon the night —
A ten-league python closing on its prey.

No guiding hand was needed for the way;
Blind speed was all.   So little Nature heeds
The fate of men, these blew as tumbleweeds
Before that dwarfing, elemental rage.
A gray wolf bounded from a clump of sage;
A rabbit left its bunchgrass nest and ran
Beside its foe; and neither dreaded Man,
The deadliest of all earth's preying things.
A passing knoll exploded into wings,
And prairie owls, befuddled by the light,
Went tumbling up like patches of the night
The burning tempest tattered.

                                        Leaning low,
The gasping riders let the ponies go,
The little buckskin leading, while the roan
Strove hard a-flank, afraid to be alone
And nickering at whiles.   And he who led,
By brief hypnotic lapses comforted,
Recalled the broad Ohio, heard the horns
The way they used to sing those summer morns
When he and Mike and —.   There the dream
        went wrong
And through his head went running, like a song

That sings itself: 'He tried so hard to come
And warn us; but the grave had made him dumb,
And 'twas to show he loved us that he smiled.'
And of the other terror made a child
Whom often, for a panic moment's span,
Projections from the conscience of the man
Pursued with glaring eyes and claws of flame.
For this the dead arose, for this he came —
That grin upon his face!

A blinding gloom
Crushed down; then, followed by a rolling boom,
There broke a scarlet hurricane of light
That swept the farthest reaches of the night
Where unsuspected hills leaped up aghast.
Already through the hollow they had passed
So recently, the hounding Terror sped!
And now the wind grew hotter. Overhead
Inverted seas of color rolled and broke,
And from the combers of the litten smoke
A stinging spindrift showered.

On they went,
Unconscious of duration or extent,
Of everything but that from which they fled.
Now, sloping to an ancient river bed,

The prairie flattened.   Plunging downward there,
The riders suddenly became aware
How surged, beneath, a mighty shadow-stream —
As though the dying Prairie dreamed a dream
Of yesterage when all her valleys flowed
With Amazons, and monster life abode
Upon her breast and quickened in her womb.
And from that rushing in the flame-smeared
     gloom
Unnumbered outcries blended in a roar.
The headlong ponies struck the sounding shore
And reared upon their haunches.   Far and near,
The valley was a-flood with elk and deer
And buffalo and wolves and antelope
And whatsoever creature slough and slope
Along the path of terror had to give.
Torrential with the common will to live,
The river of unnumbered egos swept
The ponies with it.   But the buckskin kept
The margin where the rabble frayed and thinned
And, breathing with the wheeze of broken wind,
The stallion clung to her.

                              It came to pass
The valley yawned upon a sea of grass
That seemed to heave, as waves of gloom and glare
Ran over it; and, rising here and there,

Tall buttes made islands in the living tide
That roared about them. Still with swinging
    stride
And rhythmic breath the little buckskin ran
Among the herd, that opened like a fan
And scattered. But the roan was losing ground.
His breathing gave a gurgling, hollow sound,
As though his life were gushing from his throat.
His whole frame quivered like a scuttled boat
That slowly sinks; nor did he seem to feel
Upon his flank the biting of the steel
That made him bleed. Fink cut the rifle-boot
And saddle-bags away, to give the brute
Less burden.

       Now it happened, as they neared
A lofty butte whose summit glimmered weird
Beneath the lurid boiling of the sky,
Talbeau was startled by a frantic cry
Behind him; noted that he rode alone,
And, turning in the saddle, saw the roan
Go stumbling down and wither to a heap.
And momently, between a leap and leap,
The love of self was mighty in the man;
For now the Terror left the hills and ran
With giant strides along the grassy plains.
Dear Yesterdays fought wildly for the reins,

To-morrows for the spur.   And then the mare
Heeled to the sawing bit and pawed the air
And halted, prancing.
                                  Once again Talbeau
Looked back to where the sparks were blown as
        snow
Before that blizzard blast of scorching light,
And saw Fink running down the painted night
Like some lost spirit fleeing from the Wrath.

One horse — and who should ride it?   All he
        hath
A man will give for life!   But shall he give
For living that which makes it good to live —
The consciousness of fellowship and trust?
Let fools so prize a pinch of throbbing dust!
Now Fink should ride, and let the rest be hid.
He bounded from the mare; but, as he did,
The panic-stricken pony wheeled about,
Won freedom with a lunge, and joined the
        rout
Of fleeing shadows.
                              Well, 'twas over now —
Perhaps it didn't matter anyhow —
They'd go together now and hunt for Bill!
And momently the world seemed very still

About Talbeau. Then Fink was at his side,
Blank horror in his face. "Come on!" he cried;
"The butte! We'll climb the butte!" And
    once again
Talbeau knew fear.

              Now, gripping hands, the men
Scuttled and dodged athwart the scattered flight
Of shapes that drifted in the flood of light,
A living flotsam; reached the bare butte's base,
Went scrambling up its leaning leeward face
To where the slope grew sheer, and huddled there.
And hotter, hotter, hotter grew the air,
Until their temples sang a fever tune.
The April night became an August noon.
Then, near to swooning in a blast of heat,
They heard the burning breakers boom and beat
About their lofty island, as they lay,
Their gaping mouths pressed hard against the
    clay,
And fought for every breath. Nor could they tell
How long upon a blistered scarp in hell
They gasped and clung. But suddenly at last —
An age in passing, and a moment, passed —
The torture ended, and the cool air came;
And, looking out, they saw the long slant flame
Devour the night to leeward.

By and by
Drab light came seeping through the sullen sky.
They waited there until the morning broke,
And, like a misty moon amid the smoke,
The sun came stealing up.

They found a place
Where rain had scarred the butte wall's western
    face
With many runnels; clambered upward there —
And viewed a panorama of despair.
The wind had died, and not a sound arose
Above those blackened leagues; for even crows
(The solitude embodied in a bird)
Had fled that desolation.   Nothing stirred,
Save here and there a thin gray column grew
From where some draw still smouldered.   And
    they knew
How universal quiet may appal
As violence, and, even as a wall,
Sheer vacancy confine.

No horse, no gun!
Nay, worse; no hint of water hole or run
In all the flat or back among the hills!
Mere hunger is a goad that, ere it kills,
May drive the lean far down the hardest road:
But thirst is both a snaffle and a load;

It gripped them now.   When Mike made bold to
    speak,
His tongue was like a stranger to his cheek.
"Shure, b'y," he croaked; "'tis Sunday morn in
    hell!"
The sound seemed profanation; on it fell
The vast, rebuking silence.

                      Long they gazed
About them, standing silent and amazed
Upon the summit.   West and north and east
They saw too far.   But mystery, at least,
Was in the south, where still the smoke con-
    cealed
The landscape.   Vistas of the unrevealed
Invited Hope to stray there as it please.
And presently there came a little breeze
Out of the dawn.   As of a crowd that waits
Some imminent revealment of the Fates
That toil behind the scenes, a murmur 'woke
Amid the hollow hush.   And now the smoke
Mysteriously stirs, begins to flow,
And giant shadow bulks that loom below
Seem crowding dawnward.   One by one they lift
Above the reek, and trail the ragged drift
About their flanks.   A melancholy scene!
Gray buttes and giddy gulfs that yawn between —

A Titan's labyrinth! But see afar
Where yonder canyon like a purple scar
Cuts zigzag through the waste! Is that a gleam
Of water in its deeps?

                              A stream! A stream!

Now scrambling down the runnels of the rain,
They struck across the devastated plain
Where losers of the night's mad race were strewn
To wait the wolves and crows.

                              Mid-afternoon
Beheld them stripping at the river's bank.
They wallowed in the turbid stream and drank
Delicious beakers in the liquid mud;
Nor drank alone, for here the burning flood
Had flung its panting driftage in the dark.
The valley teemed with life, as though some Ark
That rode the deluge, spewed its cargo here:
Elk, antelope, wolves, bison, rabbits, deer,
Owls, crows — the greatest mingled with the least.
And when the men had drunk, they had a feast
Of liver, bolted dripping from a cow
Dead at the water's lip.

                              Blue shadow now
Was mounting slowly up the canyon steep;
So, seeking for a better place to sleep,

They wandered down the margin of the stream.
'Twas scarce more real than walking in a dream
Of lonely craters in a lunar land
That never thrilled with roots. On either hand
The dwarfing summits soared, grotesque, austere,
And jaggéd fissures, sentinelled with fear,
Led back to mysteries of purple gloom.

They came to where a coulee, like a flume,
Rose steeply to the prairie. Thither hurled,
A roaring freshet of the herd had swirled,
Cascading to the river bed; and there,
Among the trampelled carcasses, the mare
Lay bloated near the water. She had run
With saddle, panniers, powder-horn and gun
Against the wind-thewed fillies of the fire,
And won the heat, to perish at the wire —
A plucky little brute!

VIII

VENGEANCE

They made a camp
Well up above the crawling valley damp,
And where no prowling beast might chance to
come.
There was no fuel; but a flask of rum,
Thanks to the buckskin, dulled the evening chill.
And both grew mellow. Memories of Bill
And other nights possessed the little man;
And on and on his reminiscence ran,
As 'twere the babble of a brook of tears
Gone groping for the ocean of dead years
Too far away to reach. And by and by
The low voice sharpened to an anguished cry:
"O Mike! I said you couldn't miss the cup!"

Then something snapped in Fink and, leaping up,
He seized Talbeau and shook him as a rat
Is shaken by a dog. "Enough of that!"
He yelled; "And, 'faith, I'll sind ye afther Bill
Fer wan more wurrd! Ye fool! I mint to kill!
And, moind me now, ye'd better howld yer lip!"

Talbeau felt murder shudder in the grip
That choked and shook and flung him. Faint
    and dazed,
He sprawled upon the ground. And anger blazed
Within him, like the leaping Northern Light
That gives no heat. He wished to rise and
    fight,
But could not for the horror of it all.
Wild voices thronged the further canyon wall
As Fink raved on; and every word he said
Was like a mutilation of the dead
By some demonic mob.

              And when at length
He heard Mike snoring yonder, still the strength
To rise and kill came not upon Talbeau.
So many moments of the Long Ago
Came pleading; and the gentle might thereof
United with the habit of old love
To weave a spell about the sleeping man.
Then drowsily the pondered facts began
To merge and group, as running colors will,
In new and vaguer patterns. Mike and Bill
Were bickering again. And someone said:
"Let's flip a copper; if it's tails, he's dead;
If heads, he's living. That's the way to tell!"
A spinning copper jangled like a bell.

But even as he stooped to pick it up,
Behold! the coin became a whisky cup
Bored smoothly through the center! "Look at
    this!"
He seemed to shout: "I knew Mike couldn't
    miss!
Bill only played at dying for a joke!"

Then laughter filled his dream, and he awoke.
The dawn was like a stranger's cold regard
Across the lifeless land, grotesquely scarred
As by old sorrow; and the man's dull sense
Of woe, become objective and immense,
Seemed waiting there to crush him.

                              Fink still slept;
And even now, it seemed, his loose mouth kept
A shape for shameless words, as though a breath,
Deep drawn, might set it gloating o'er the death
Of one who loved its jesting and its song.
And while Talbeau sat pondering the wrong
So foully done, and all that had been killed,
And how the laughter of the world was stilled
And all its wine poured out, he seemed to hear
As though a spirit whispered in his ear:
You won't forget I gave my gun to you!
And instantly the deep conviction grew

That 'twas a plea for justice from the slain.
Ah, not without a hand upon the rein,
Nor with an empty saddle, had the mare
Outrun the flame that she might carry there
The means of vengeance!

                        Yet — if Mike were dead!
He shuddered, gazing where the gray sky bled
With morning, like a wound.   He couldn't kill;
Nor did it seem to be the way of Bill
To bid him do it.   Yet the gun was sent.
For what? — To make Mike suffer and repent?
But how?

            Awhile his apathetic gaze
Explored yon thirst- and hunger-haunted maze,
As though he might surprise the answer there.
The answer came.   That region of despair
Should be Mike's Purgatory!   More than Chance
Had fitted circumstance to circumstance
That this should be!   He knew it!   And the plan,
Thus suddenly conceived, possessed the man.
It seemed the might of Bill had been reborn
In him.

            He took the gun and powder horn,
The water flasks and sun-dried bison meat
The panniers gave; then climbing to a seat

Above the sleeper, shouted down to him:
"Get up!"   Along the further canyon rim
A multitude of voices swelled the shout.
Fink started up and yawned and looked about,
Bewildered.   Once again the clamor ran
Along the canyon wall.   The little man,
Now squinting down the pointed rifle, saw
The lifted face go pale, the stubborn jaw
Droop nervelessly.   A twinge of pity stirred
Within him, and he marvelled as he heard
His own voice saying what he wished unsaid:
"It's Bill's own rifle pointing at your head;
Go east, and think of all the wrong you've
      done!"

Fink glanced across his shoulder where the sun
Shone level on the melancholy land;
And, feigning that he didn't understand,
Essayed a careless grin that went awry.
"Bejasus, and we'll not go there, me b'y,"
He said; "for shure 'tis hell widout the lights!"
That one-eyed stare along the rifle sights
Was narrowed to a slit.   A sickening shock
Ran through him at the clucking of the lock.
He clutched his forehead, stammering: "Tal
      beau,
I've been yer frind —."

"I'll give you three to go,"
The other said, "or else you'll follow Bill!
One — two —."

Fink turned and scuttled down the hill;
And at the sight the watcher's eyes grew dim,
For something old and dear had gone from him —
His pride in one who made a clown of Death.
Alas, how much the man would give for breath!
How easily Death made of him the clown!

Now scrambling for a grip, now rolling down,
Mike landed at the bottom of the steep,
And, plunging in the river belly deep,
Struck out in terror for the other shore.
At any moment might the rifle's roar
Crash through that rearward silence, and the
      lead
Come snarling like a hornet at his head —
He felt the spot! Then presently the flood
Began to cool the fever in his blood,
And furtive self-derision stung his pride.
He clambered dripping up the further side
And felt himself a fool! He wouldn't go!
That little whiffet yonder was Talbeau!
And who was this that he, Mike Fink, had feared?
He'd go and see.

A spurt of smoke appeared
Across the river, and a bullet struck —
Spat ping — beside him, spewing yellow muck
Upon his face.   Then every cliff and draw
Rehearsed the sullen thunders of the law
He dared to question.   Stricken strangely weak,
He clutched the clay and watched the powder reek
Trail off with glories of the level sun.
He saw Talbeau pour powder in his gun
And ram the wad.   A second shot might kill!
That brooding like a woman over Bill
Had set the fellow daft.   *A crazy man!*
The notion spurred him.   Springing up, he ran
To where a gully cleft the canyon rim
And, with that one-eyed fury after him,
Fled east.

The very buttes, grotesque and weird,
Seemed startled at the sight of what he feared
And powerless to shield him in his need.
'Twas more than man he fled from; 'twas a deed,
Become alive and subtle as the air,
That turned upon the doer.   Everywhere
It gibbered in the echoes as he fled.
A stream of pictures flitted through his head:
The quiet body in the hearth-lit hall,
The grinning ghost, the flight, the stallion's fall,

The flame girt isle, the spectral morning sun,
And then the finding of the dead man's gun
Beside the glooming river.   Flowing by,
These fused and focused in the deadly eye
He felt behind him.

                    Suddenly the ground
Heaved up and smote him with a crashing
        sound;
And in the vivid moment of his fall
He thought he heard the snarling rifle ball
And felt the one-eyed fury crunch its mark.
Expectant of the swooping of the dark,
He raised his eyes. — The sun was shining
        still;
It peeped about the shoulder of a hill
And viewed him with a quizzifying stare.
He looked behind him.   Nothing followed
        there;
But Silence, big with dread-begotten sound,
Dismayed him; and the steeps that hemmed him
        round
Seemed plotting with a more than human guile.
He rose and fled; but every little while
A sense of eyes behind him made him pause;
And always down the maze of empty draws
It seemed a sound of feet abruptly ceased.

Now trotting, walking now, he labored east;
And when at length the burning zenith beat
Upon him, and the summits swam with heat,
And on the winding gullies fell no shade,
He came to where converging gulches made
A steep-walled basin for the blinding glare.
Here, fanged and famished, crawled the prickly
    pear;
Malevolent with thirst, the soap weed thrust
Its barbed stilettos from the arid dust,
Defiant of the rain-withholding blue:
And in the midst a lonely scrub oak grew,
A crooked dwarf that, in the pictured bog
Of its own shadow, squatted like a frog.
Fink, panting, flung himself beneath its boughs.
A mighty magic in the noonday drowse
Allayed the driving fear.   A waking dream
Fulfilled a growing wish.   He saw the stream
Far off as from a space-commanding height.
And now a phantasy of rapid flight
Transported him above the sagging land,
And with a sudden swoop he seemed to stand
Once more upon the shimmering river's brink.
His eyes drank deep; but when his mouth would
    drink,
A giant hornet from the other shore —
The generating center of a roar
That shook the world — snarled by.

He started up,
And saw the basin filling as a cup
With purple twilight! Gazing all around
Where still the flitting ghost of some great sound
Troubled the crags a moment, then was mute,
He saw along the shoulder of a butte,
A good three hundred paces from the oak,
A slowly spreading streak of rifle smoke
And knew the deadly eye was lurking there.
He fled again.

About him everywhere
Amid the tangled draws now growing dim,
Weird witnesses took cognizance of him
And told abroad the winding way he ran.
He halted only when his breath began
To stab his throat. And lo, the staring eye
Was quenched with night! No further need he
    fly
Till dawn. And yet —. He held his breath to
    hear
If footsteps followed. Silence smote his ear,
The gruesome silence of the hearth-lit hall,
More dread than sound. Against the gully wall
He shrank and huddled with his eyes shut tight,
For fear a presence, latent in the night,
Should walk before him.

                              Then it seemed he ran
Through regions alien to the feet of Man,
A weary way despite the speed of sleep,
And came upon a river flowing deep
Between black crags that made the sky a well.
And eerily the feeble starlight fell
Upon the flood with water lilies strown.
But when he stooped, the stream began to moan,
And suddenly from every lily pad
A white face bloomed, unutterably sad
And bloody browed.

                              A swift, erasing flame
Across the dusky picture, morning came.
Mike lay a moment, blinking at the blue;
And then the fear of yesterday broke through
The clinging drowse.   For lo, on every side
The paling summits watched him, Argus-eyed,
In hushed anticipation of a roar.
He fled.

                     All day, intent to see once more
The open plain before the night should fall,
He labored on.   But many a soaring wall
Annulled some costly distance he had won;
And misdirected gullies, white with sun,
Seemed spitefully to baffle his desire.

The deeps went blue; on mimic dome and spire
The daylight faded to a starry awe.
Mike slept; and lo, they marched along the
    draw —
Or rather burned — tall, radiantly white!
A hushed procession, tunnelling the night,
They came, with lips that smiled and brows that
    bled,
And each one bore a tin cup on its head,
A brimming cup.   But ever as they came
Before him, like a draught-struck candle flame
They shuddered and were snuffed.

                        'Twas deep night yet
When Mike awoke and felt the terror sweat
Upon his face, the prickling of his hair.
Afraid to sleep, he paced the gully there
Until the taller buttes were growing gray.
He brooded much on flowing streams that day.
As with a weight, he stooped; his feet were slow;
He shuffled.   Less and less he feared Talbeau
Behind him.   More and more he feared the
    night
Before him.   Any hazard in the light,
Or aught that might befall 'twixt living men,
Were better than to be alone again
And meet that dream!

                          The deeps began to fill
With purple haze.   Bewildered, boding ill,
A moaning wind awoke.   'Twould soon be dark.
Mike pondered.   Twice Talbeau had missed the
     mark.
Perhaps he hadn't really meant to hit.
And surely now that flaring anger fit
Had burned away.   It wasn't like the man
To hold a grudge.   Mike halted, and began
To grope for words regretful of the dead,
Persuasive words about a heart that bled
For Bill.   'Twas all a terrible mistake.
"Plase now, a little dhrop fer owld toime's sake!"
With troublesome insistence, that refrain
Kept running through the muddle of his brain
And disarranged the words he meant to speak.
The trickle of a tear along his cheek
Consoled him.   Soon his suffering would end.
Talbeau would see him weeping for his friend —
Talbeau had water!

                          Now the heights burned red
To westward.   With a choking clutch of dread
He noted how the dusk was gathering
Along the draws — a trap about to spring.
He cupped his hands about his mouth and cried:
"Talbeau! Talbeau!"   Despairing voices died

Among the summits, and the lost wind pined.
It made Talbeau seem infinitely kind —
The one thing human in a ghostly land.
Where was he ? Just a touch of that warm hand
Would thwart the dark ! Mike sat against a wall
And brooded.

       By and by a skittering fall
Of pebbles at his back aroused the man.
He scrambled to his feet and turned to scan
The butte that sloped above him. Where the
    glow
Still washed the middle height, he saw Talbeau
Serenely perched upon a ledge of clay !
And Mike forgot the words he meant to say,
The fitted words, regretful of his deed.
A forthright, stark sincerity of need
Rough hewed the husky, incoherent prayer
He shouted to that Lord of water there
Above the gloom. A little drop to drink
For old time's sake !

       Talbeau regarded Fink
Awhile in silence ; then his thin lips curled.
"You spilled the only drink in all the world !
Go on," he said, "and think of what you've
    done !"
Beyond the pointed muzzle of his gun

He saw the big man wither to a squat
And tremble, like a bison when the shot
Just nips the vital circle.   Then he saw
A stooping figure hurry down the draw,
Grow dim, and vanish in the failing light.

'Twas long before Talbeau could sleep that night.
Some questioner, insistently perverse,
Assailed him and compelled him to rehearse
The justifying story of the friend
Betrayed and slain.   But when he reached the
      end,
Still unconvinced the questioner was there
To taunt him with that pleading of despair —
For old time's sake!   Sleep brought him little
      rest;
For what the will denied, the heart confessed
In mournful dreams.   And when the first faint
      gray
Aroused him, and he started on his way,
He knew the stubborn questioner had won.
No brooding on the wrong that Mike had done
Could still that cry: "Plase now, fer owld
      toime's sake,
A little dhrop!"   It made his eyeballs ache
With tears of pity that he couldn't shed.
No other dawn, save that when Bill lay dead

And things began to stare about the hall,
Had found the world so empty.   After all,
What man could know the way another trod?
And who was he, Talbeau, to play at God?
Let one who curbs the wind and brews the
          rain
Essay the subtler portioning of pain
To souls that err!   Talbeau would make amends!
Once more they'd drink together and be friends.
How often they had shared!

                              He struck a trot,
Eyes fixed upon the trail.   The sun rose hot;
Noon poured a blinding glare along the draws;
And still the trail led on, without a pause
To show where Mike had rested.   Thirst began
To be a burden on the little man;
His progress dwindled to a dragging pace.
But when he tipped the flask, that pleading
          face
Arose before him, and a prayer denied
Came mourning back to thrust his need aside —
A little drop!   How Mike must suffer now!
"I'm not so very thirsty, anyhow,"
He told himself.   And almost any bend
Might bring him on a sudden to his friend.
He'd wait and share the water.

                              Every turn
Betrayed a hope.   The west began to burn;
Flared red; went ashen; and the stars came out
Dreams, colored by an unacknowledged doubt,
Perplexed the trail he followed in his sleep;
And dreary hours before the tallest steep
Saw dawn, Talbeau was waiting for the day.

Till noon he read a writing in the clay
That bade him haste; for now from wall to wall
The footmarks wandered, like the crabbéd scrawl
An old man writes.   They told a gloomy tale.
And then the last dim inkling of a trail
Was lost upon a patch of hardened ground!

The red west saw him, like a nervous hound
That noses vainly for the vanished track,
Still plunging into gullies, doubling back,
And pausing now and then to hurl a yell
Among the ululating steeps.   Night fell.
The starlit buttes still heard him panting by,
And summits weird with midnight caught his cry
To answer, mocking.

                       Morning brought despair;
Nor did he get much comfort of his prayer:
"God, let me find him!   Show me where to go!"
Some greater, unregenerate Talbeau

Was God that morning; for the lesser heard
His own bleak answer echoed word for word:
Go on, and think of all the wrong you've done!

His futile wish to hasten sped the sun.
That day, as he recalled it in the dark,
Was like the spinning of a burning arc.
He nodded, and the night was but a swoon;
And morning neighbored strangely with the noon;
And evening was the noon's penumbral haze.

No further ran the reckoning of days.
'Twas evening when at last he stooped to stare
Upon a puzzling trail. A wounded bear,
It seemed, had dragged its rump across the sands
That floored the gullies now. But sprawling
    hands
Had marked the margin! Why was that? No
    doubt
Mike too had tarried here to puzzle out
What sort of beast had passed. And yet — how
    queer —
'Twas plain no human feet had trodden here!
A trail of hands! That throbbing in his brain
Confused his feeble efforts to explain;
And hazily he wondered if he slept
And dreamed again. Tenaciously he kept

His eyes upon the trail and labored on,
Lest, swooping like a hawk, another dawn
Should snatch that hope away.

                                    A sentry crow,
Upon a sunlit summit, saw Talbeau
And croaked alarm.   The noise of many wings,
In startled flight, and raucous chatterings
Arose.   What feast was interrupted there
A little way ahead ?   'Twould be the bear!
He plodded on.   The intervening space
Sagged under him;   and, halting at the place
Where late the flock had been, he strove to break
A grip of horror.   Surely now he'd wake
And see the morning quicken in the skies !

The thing remained ! — It hadn't any eyes —
The pilfered sockets bore a pleading stare !

A long, hoarse wail of anguish and despair
Aroused the echoes.   Answering, arose
Once more the jeering chorus of the crows.

THE SONG OF HUGH GLASS

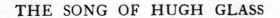

TO SIGURD, SCARCELY THREE

When you are old enough to know
The joys of kite and boat and bow
And other suchlike splendid things
That boyhood's rounded decade brings,
I shall not give you tropes and rhymes ;
But, rising to those rousing times,
I shall ply well the craft I know
Of shaping kite and boat and bow,
For you shall teach me once again
The goodly art of being ten.

Meanwhile, as on a rainy day
When 'tis not possible to play,
The while you do your best to grow
I ply the other craft I know
And strive to build for you the mood
Of daring and of fortitude
With fitted word and shapen phrase,
Against those later wonder-days
When first you glimpse the world of men
Beyond the bleaker side of ten.

SONG OF HUGH GLASS

I

GRAYBEARD AND GOLDHAIR

The year was eighteen hundred twenty three.

'Twas when the guns that blustered at the Ree
Had ceased to brag, and ten score martial clowns
Retreated from the unwhipped river towns,
Amid the scornful laughter of the Sioux.
A withering blast the arid South still blew,
And creeks ran thin beneath the glaring sky;
For 'twas a month ere honking geese would fly
Southward before the Great White Hunter's face:
And many generations of their race,
As bow-flung arrows, now have fallen spent.

It happened then that Major Henry went
With eighty trappers up the dwindling Grand,
Bound through the weird, unfriending barren-land
For where the Big Horn meets the Yellowstone;
And old Hugh Glass went with them.
                                          Large of bone,

129

Deep-chested, that his great heart might have
    play,
Gray-bearded, gray of eye and crowned with gray
Was Glass.   It seemed he never had been young;
And, for the grudging habit of his tongue,
None knew the place or season of his birth.
Slowly he 'woke to anger or to mirth;
Yet none laughed louder when the rare mood
    fell,
And hate in him was like a still, white hell,
A thing of doom not lightly reconciled.
What memory he kept of wife or child
Was never told; for when his comrades sat
About the evening fire with pipe and chat,
Exchanging talk of home and gentler days,
Old Hugh stared long upon the pictured blaze,
And what he saw went upward in the smoke.

But once, as with an inner lightning stroke,
The veil was rent, and briefly men discerned
What pent-up fires of selfless passion burned
Beneath the still gray smoldering of him.
There was a rakehell lad, called Little Jim,
Jamie or Petit Jacques; for scarce began
The downy beard to mark him for a man.
Blue-eyed was he and femininely fair.
A maiden might have coveted his hair

That trapped the sunlight in its tangled skein:
So, tardily, outflowered the wild blond strain
That gutted Rome grown overfat in sloth.
A Ganymedes haunted by a Goth
Was Jamie.   When the restive ghost was laid,
He seemed some fancy-ridden child who played
At manliness 'mid all those bearded men.
The sternest heart was drawn to Jamie then.
But his one mood ne'er linked two hours together.
To schedule Jamie's way, as prairie weather,
Was to get fact by wedding doubt and whim;
For very lightly slept that ghost in him.
No cloudy brooding went before his wrath
That, like a thunder-squall, recked not its path,
But raged upon what happened in its way.
Some called him brave who saw him on that day
When Ashley stormed a bluff town of the Ree,
And all save beardless Jamie turned to flee
For shelter from that steep, lead-harrowed slope.
Yet, hardly courage, but blind rage agrope
Inspired the foolish deed.

                                'Twas then old Hugh
Tore off the gray mask, and the heart shone
        through.
For, halting in a dry, flood-guttered draw,
The trappers rallied, looked aloft and saw

That travesty of war against the sky.
Out of a breathless hush, the old man's cry
Leaped shivering, an anguished cry and wild
As of some mother fearing for her child,
And up the steep he went with mighty bounds.
Long afterward the story went the rounds,
How old Glass fought that day. With gun for
     club,
Grim as a grizzly fighting for a cub,
He laid about him, cleared the way, and so,
Supported by the firing from below,
Brought Jamie back. And when the deed was
     done,
Taking the lad upon his knee: "My Son,
Brave men are not ashamed to fear," said Hugh,
"And I've a mind to make a man of you;
So here's your first acquaintance with the law!"
Whereat he spanked the lad with vigorous paw
And, having done so, limped away to bed;
For, wounded in the hip, the old man bled.

It was a month before he hobbled out,
And Jamie, like a fond son, hung about
The old man's tent and waited upon him.
And often would the deep gray eyes grow dim
With gazing on the boy; and there would go —
As though Spring-fire should waken out of snow —

A wistful light across that mask of gray.
And once Hugh smiled his enigmatic way,
While poring long on Jamie's face, and said:
"So with their sons are women brought to bed,
Sore wounded!"
                    Thus united were the two:
And some would dub the old man 'Mother Hugh';
While those in whom all living waters sank
To some dull inner pool that teemed and stank
With formless evil, into that morass
Gazed, and saw darkly there, as in a glass,
The foul shape of some weakly envied sin.
For each man builds a world and dwells therein.
Nor could these know what mocking ghost of
        Spring
Stirred Hugh's gray world with dreams of blossom-
        ing
That wooed no seed to swell or bird to sing.
So might a dawn-struck digit of the moon
Dream back the rain of some old lunar June
And ache through all its craters to be green.
Little they know what life's one love can mean,
Who shrine it in a bower of peace and bliss:
Pang dwelling in a puckered cicatrice
More truly figures this belated love.
Yet very precious was the hurt thereof,
Grievous to bear, too dear to cast away.

Now Jamie went with Hugh; but who shall say
If 'twas a warm heart or a wind of whim,
Love, or the rover's teasing itch in him,
Moved Jamie? Howsoe'er, 'twas good to see
Graybeard and Goldhair riding knee to knee,
One age in young adventure. One who saw
Has likened to a February thaw
Hugh's mellow mood those days; and truly so,
For when the tempering Southwest wakes to blow
A phantom April over melting snow,
Deep in the North some new white wrath is
        brewed.
Out of a dim-trailed inner solitude
The old man summoned many a stirring story,
Lived grimly once, but now shot through with
        glory
Caught from the wondering eyes of him who
        heard —
Tales jaggéd with the bleak unstudied word,
Stark saga-stuff. "A fellow that I knew,"
So nameless went the hero that was Hugh —
A mere pelt merchant, as it seemed to him;
Yet trailing epic thunders through the dim,
Whist world of Jamie's awe.
                                    And so they went,
One heart, it seemed, and that heart well content
With tale and snatch of song and careless laughter.

Never before, and surely never after,
The gray old man seemed nearer to his youth —
That myth that somehow had to be the truth,
Yet could not be convincing any more.

Now when the days of travel numbered four
And nearer drew the barrens with their need,
On Glass, the hunter, fell the task to feed
Those four score hungers when the game should
　　fail.
For no young eye could trace so dim a trail,
Or line the rifle sights with speed so true.
Nor might the wistful Jamie go with Hugh;
"For," so Hugh chaffed, "my trick of getting
　　game
Might teach young eyes to put old eyes to
　　shame.
An old dog never risks his only bone."
'Wolves prey in packs, the lion hunts alone'
Is somewhat nearer what he should have meant.

And so with merry jest the old man went;
And so they parted at an unseen gate
That even then some gust of moody fate
Clanged to betwixt them; each a tale to spell —
One in the nightmare scrawl of dreams from hell,
One in the blistering trail of days a-crawl,

Venomous footed.   Nor might it ere befall
These two should meet in after days and be
Graybeard and Goldhair riding knee to knee,
Recounting with a bluff, heroic scorn
The haps of either tale.

                    'Twas early morn
When Hugh went forth, and all day Jamie rode
With Henry's men, while more and more the
    goad
Of eager youth sore fretted him, and made
The dusty progress of the cavalcade
The journey of a snail flock to the moon;
Until the shadow-weaving afternoon
Turned many fingers nightward — then he fled,
Pricking his horse, nor deigned to turn his head
At any dwindling voice of reprimand;
For somewhere in the breaks along the Grand
Surely Hugh waited with a goodly kill.
Hoofbeats of ghostly steeds on every hill,
Mysterious, muffled hoofs on every bluff!
Spurred echo horses clattering up the rough
Confluent draws!   These flying Jamie heard.
The lagging air droned like the drowsy word
Of one who tells weird stories late at night.
Half headlong joy and half delicious fright,
His day-dream's pace outstripped the plunging
    steed's.

Lean galloper in a wind of splendid deeds,
Like Hugh's, he seemed unto himself, until,
Snorting, a-haunch above a breakneck hill,
The horse stopped short — then Jamie was aware
Of lonesome flatlands fading skyward there
Beneath him, and, zigzag on either hand,
A purple haze denoted how the Grand
Forked wide 'twixt sunset and the polar star.

A-tiptoe in the stirrups, gazing far,
He saw no Hugh nor any moving thing,
Save for a welter of cawing crows, a-wing
About some banquet in the further hush.
One faint star, set above the fading blush
Of sunset, saw the coming night, and grew.
With hand for trumpet, Jamie gave halloo;
And once again.   For answer, the horse neighed.
Some vague mistrust now made him half afraid —
Some formless dread that stirred beneath the will
As far as sleep from waking.
                                        Down the hill,
Close-footed in the skitter of the shale,
The spurred horse floundered to the solid vale
And galloped to the northwest, whinnying.
The outstripped air moaned like a wounded thing,
But Jamie gave the lie unto his dread.
"The old man's camping out to-night," he said,

"Somewhere about the forks, as like as not;
And there'll be hunks of fresh meat steaming hot,
And fighting stories by a dying fire!"

The sunset reared a luminous phantom spire
That, crumbling, sifted ashes down the sky.

Now, pausing, Jamie sent a searching cry
Into the twilit river-skirting brush,
And in the vast denial of the hush
The champing of the snaffled horse seemed loud.

Then, startling as a voice beneath a shroud,
A muffled boom woke somewhere up the stream
And, like vague thunder hearkened in a dream,
Drawled back to silence. Now, with heart a-
    bound,
Keen for the quarter of the perished sound,
The lad spurred gaily; for he doubted not
His cry had brought Hugh's answering rifle shot.
The laggard air was like a voice that sang,
And Jamie half believed he sniffed the tang
Of woodsmoke and the smell of flesh a-roast;
When presently before him, like a ghost,
Upstanding, huge in twilight, arms flung wide,
A gray form loomed. The wise horse reared and
    shied,

Snorting his inborn terror of the bear!
And in the whirlwind of a moment there,
Betwixt the brute's hoarse challenge and the
    charge,
The lad beheld, upon the grassy marge
Of a small spring that bullberries stooped to scan,
A ragged heap that should have been a man,
A huddled, broken thing — and it was Hugh!

There was no need for any closer view.
As, on the instant of a lightning flash
Ere yet the split gloom closes with a crash,
A landscape stares with every circumstance
Of rock and shrub — just so the fatal chance
Of Hugh's one shot, made futile with surprise,
Was clear to Jamie.   Then before his eyes
The light whirled in a giddy dance of red;
And, doubting not the crumpled thing was dead
That was a friend, with but a skinning knife
He would have striven for the hated life
That triumphed there: but with a shriek of fright
The mad horse bolted through the falling night,
And Jamie, fumbling at his rifle boot,
Heard the brush crash behind him where the brute
Came headlong, close upon the straining flanks.
But when at length low-lying river banks —
White rubble in the gloaming — glimmered near,

A swift thought swept the mind of Jamie clear
Of anger and of anguish for the dead.
Scarce seemed the raging beast a thing to dread,
But some foul-playing braggart to outwit.
Now hurling all his strength upon the bit,
He sank the spurs, and with a groan of pain
The plunging horse, obedient to the rein,
Swerved sharply streamward.   Sliddering in the
        sand,
The bear shot past.   And suddenly the Grand
Loomed up beneath and rose to meet the pair
That rode a moment upon empty air,
Then smote the water in a shower of spray.
And when again the slowly ebbing day
Came back to them, a-drip from nose to flank,
The steed was scrambling up the further bank,
And Jamie saw across the narrow stream,
Like some vague shape of fury in a dream,
The checked beast ramping at the water's rim.
Doubt struggled with a victor's thrill in him,
As, hand to buckle of the rifle-sheath,
He thought of dampened powder; but beneath
The rawhide flap the gun lay snug and dry.
Then as the horse wheeled and the mark went by—
A patch of shadow dancing upon gray —
He fired.   A sluggish thunder trailed away;
The spreading smoke-rack lifted slow, and there,

Floundering in a seethe of foam, the bear
Hugged yielding water for the foe that slew!

Triumphant, Jamie wondered what old Hugh
Would think of such a "trick of getting game"!
"Young eyes" indeed! — And then that memory
    came,
Like a dull blade thrust back into a wound.
One moment 'twas as though the lad had swooned
Into a dream-adventure, waking there
To sicken at the ghastly land, a-stare
Like some familiar face gone strange at last.
But as the hot tears came, the moment passed.
Song snatches, broken tales — a troop forlorn,
Like merry friends of eld come back to mourn —
O'erwhelmed him there.   And when the black
    bulk churned
The star-flecked stream no longer, Jamie turned,
Recrossed the river and rode back to Hugh.

A burning twist of valley grasses threw
Blear light about the region of the spring.
Then Jamie, torch aloft and shuddering,
Knelt there beside his friend, and moaned: "O
    Hugh,
If I had been with you — just been with you!
We might be laughing now — and you are dead."

With gentle hand he turned the hoary head
That he might see the good gray face again.
The torch burned out, the dark swooped back, and
    then
His grief was frozen with an icy plunge
In horror. 'Twas as though a bloody sponge
Had wiped the pictured features from a slate!
So, pillaged by an army drunk with hate,
Home stares upon the homing refugee.
A red gout clung where either brow should be;
The haughty nose lay crushed amid the beard,
Thick with slow ooze, whence like a devil leered
The battered mouth convulsed into a grin.

Nor did the darkness cover, for therein
Some torch, unsnuffed, with blear funereal flare,
Still painted upon black that alien stare
To make the lad more terribly alone.

Then in the gloom there rose a broken moan,
Quick stifled; and it seemed that something stirred
    stirred
About the body. Doubting that he heard,
The lad felt, with a panic catch of breath,
Pale vagrants from the legendry of death
Potential in the shadows there. But when
The motion and the moaning came again,

Hope, like a shower at daybreak, cleansed the
      dark,
And in the lad's heart something like a lark
Sang   morning.   Bending   low,   he   crooned:
      "Hugh, Hugh,
It's Jamie — don't you know? — I'm here with
      you."

As one who in a nightmare strives to tell —
Shouting across the gap of some dim hell —
What things assail him; so it seemed Hugh heard,
And flung some unintelligible word
Athwart the muffling distance of his swoon.

Now kindled by the yet unrisen moon,
The East went pale; and like a naked thing
A little wind ran vexed and shivering
Along the dusk, till Jamie shivered too
And worried lest 'twere bitter cold where Hugh
Hung clutching at the bleak, raw edge of life.
So Jamie rose, and with his hunting-knife
Split wood and built a fire.   Nor did he fear
The staring face now, for he found it dear
With the warm presence of a friend returned.
The fire made cozy chatter as it burned,
And reared a tent of light in that lone place.
Then Jamie set about to bathe the face

With water from the spring, oft crooning low,
"It's Jamie here beside you — don't you know?"
Yet came no answer save the labored breath
Of one who wrestled mightily with Death
Where watched no referee to call the foul.

The moon now cleared the world's end, and the
    owl
Gave voice unto the wizardry of light;
While in some dim-lit chancel of the night,
Snouts to the goddess, wolfish corybants
Intoned their wild antiphonary chants —
The oldest, saddest worship in the world.

And Jamie watched until the firelight swirled
Softly about him.   Sound and glimmer merged
To make an eerie void, through which he urged
With frantic spur some whirlwind of a steed
That made the way as glass beneath his speed,
Yet scarce kept pace with something dear that fled
On, ever on — just half a dream ahead:
Until it seemed, by some vague shape dismayed,
He cried aloud for Hugh, and the steed neighed —
A neigh that was a burst of light, not sound.
And Jamie, sprawling on the dewy ground,
Knew that his horse was sniffing at his hair,
While, mumbling through the early morning air,

There came a roll of many hoofs — and then
He saw the swinging troop of Henry's men
A-canter up the valley with the sun.

Of all Hugh's comrades crowding round, not one
But would have given heavy odds on Death;
For, though the graybeard fought with sobbing
        breath,
No man, it seemed, might break upon the hip
So stern a wrestler with the strangling grip
That made the neck veins like a purple thong
Tangled with knots.   Nor might Hugh tarry long
There where the trail forked outward far and
        dim;
Or so it seemed.   And when they lifted him,
His moan went treble like a song of pain,
He was so tortured.   Surely it were vain
To hope he might endure the toilsome ride
Across the barrens.   Better let him bide
There on the grassy couch beside the spring.
And, furthermore, it seemed a foolish thing
That eighty men should wait the issue there;
For dying is a game of solitaire
And all men play the losing hand alone.

But when at noon he had not ceased to moan,
And fought still like the strong man he had been,

There grew a vague mistrust that he might win,
And all this be a tale for wondering ears.
So Major Henry called for volunteers,
Two men among the eighty who would stay
To wait on Glass and keep the wolves away
Until he did whatever he should do.
All quite agreed 'twas bitter bread for Hugh,
Yet none, save Jamie, felt in duty bound
To run the risk — until the hat went round,
And pity wakened, at the silver's clink,
In Jules Le Bon.

        'He would not have them think
That mercenary motives prompted him.
But somehow just the grief of Little Jim
Was quite sufficient — not to mention Hugh.
He weighed the risk.   As everybody knew,
The Rickarees were scattered to the West:
The late campaign had stirred a hornet's nest
To fill the land with stingers (which was so),
And yet —'
        Three days a southwest wind may blow
False April with no drop of dew at heart.
So Jules ran on, while, ready for the start,
The pawing horses nickered and the men,
Impatient in their saddles, yawned.   And then,
With brief advice, a round of bluff good-byes

And some few reassuring backward cries,
The troop rode up the valley with the day.

Intent upon his friend, with naught to say,
Sat Jamie; while Le Bon discussed at length
The reasonable limits of man's strength —
A self-conducted dialectic strife
That made absurd all argument for life
And granted but a fresh-dug hole for Hugh.
'Twas half like murder.   Yet it seemed Jules knew
Unnumbered tales accordant with the case,
Each circumstantial as to time and place
And furnished with a death's head colophon.

Vivaciously despondent, Jules ran on.
'Did he not share his judgment with the rest?
You see, 'twas some contusion of the chest
That did the trick — heart, lungs and all that,
     mixed
In such a way they never could be fixed.
A bear's hug — ugh!'
                            And often Jamie winced
At some knife-thrust of reason that convinced
Yet left him sick with unrelinquished hope.
As one who in a darkened room might grope
For some belovéd face, with shuddering
Anticipation of a clammy thing;

So in the lad's heart sorrow fumbled round
For some old joy to lean upon, and found
The stark, cold something Jamie knew was there.
Yet, womanlike, he stroked the hoary hair
Or bathed the face; while Jules found tales to
    tell —
Lugubriously garrulous.
                        Night fell.
At sundown, day-long winds are like to veer;
So, summoning a mood of relished fear,
Le Bon remembered dire alarms by night —
The swoop of savage hordes, the desperate fight
Of men outnumbered: and, like him of old,
In all that made Jules shudder as he told,
His the great part — a man by field and flood
Fate-tossed.   Upon the gloom he limned in blood
Their situation's possibilities:
Two men against the fury of the Rees —
A game in which two hundred men had failed!
He pointed out how little it availed
To run the risk for one as good as dead;
Yet, Jules Le Bon meant every word he said,
And had a scalp to lose, if need should be.

That night through Jamie's dreaming swarmed
    the Ree.
Gray-souled, he wakened to a dawn of gray,

And felt that something strong had gone away,
Nor knew what thing.   Some whisper of the will
Bade him rejoice that Hugh was living still;
But Hugh, the real, seemed somehow otherwhere.
Jules, snug and snoring in his blanket there,
Was half a life the nearer.   Just so, pain
Is nearer than the peace we seek in vain,
And by its very sting compells belief.
Jules woke, and with a fine restraint of grief
Saw early dissolution.   'One more night,
And then the poor old man would lose the fight —
Ah, such a man!'
                         A day and night crept by,
And yet the stubborn fighter would not die,
But grappled with the angel.   All the while,
With some conviction, but with more of guile,
Jules colonized the vacancy with Rees;
Till Jamie felt that looseness of the knees
That comes of oozing courage.   Many men
May tower for a white-hot moment, when
The wild blood surges at a sudden shock;
But when, insistent as a ticking clock,
Blind peril haunts and whispers, fewer dare.
Dread hovered in the hushed and moony air
The long night through; nor might a fire be lit,
Lest some far-seeing foe take note of it.
And day-long Jamie scanned the blank sky rim

For hoof-flung dust clouds; till there woke in him
A childish anger — dumb for ruth and shame —
That Hugh so dallied.
                    But the fourth dawn came
And with it lulled the fight, as on a field
Where broken armies sleep but will not yield.
Or had one conquered? Was it Hugh or Death?
The old man breathed with faintly fluttering
      breath,
Nor did his body shudder as before.
Jules triumphed sadly. 'It would soon be o'er;
So men grew quiet when they lost their grip
And did not care. At sundown he would slip
Into the deeper silence.'
                    Jamie wept,
Unwitting how a furtive gladness crept
Into his heart that gained a stronger beat.
So cities, long beleaguered, take defeat —
Unto themselves half traitors.
                    Jules began
To dig a hole that might conceal a man;
And, as his sheath knife broke the stubborn sod,
He spoke in kindly vein of Life and God
And Mutability and Rectitude.
The immemorial funerary mood
Brought tears, mute tribute to the mother-dust;
And Jamie, seeing, felt each cutting thrust
Less like a stab into the flesh of Hugh.

The sun crept up and down the arc of blue
And through the air a chill of evening ran;
But, though the grave yawned, waiting for the
    man,
The man seemed scarce yet ready for the grave.

Now prompted by a coward or a knave
That lurked in him, Le Bon began to hear
Faint sounds that to the lad's less cunning ear
Were silence; more like tremors of the ground
They were, Jules said, than any proper sound —
Thus one detected horsemen miles away.
For many moments big with fate, he lay,
Ear pressed to earth; then rose and shook his
    head
As one perplexed. "There's something wrong,"
    he said.
And — as at daybreak whiten winter skies,
Agape and staring with a wild surmise —
The lad's face whitened at the other's word.
Jules could not quite interpret what he heard;
A hundred horse might noise their whereabouts
In just that fashion; yet he had his doubts.
It could be bison moving, quite as well.
But if 'twere Rees — there'd be a tale to tell
That two men he might name should never hear.
He reckoned scalps that Fall were selling dear,

In keeping with the limited supply.
Men, fit to live, were not afraid to die!

Then, in that caution suits not courage ill,
Jules saddled up and cantered to the hill,
A white dam set against the twilight stream;
And as a horseman riding in a dream
The lad beheld him; watched him clamber up
To where the dusk, as from a brimming cup,
Ran over; saw him pause against the gloom,
Portentous, huge — a brooder upon doom.
What did he look upon?

                Some moments passed;
Then suddenly it seemed as though a blast
Of wind, keen-cutting with the whips of sleet,
Smote horse and rider. Haunched on huddled feet,
The steed shrank from the ridge, then, rearing,
    wheeled
And took the rubbly incline fury-heeled.

Those days and nights, like seasons creeping slow,
Had told on Jamie. Better blow on blow
Of evil hap, with doom seen clear ahead,
Than that monotonous, abrasive dread,
Blind gnawer at the soul-thews of the blind.
Thin-worn, the last heart-string that held him
    kind;

Strung taut, the final tie that kept him true
Now snapped in Jamie, as he saw the two
So goaded by some terrifying sight.
Death riding with the vanguard of the Night,
Life dwindling yonder with the rear of Day!
What choice for one whom panic swept away
From moorings in the sanity of will?

Jules came and summed the vision of the hill
In one hoarse cry that left no word to say:
"Rees! Saddle up! We've got to get away!"

Small wit had Jamie left to ferret guile,
But fumblingly obeyed Le Bon; the while
Jules knelt beside the man who could not flee:
For big hearts lack not time for charity
However thick the blows of fate may fall.
Yet, in that Jules Le Bon was practical,
He could not quite ignore a hunting knife,
A flint, a gun, a blanket — gear of life
Scarce suited to the customs of the dead!

And Hugh slept soundly in his ample bed,
Star-canopied and blanketed with night,
Unwitting how Venality and Fright
Made hot the westward trail of Henry's men.

II

THE AWAKENING

No one may say what time elapsed, or when
The slumberous shadow lifted over Hugh:
But some globose immensity of blue
Enfolded him at last, within whose light
He seemed to float, as some faint swimmer might,
A deep beneath and overhead a deep.
So one late plunged into the lethal sleep,
A spirit diver fighting for his breath,
Swoops through the many-fathomed glooms of
    death,
Emerging in a daylight strange and new.

Rousing a languid wonder, came on Hugh
The quiet, steep-arched splendor of the day.
Agrope for some dim memory, he lay
Upon his back, and watched a lucent fleece
Fade in the blue profundity of peace
As did the memory he sought in vain.
Then with a stirring of mysterious pain,

Old habit of the body bade him rise;
But when he would obey, the hollow skies
Broke as a bubble punctured, and went out.

Again he woke, and with a drowsy doubt,
Remote unto his horizontal gaze
He saw the world's end kindle to a blaze
And up the smoky steep pale heralds run.
And when at length he knew it for the sun,
Dawn found the darkling reaches of his mind,
Where in the twilight he began to find
Strewn shards and torsos of familiar things.
As from the rubble in a place of kings
Men school the dream to build the past anew,
So out of dream and fragment builded Hugh,
And came upon the reason of his plight:
The bear's attack — the shot — and then the
     night
Wherein men talked as ghosts above a grave.

Some consciousness of will the memory gave:
He would get up.   The painful effort spent
Made the wide heavens billow as a tent
Wind-struck, the shaken prairie sag and roll.
Some moments with an effort at control
He swayed, half raised upon his arms, until
The dizzy cosmos righted, and was still.

Then would he stand erect and be again
The man he was: an overwhelming pain
Smote him to earth, and one unruly limb
Refused the weight and crumpled under him.

Sickened with torture he lay huddled there,
Gazing about him with a great despair
Proportioned to the might that felt the chain.
Far-flung as dawn, collusive sky and plain
Stared bleak denial back.
                                          Why strive at all? —
That vacancy about him like a wall,
Yielding as light, a granite scarp to climb!
Some little waiting on the creep of time,
Abandonment to circumstance; and then —

Here flashed a sudden thought of Henry's men
Into his mind and drove the gloom away.
They would be riding westward with the day!
How strange he had forgot! That battered leg
Or some scalp wound, had set his wits a-beg!
Was this Hugh Glass to whimper like a squaw?
Grimly amused, he raised his head and saw —
The empty distance: listened long and heard —
Naught but the twitter of a lonely bird
That emphasized the hush.
                                          Was something wrong?

'Twas not the Major's way to dally long,
And surely they had camped not far behind.
Now woke a query in his troubled mind —
Where was his horse?   Again came creeping back
The circumstances of the bear's attack.
He had dismounted, thinking at the spring
To spend the night — and then the grisly thing —
Of course the horse had bolted; plain enough!
But why was all the soil about so rough
As though a herd of horses had been there?
The riddle vexed him till his vacant stare
Fell on a heap of earth beside a pit.
What did that mean?   He wormed his way to it,
The newly wakened wonder dulling pain.
No paw of beast had scooped it — that was plain.
'Twas squared; indeed, 'twas like a grave, he
        thought.
A grave — a grave — the mental echo wrought
Sick fancies!   Who had risen from the dead?
Who, lying there, had heard above his head
The ghostly talkers deaf unto his shout?

Now searching all the region round about,
As though the answer were a lurking thing,
He saw along the margin of the spring
An ash-heap and the litter of a camp.
Suspicion, like a little smoky lamp

That daubs the murk but cannot fathom it,
Flung blear grotesques before his groping wit.
Had Rees been there? And he alive? Who
    then?
And were he dead, it might be Henry's men!
How many suns had risen while he slept?
The smoky glow flared wildly, and he crept,
The dragged limb throbbing, till at length he
    found
The trail of many horses westward bound;
And in one breath the groping light became
A gloom-devouring ecstasy of flame,
A dazing conflagration of belief!

Plunged deeper than the seats of hate and grief,
He gazed about for aught that might deny
Such baseness: saw the non-committal sky,
The prairie apathetic in a shroud,
The bland complacence of a vagrant cloud —
World-wide connivance! Smilingly the sun
Approved a land wherein such deeds were done;
And careless breezes, like a troop of youth,
Unawed before the presence of such truth,
Went scampering amid the tousled brush.
Then bye and bye came on him with a rush
His weakness and the consciousness of pain,
While, with the chill insistence of a rain

That pelts the sodden wreck of Summer's end,
His manifest betrayal by a friend
Beat in upon him.   Jamie had been there;
And Jamie — Jamie — Jamie did not care!

What no man yet had witnessed, the wide sky
Looked down and saw; a light wind idling by
Heard what no ear of mortal yet had heard:
For he — whose name was like a magic word
To conjure the remote heroic mood
Of valiant deed and splendid fortitude,
Wherever two that shared a fire might be, —
Gave way to grief and wept unmanfully.
Yet not as they for whom tears fall like dew
To green a frosted heart again, wept Hugh.
So thewed to strive, so engined to prevail
And make harsh fate the zany of a tale,
His own might shook and tore him.
                                    For a span
He lay, a gray old ruin of a man
With all his years upon him like a snow.
And then at length, as from the long ago,
Remote beyond the other side of wrong,
The old love came like some remembered song
Whereof the strain is sweet, the burden sad.
A retrospective vision of the lad
Grew up in him, as in a foggy night

The witchery of semilunar light
Mysteriously quickens all the air.
Some memory of wind-blown golden hair,
The boyish laugh, the merry eyes of blue,
Wrought marvelously in the heart of Hugh,
As under snow the dæmon of the Spring.
And momently it seemed a little thing
To suffer; nor might treachery recall
The miracle of being loved at all,
The privilege of loving to the end.
And thereupon a longing for his friend
Made life once more a struggle for a prize —
To look again upon the merry eyes,
To see again the wind-blown golden hair.
Aye, one should lavish very tender care
Upon the vessel of a hope so great,
Lest it be shattered, and the precious freight,
As water on the arid waste, poured out.
Yet, though he longed to live, a subtle doubt
Still turned on him the weapon of his pain:
Now, as before, collusive sky and plain
Outstared his purpose for a puny thing.

Praying to live, he crawled back to the spring,
With something in his heart like gratitude
That by good luck his gun might furnish food,
His blanket, shelter, and his flint, a fire.

For, after all, what thing do men desire
To be or have, but these condition it?
These with a purpose and a little wit,
And howsoever smitten, one might rise,
Push back the curtain of the curving skies,
And come upon the living dream at last.

Exhausted, by the spring he lay and cast
Dull eyes about him. What did it portend?
Naught but the footprints of a fickle friend,
A yawning grave and ashes met his eyes!
Scarce feeling yet the shock of a surprise,
He searched about him for his flint and knife;
Knew vaguely that his seeking was for life,
And that the place was empty where he sought.
No food, no fire, no shelter! Dully wrought
The bleak negation in him, slowly crept
To where, despite the pain, his love had kept
A shrine for Jamie undefiled of doubt.
Then suddenly conviction, like a shout,
Aroused him.   Jamie — Jamie was a thief!
The very difficulty of belief
Was fuel for the simmering of rage,
That grew and grew, the more he strove to gage
The underlying motive of the deed.
Untempered youth might fail a friend in need;
But here had wrought some devil of the will,

Some heartless thing, too cowardly to kill,
That left to Nature what it dared not do!

So bellowsed, all the kindled soul of Hugh
Became a still white hell of brooding ire,
And through his veins regenerating fire
Ran, driving out the lethargy of pain.
Now once again he scanned the yellow plain,
Conspirant with the overbending skies;
And lo, the one was blue as Jamie's eyes,
The other of the color of his hair —
Twin hues of falseness merging to a stare,
As though such guilt, thus visibly immense,
Regarded its effect with insolence!

Alas for those who fondly place above
The act of loving, what they chance to love;
Who prize the goal more dearly than the way!
For time shall plunder them, and change betray,
And life shall find them vulnerable still.

A bitter-sweet narcotic to the will,
Hugh's love increased the peril of his plight;
But anger broke the slumber of his might,
Quickened the heart and warmed the blood that
    ran
Defiance for the treachery of Man,

Defiance for the meaning of his pain,
Defiance for the distance of the plain
That seemed to gloat, 'You can not master me.'
And for one burning moment he felt free
To rise and conquer in a wind of rage.
But as a tiger, conscious of the cage,
A-smoulder with a purpose, broods and waits,
So with the sullen patience that is hate's
Hugh taught his wrath to bide expedience.

Now cognizant of every quickened sense,
Thirst came upon him.   Leaning to the spring,
He stared with fascination on a thing
That rose from giddy deeps to share the draught—
A face, it was, so tortured that it laughed,
A ghastly mask that Murder well might wear;
And while as one they drank together there,
It was as though the deed he meant to do
Took shape and came to kiss the lips of Hugh,
Lest that revenge might falter.   Hunger woke;
And from the bush with leafage gray as smoke,
Wherein like flame the bullberries glinted red
(Scarce sweeter than the heart of him they fed),
Hugh feasted.
                    And the hours of waiting crept,
A-gloom, a-glow; and though he waked or slept,
The pondered purpose or a dream that wrought,

By night, the murder of his waking thought,
Sustained him till he felt his strength returned.
And then at length the longed-for morning burned
And beckoned down the vast way he should crawl—
That waste to be surmounted as a wall,
Sky-rims and yet more sky-rims steep to climb —
That simulacrum of enduring Time —
The hundred empty miles 'twixt him and where
The stark Missouri ran!
                                        Yet why not dare?
Despite the useless leg, he could not die
One hairsbreadth farther from the earth and sky,
Or more remote from kindness.

III

THE CRAWL

STRAIGHT away

Beneath the flare of dawn, the Ree land lay,
And through it ran the short trail to the goal.
Thereon a grim turnpikeman waited toll:
But 'twas so doomed that southering geese should
    flee
Nine times, ere yet the vengeance of the Ree
Should make their foe the haunter of a tale.

Midway to safety on the northern trail
The scoriac region of a hell burned black
Forbade the crawler. And for all his lack,
Hugh had no heart to journey with the suns:
No suppliant unto those faithless ones
Should bid for pity at the Big Horn's mouth.

The greater odds for safety in the South
Allured him; so he felt the midday sun
Blaze down the coulee of a little run

That dwindled upward to the watershed
Whereon the feeders of the Moreau head —
Scarce more than deep-carved runes of vernal
    rain.
The trailing leg was like a galling chain,
And bound him to a doubt that would not pass.
Defiant clumps of thirst-embittered grass
That bit parched earth with bared and fang-like
    roots;
Dwarf thickets, jealous for their stunted fruits,
Harsh-tempered by their disinheritance —
These symbolized the enmity of Chance
For him who, with his fate unreconciled,
Equipped for travel as a weanling child,
Essayed the journey of a mighty man.

Like agitated oil the heat-waves ran
And made the scabrous gulch appear to shake
As some reflected landscape in a lake
Where laggard breezes move.   A taunting reek
Rose from the grudging seepage of the creek,
Whereof Hugh drank and drank, and still would
    drink.
And where the mottled shadow dripped as ink
From scanty thickets on the yellow glare,
The crawler faltered with no heart to dare
Again the torture of that toil, until

The master-thought of vengeance 'woke the will
To goad him forth. And when the sun quiesced
Amid ironic heavens in the West —
The region of false friends — Hugh gained a rise
Whence to the fading cincture of the skies
A purpling panorama swept away.
Scarce farther than a shout might carry, lay
The place of his betrayal. He could see
The yellow blotch of earth where treachery
Had digged his grave. O futile wrath and toil!
Tucked in beneath yon coverlet of soil,
Turned back for him, how soundly had he slept!
Fool, fool! to struggle when he might have crept
So short a space, yet farther than the flight
Of swiftest dreaming through the longest night,
Into the quiet house of no false friend.

Alas for those who seek a journey's end —
They have it ever with them like a ghost:
Nor shall they find, who deem they seek it most,
But crave the end of human ends — as Hugh.

Now swoopingly the world of dream broke through
The figured wall of sense. It seemed he ran
As wind above the creeping ways of man,
And came upon the place of his desire,
Where burned, far-luring as a beacon-fire,

The face of Jamie.   But the vengeful stroke
Bit air.   The darkness lifted like a smoke —
And it was early morning.
                                   Gazing far,
From where the West yet kept a pallid star
To thinner sky where dawn was wearing through,
Hugh shrank with dread, reluctant to renew
The war with that serene antagonist.
More fearsome than a smashing iron fist
Seemed that vast negativity of might;
Until the frustrate vision of the night
Came moonwise on the gloom of his despair.
And lo, the foe was naught but yielding air,
A vacancy to fill with his intent!
So from his spacious bed he 'rose and went
Three-footed; and the vision goaded him.

All morning southward to the bare sky rim
The rugged coulee zigzagged, mounting slow;
And ever as it 'rose, the lean creek's flow
Dwindled and dwindled steadily, until
At last a scooped-out basin would not fill;
And thenceforth 'twas a way of mocking dust.
But, in that Hugh still kept the driving lust
For vengeance, this new circumstance of fate
Served but to brew more venom for his hate,
And nerved him to avail the most with least.

Ere noon the crawler chanced upon a feast
Of bread-root sunning in a favored draw.
A sentry gopher from his stronghold saw
Some three-legged beast, bear-like, yet not a bear,
With quite misguided fury digging where
No hapless brother gopher might be found.
And while, with stripéd nose above his mound,
The sentinel chirped shrilly to his clan
Scare-tales of that anomaly, the man
Devoured the chance-flung manna of the plains
That some vague reminiscence of old rains
Kept succulent, despite the burning drouth.

So with new vigor Hugh assailed the South,
His pockets laden with the precious roots
Against that coming traverse, where no fruits
Of herb or vine or shrub might brave the land
Spread rooflike 'twixt the Moreau and the Grand.

The coulee deepened; yellow walls flung high,
Sheer to the ragged strip of blinding sky,
Dazzled and sweltered in the glare of day.
Capricious draughts that woke and died away
Into the heavy drowse, were breatht as flame.
And midway down the afternoon, Hugh came
Upon a little patch of spongy ground.
His thirst became a rage. He gazed around,

Seeking a spring; but all about was dry
As strewn bones bleaching to a desert sky;
Nor did a clawed hole, bought with needed
    strength,
Return a grateful ooze. And when at length
Hugh sucked the mud, he spat it in disgust.
It had the acrid tang of broken trust,
The sweetish, tepid taste of feigning love!

Still hopeful of a spring somewhere above,
He crawled the faster for his taunted thirst.
More damp spots, no less grudging than the first,
Occurred with growing frequence on the way,
Until amid the purple wane of day
The crawler came upon a little pool!
Clear as a friend's heart, 'twas, and seeming cool —
A crystal bowl whence skyey deeps looked up.
So might a god set down his drinking cup
Charged with a distillation of haut skies.
As famished horses, thrusting to the eyes
Parched muzzles, take a long-sought water-hole,
Hugh plunged his head into the brimming bowl
As though to share the joy with every sense.
And lo, the tang of that wide insolence
Of sky and plain was acrid in the draught!
How ripplingly the lying water laughed!
How like fine sentiment the mirrored sky

Won credence for a sink of alkali!
So with false friends. And yet, as may accrue
From specious love some profit of the true,
One gift of kindness had the tainted sink.
Stripped of his clothes, Hugh let his body drink
At every thirsting pore. Through trunk and
    limb
The elemental blessing solaced him;
Nor did he rise till, vague with stellar light,
The lone gulch, buttressing an arch of night,
Was like a temple to the Holy Ghost.
As priests in slow procession with the Host,
A gusty breeze intoned — now low, now loud,
And now, as to the murmur of a crowd,
Yielding the dim-torched wonder of the nave.
Aloft along the dusky architrave
The wander-tale of drifting stars evolved;
And Hugh lay gazing till the whole resolved
Into a haze.
          It seemed that Little Jim
Had come to share a merry fire with him,
And there had been no trouble 'twixt the two.
And Jamie listened eagerly while Hugh
Essayed a tangled tale of bears and men,
Bread-root and stars. But ever now and then
The shifting smoke-cloud dimmed the golden hair,
The leal blue eyes; until with sudden flare

The flame effaced them utterly — and lo,
The gulch bank-full with morning!

                                    Loath to go,
Hugh lay beside the pool and pondered fate.
He saw his age-long pilgrimage of hate
Stretch out — a fool's trail; and it made him
        cringe;
For still amid the nightly vision's fringe
His dull wit strayed, companioned with regret.
But when the sun, a tilted cauldron set
Upon the gulch rim, poured a blaze of day,
He rose and bathed again, and went his way,
Sustaining wrath returning with the toil.

At noon the gulch walls, hewn in lighter soil,
Fell back; and coulees dense with shrub and vine
Climbed zigzag to the sharp horizon line,
Whence one might choose the pilotage of crows.
He labored upward through the noonday doze.
Of breathless shade, where plums were turning
        red
In tangled bowers, and grapevines overhead
Purpled with fruit to taunt the crawler's thirst.
With little effort Hugh attained the first;
The latter bargained sharply ere they sold
Their luscious clusters for the hoarded gold
Of strength that had so very much to buy.

Now, having feasted, it was sweet to lie
Beneath a sun-proof canopy; and sleep
Came swiftly.

        Hugh awakened to some deep
Star-snuffing well of night. Awhile he lay
And wondered what had happened to the day
And where he was and what were best to do.
But when, fog-like, the drowse dispersed, he knew
How from the rim above the plain stretched far
To where the evening and the morning are,
And that 'twere better he should crawl by night,
Sleep out the glare. With groping hands for
    sight,
Skyward along the broken steep he crawled,
And saw at length, immense and purple-walled —
Or sensed — the dusky mystery of plain.
Gazing aloft, he found the capsized Wain
In mid-plunge down the polar steep. Thereto
He set his back; and far ahead there grew,
As some pale blossom from a darkling root,
The star-blanched summit of a lonely butte,
And thitherward he dragged his heavy limb.

It seemed naught moved. Time hovered over
    him,
An instant of incipient endeavor.
'Twas ever thus, and should be thus forever —

This groping for the same armful of space,
An insubstantial essence of one place,
Extentless on a weird frontier of sleep.
Sheer deep upon unfathomable deep
The flood of dusk bore down without a sound,
As ocean on the spirits of the drowned
Awakened headlong leagues beneath the light.

So lapsed the drowsy æon of the night —
A strangely tensile moment in a trance.
And then, as quickened to somnambulance,
The heavens, imperceptibly in motion,
Were altered as the upward deeps of ocean
Diluted with a seepage of the moon.
The butte-top, late a gossamer balloon
In mid-air tethered hovering, grew down
And rooted in a blear expanse of brown,
That, lifting slowly with the ebb of night,
Took on the harsh solidity of light —
And day was on the prairie like a flame.

Scarce had he munched the hoarded roots, when
    came
A vertigo of slumber.   Snatchy dreams
Of sick pools, inaccessible cool streams,
Lured on through giddy vacancies of heat
In swooping flights; now hills of roasting meat

Made savory the oven of the world,
Yet kept remote peripheries and whirled
About a burning center that was Hugh.
Then all were gone, save one, and it turned blue
And was a heap of cool and luscious fruit,
Until at length he knew it for the butte
Now mantled with a weaving of the gloam.
    It was the hour when cattle straggle home.
Across the clearing in a hush of sleep
They saunter, lowing; loiter belly-deep
Amid the lush grass by the meadow stream.
How like the sound of water in a dream
The intermittent tinkle of yon bell.
A windlass creaks contentment from a well,
And cool deeps gurgle as the bucket sinks.
Now blowing at the trough the plow-team drinks;
The shaken harness rattles. Sleepy quails
Call far. The warm milk hisses in the pails
There in the dusky barn-lot. Crickets cry.
The meadow twinkles with the glowing fly.
One hears the horses munching at their oats.
The green grows black. A veil of slumber floats
Across the haunts of home-enamored men.

Some freak of memory brought back again
The boyhood world of sight and scent and sound:
It perished, and the prairie ringed him round,

Blank as the face of fate.   In listless mood
Hugh set his face against the solitude
And met the night. The new moon, low and
      far,
A frail cup tilted, nor the high-swung star,
It seemed, might glint on any stream or spring
Or touch with silver any toothsome thing.
The kiote voiced the universal lack.
As from a nether fire, the plain gave back
The swelter of the noon-glare to the gloom.
In the hot hush Hugh heard his temples boom.
Thirst tortured.   Motion was a languid pain.
Why seek some further nowhere on the plain?
Here might the kiotes feast as well as there.
So spoke some loose-lipped spirit of despair;
And still Hugh moved, volitionless — a weight
Submissive to that now unconscious hate,
As darkling water to the hidden moon.

    Now when the night wore on in middle swoon,
The crawler, roused from stupor, was aware
Of some strange alteration in the air.
To breathe became an act of conscious will.
The starry waste was ominously still.
The far-off kiote's yelp came sharp and clear
As through a tunnel in the atmosphere —
A ponderable, resonating mass.

The limp leg dragging on the sun-dried grass
Produced a sound unnaturally loud.

Crouched, panting, Hugh looked up but saw no
    cloud.
An oily film seemed spread upon the sky
Now dully staring as the open eye
Of one in fever. Gasping, choked with thirst,
A childish rage assailed Hugh, and he cursed:
'Twas like a broken spirit's outcry, tossed
Upon hell's burlesque sabbath for the lost,
And briefly space seemed crowded with the voice.

To wait and die, to move and die — what
    choice?
Hugh chose not, yet he crawled; though more
    and more
He felt the futile strife was nearly o'er.
And as he went, a muffled rumbling grew,
More felt than heard; for long it puzzled Hugh.
Somehow 'twas coextensive with his thirst,
Yet boundless; swollen blood-veins ere they burst
Might give such warning, so he thought. And
    still
The drone seemed heaping up a phonic hill
That towered in a listening profound.
Then suddenly a mountain peak of sound

Came toppling to a heaven-jolting fall!
The prairie shuddered, and a raucous drawl
Ran far and perished in the outer deep.

As one too roughly shaken out of sleep,
Hugh stared bewildered.   Still the face of night
Remained the same, save where upon his right
The moon had vanished 'neath the prairie rim.
Then suddenly the meaning came to him.
He turned and saw athwart the northwest sky,
Like some black eyelid shutting on an eye,
A coming night to which the night was day!
Star-hungry, ranged in regular array,
The lifting mass assailed the Dragon's lair,
Submerged the region of the hounded Bear,
Out-topped the tall Ox-Driver and the Pole.
And all the while there came a low-toned roll,
Less sound in air than tremor in the earth,
From where, like flame upon a windy hearth,
Deep in the further murk sheet-lightning flared.
And still the southern arc of heaven stared,
A half-shut eye, near blind with fever rheum;
And still the plain lay tranquil as a tomb
Wherein the dead reck not a menaced world.

What turmoil now?   Lo, ragged columns hurled
Pell-mell up stellar slopes!   Swift blue fires leap

Above the wild assailants of the steep!
Along the solid rear a dull boom runs!
So light horse squadrons charge beneath the guns.
Now once again the night is deathly still.
What ghastly peace upon the zenith hill,
No longer starry? Not a sound is heard.
So poised the hush, it seems a whispered word
Might loose all noises in an avalanche.
Only the black mass moves, and far glooms blanch
With fitful flashes. The capricious flare
Reveals the butte-top tall and lonely there
Like some gray prophet contemplating doom.

But hark! What spirits whisper in the gloom?
What sibilation of conspiracies
Ruffles the hush — or murmuring of trees,
Ghosts of the ancient forest — or old rain,
In some hallucination of the plain,
A frustrate phantom mourning? All around,
That e'er evolving, ne'er resolving sound
Gropes in the stifling hollow of the night.

Then — once — twice — thrice — a   blade   of
    blinding light
Ripped up the heavens, and the deluge came —
A burst of wind and water, noise and flame
That hurled the watcher flat upon the ground.

A moment past Hugh famished; now, half
    drowned,
He gasped for breath amid the hurtling drench.

So might a testy god, long sought to quench
A puny thirst, pour wassail, hurling after
The crashing bowl with wild sardonic laughter
To see man wrestle with his answered prayer!

Prone to the roaring flaw and ceaseless flare,
The man drank deeply with the drinking grass;
Until it seemed the storm would never pass
But ravin down the painted murk for aye.
When had what dreamer seen a glaring day
And leagues of prairie pantingly aquiver?
Flame, flood, wind, noise and darkness were a
    river
Tearing a cosmic channel to no sea.

The tortured night wore on; then suddenly
Peace fell. Remotely the retreating Wrath
Trailed dull, reluctant thunders in its path,
And up along a broken stair of cloud
The Dawn came creeping whitely. Like a
    shroud
Gray vapors clung along the sodden plain.
Up rose the sun to wipe the final stain

Of fury from the sky and drink the mist.
Against a flawless arch of amethyst
The butte soared, like a soul serene and white
Because of the katharsis of the night.

All day Hugh fought with sleep and struggled on
Southeastward; for the heavy heat was gone
Despite the naked sun. The blank Northwest
Breathed coolly; and the crawler thought it best
To move while yet each little break and hollow
And shallow basin of the bison-wallow
Begrudged the earth and air its dwindling store.
But now that thirst was conquered, more and
    more
He felt the gnaw of hunger like a rage.
And once, from dozing in a clump of sage,
A lone jackrabbit bounded. As a flame
Hope flared in Hugh, until the memory came
Of him who robbed a sleeping friend and fled.
Then hate and hunger merged; the man saw red,
And momently the hare and Little Jim
Were one blurred mark for murder unto him —
Elusive, taunting, sweet to clutch and tear.
The rabbit paused to scan the crippled bear
That ground its teeth as though it chewed a
    root.
But when, in witless rage, Hugh drew his boot

And hurled it with a curse, the hare loped off,
Its critic ears turned back, as though to scoff
At silly brutes that threw their legs away.

Night like a shadow on enduring day
Swooped by. The dream of crawling and the
    act
Were phases of one everlasting fact:
Hugh woke, and he was doing what he dreamed.
The butte, outstripped at eventide, now seemed
Intent to follow.   Ever now and then
The crawler paused to calculate again
What dear-bought yawn of distance dwarfed the
    hill.
Close in the rear it soared, a Titan still,
Whose hand-in-pocket saunter kept the pace.

Distinct along the southern rim of space
A low ridge lay, the crest of the divide.
What rest and plenty on the other side!
Through what lush valleys ran what crystal
    brooks!
And there in virgin meadows wayside nooks
With leaf and purple cluster dulled the light!

All day it seemed that distant Pisgah Height
Retreated, and the tall butte dogged the rear.

At eve a stripéd gopher chirping near
Gave Hugh an inspiration.   Now, at least,
No thieving friend should rob him of a feast.
His great idea stirred him as a shout.
Off came a boot, a sock was ravelled out.
The coarse yarn, fashioned to a running snare,
He placed about the gopher's hole with care,
And then withdrew to hold the yarn and wait.
The nightbound moments, ponderous with fate,
Crept slowly by.   The battered gray face leered
In expectation.   Down the grizzled beard
Ran slaver from anticipating jaws.
Evolving twilight hovered to a pause.
The light wind fell.   Again and yet again
The man devoured his fancied prey: and then
Within the noose a timid snout was thrust.
His hand unsteadied with the hunger lust,
Hugh jerked the yarn.   It broke.

                Down swooped the night,
A shadow of despair.   Bleak height on height,
It seemed, a sheer abyss enclosed him round.
Clutching a strand of yarn, he heard the sound
Of some infernal turmoil under him.
Grimly he strove to reach the ragged rim
That snared a star, until the skyey space
Was darkened with a roof of Jamie's face.

And then the yarn was broken, and he fell.
A-tumble like a stricken bat, his yell
Woke hordes of laughers down the giddy yawn
Of that black pit — and suddenly 'twas dawn.

Dream-dawn, dream-noon, dream-twilight! Yet,
    possest
By one stern dream more clamorous than the
    rest,
Hugh headed for a gap that notched the hills,
Wherethrough a luring murmur of cool rills,
A haunting smell of verdure seemed to creep.
By fits the wild adventure of his sleep
Became the cause of all his waking care,
And he complained unto the empty air
How Jamie broke the yarn.

             The sun and breeze
Had drunk all shallow basins to the lees,
But now and then some gully, choked with mud,
Retained a turbid relict of the flood.
Dream-dawn, dream-noon, dream-night! And
    still obsessed
By that one dream more clamorous than the rest,
Hugh struggled for the crest of the divide.
And when at length he saw the other side,
'Twas but a rumpled waste of yellow hills!

The deep-sunk, wiser self had known the rills
And nooks to be the facture of a whim;
Yet had the pleasant lie befriended him,
And now the brutal fact had come to stare.

Succumbing to a langorous despair,
He mourned his fate with childish uncontrol
And nursed that deadly adder of the soul,
Self-pity. Let the crows swoop down and feed,
Aye, batten on a thing that died of need,
A poor old wretch betrayed of God and Man!
So peevishly his broken musing ran,
Till, glutted with the luxury of woe,
He turned to see the butte, that he might know
How little all his striving could avail
Against ill-luck. And lo, a finger-nail,
At arm-length held, could blot it out of space!
A goading purpose and a creeping pace
Had dwarfed the Titan in a haze of blue!
And suddenly new power came to Hugh
With gazing on his masterpiece of will.
So fare the wise on Pisgah.

                              Down the hill,
Unto the higher vision consecrate,
Now sallied forth the new triumvirate —
A Weariness, a Hunger and a Glory —

Against tyrannic Chance.   As in a story
Some higher Hugh observed the baser part.
So sits the artist throned above his art,
Nor recks the travail so the end be fair.
It seemed the wrinkled hills pressed in to stare,
The arch of heaven was an eye a-gaze.
And as Hugh went, he fashioned many a phrase
For use when, by some friendly ember-light,
His tale of things endured should speed the night
And all this gloom grow golden in the sharing.
So wrought the old evangel of high daring,
The duty and the beauty of endeavor,
The privilege of going on forever,
A victor in the moment.

                            Ah, but when
The night slipped by and morning came again,
The sky and hill were only sky and hill
And crawling but an agony of will.
So once again the old triumvirate,
A buzzard Hunger and a viper Hate
Together with the baser part of Hugh,
Went visionless.

                  That day the wild geese flew,
Vague in a gray profundity of sky;
And on into the night their muffled cry
Haunted the moonlight like a far farewell.
It made Hugh homesick, though he could not tell

For what he yearned; and in his fitful sleeping
The cry became the sound of Jamie weeping,
Immeasurably distant.
                    Morning broke,
Blear, chilly, through a fog that drove as smoke
Before the booming Northwest.   Sweet and sad
Came creeping back old visions of the lad —
Some trick of speech, some merry little lilt,
The brooding blue of eyes too clear for guilt,
The wind-blown golden hair.   Hate slept that
        day,
And half of Hugh was half a life away,
A wandering spirit wistful of the past;
And half went drifting with the autumn blast
That mourned among the melancholy hills;
For something of the lethargy that kills
Came creeping close upon the ebb of hate.
Only the raw wind, like the lash of Fate,
Could have availed to move him any more.
At last the buzzard beak no longer tore
His vitals, and he ceased to think of food.
The fighter slumbered, and a maudlin mood
Foretold the dissolution of the man.
He sobbed, and down his beard the big tears ran.
And now the scene is changed; the bleak wind's
        cry
Becomes a flight of bullets snarling by

From where on yonder summit skulk the Rees.
Against the sky, in silhouette, he sees
The headstrong Jamie in the leaden rain.
And now serenely beautiful and slain
The dear lad lies within a gusty tent.

Thus vexed with doleful whims the crawler went
Adrift before the wind, nor saw the trail;
Till close on night he knew a rugged vale
Had closed about him; and a hush was there,
Though still a moaning in the upper air
Told how the gray-winged gale blew out the day.
Beneath a clump of brush he swooned away
Into an icy void; and waking numb,
It seemed the still white dawn of death had come
On this, some cradle-valley of the soul.
He saw a dim, enchanted hollow roll
Beneath him, and the brush thereof was fleece;
And, like the body of the perfect peace
That thralled the whole, abode the break of day.
It seemed no wind had ever come that way,
Nor sound dwelt there, nor echo found the place.
And Hugh lay lapped in wonderment a space,
Vexed with a snarl whereof the ends were lost,
Till, shivering, he wondered if a frost
Had fallen with the dying of the blast.
So, vaguely troubled, listlessly he cast

A gaze about him : lo, above his head
The gray-green curtain of his chilly bed
Was broidered thick with plums !   Or so it seemed,
For he was half persuaded that he dreamed ;
And with a steady stare he strove to keep
That treasure for the other side of sleep.

Returning hunger bade him rise ; in vain
He struggled with a fine-spun mesh of pain
That trammelled him, until a yellow stream
Of day flowed down the white vale of a dream
And left it disenchanted in the glare.
Then, warmed and soothed, Hugh rose and
      feasted there,
And thought once more of reaching the Moreau.

To southward with a painful pace and slow
He went stiff-jointed ; and a gnawing ache
In that hip-wound he had for Jamie's sake
Oft made him groan — nor wrought a tender
      mood :
The rankling weapon of ingratitude
Was turned again with every puckering twinge.

Far down the vale a narrow winding fringe
Of wilted green betokened how a spring
There sent a little rill meandering ;

And Hugh was greatly heartened, for he knew
What fruits and herbs might flourish in the
    slough,
And thirst, henceforth, should torture not again.

So day on day, despite the crawler's pain,
All in the windless, golden autumn weather,
These two, as comrades, struggled south to-
    gether —
The homeless graybeard and the homing rill:
And one was sullen with the lust to kill,
And one went crooning of the moon-wooed
    vast;
For each the many-fathomed peace at last,
But oh the boon of singing on the way!
So came these in the golden fall of day
Unto a sudden turn in the ravine,
Wherefrom Hugh saw a flat of cluttered green
Beneath the further bluffs of the Moreau.

With sinking heart he paused and gazed below
Upon the goal of so much toil and pain.
Yon green had seemed a paradise to gain
The while he thirsted where the lonely butte
Looked far and saw no toothsome herb or fruit
In all that yellow barren dim with heat.
But now the wasting body cried for meat,

And sickness was upon him. Game should pass,
Nor deign to fear the mighty hunter Glass,
But curiously sniffing, pause to stare.

Now while thus musing, Hugh became aware
Of some low murmur, phasic and profound,
Scarce risen o'er the border line of sound.
It might have been the coursing of his blood,
Or thunder heard remotely, or a flood
Flung down a wooded valley far away.
Yet that had been no weather-breeding day;
'Twould frost that night; amid the thirsty land
All streams ran thin; and when he pressed a
    hand
On either ear, the world seemed very still.

The deep-worn channel of the little rill
Here fell away to eastward, rising, rough
With old rain-furrows, to a lofty bluff
That faced the river with a yellow wall.
Thereto, perplexed, Hugh set about to crawl,
Nor reached the summit till the sun was low.
Far-spread, shade-dimpled in the level glow,
The still land told not whence the murmur grew;
But where the green strip melted into blue
Far down the winding valley of the stream,
Hugh saw what seemed the tempest of a dream

At mimic havoc in the timber-glooms.
As from the sweeping of gigantic brooms,
A dust cloud deepened down the dwindling river;
Upon the distant tree-tops ran a shiver
And huddled thickets writhed as in a gale.

On creeps the windless tempest up the vale,
The while the murmur deepens to a roar,
As with the wider yawning of a door.
And now the agitated green gloom gapes
To belch a flood of countless dusky shapes
That mill and wrangle in a turbid flow —
Migrating myriads of the buffalo
Bound for the winter pastures of the Platte!

Exhausted, faint with need of meat, Hugh sat
And watched the mounting of the living flood.
Down came the night, and like a blot of blood
The lopped moon weltered in the dust-bleared
    East.
Sleep came and gave a Barmecidal feast.
About a merry flame were simmering
Sweet haunches of the calving of the Spring,
And tender tongues that never tasted snow,
And marrow bones that yielded to a blow
Such treasure!   Hugh awoke with gnashing teeth,
And heard the mooing drone of cows beneath,

The roll of hoofs, the challenge of the bull.
So sounds a freshet when the banks are full
And bursting brush-jams bellow to the croon
Of water through green leaves. The ragged
    moon
Now drenched the valley in an eerie rain:
Below, the semblance of a hurricane;
Above, the perfect calm of brooding frost,
Through which the wolves in doleful tenson
    tossed
From hill to hill the ancient hunger-song.
In broken sleep Hugh rolled the chill night long,
Half conscious of the flowing flesh below.
And now he trailed a bison in the snow
That deepened till he could not lift his feet.
Again, he battled for a chunk of meat
With some gray beast that fought with icy
    fang.
And when he woke, the wolves no longer sang;
White dawn athwart a white world smote the
    hill,
And thunder rolled along the valley still.

Morn, wiping up the frost as with a sponge,
Day on the steep and down the nightward plunge,
And Twilight saw the myriads moving on.
Dust to the westward where the van had gone,

And dust and muffled thunder in the east!
Hugh starved while gazing on a Titan feast.
The tons of beef, that eddied there and swirled,
Had stilled the crying hungers of the world,
Yet not one little morsel was for him.

The red sun, pausing on the dusty rim,
Induced a panic aspect of his plight:
The herd would pass and vanish in the night
And be another dream to cling and flout.
Now scanning all the summit round about,
Amid the rubble of the ancient drift
He saw a bowlder.   'Twas too big to lift,
Yet he might roll it.   Painfully and slow
He worked it to the edge, then let it go
And breathlessly expectant watched it fall.
It hurtled down the leaning yellow wall,
And bounding from a brushy ledge's brow,
It barely grazed the buttocks of a cow
And made a moment's eddy where it struck.

In peevish wrath Hugh cursed his evil luck,
And seizing rubble, gave his fury vent
By pelting bison till his strength was spent:
So might a child assail the crowding sea!
Then, sick at heart and musing bitterly,
He shambled down the steep way to the creek,
And having stayed the tearing buzzard beak

With breadroot and the waters of the rill,
Slept till the white of morning o'er the hill
Was like a whisper groping in a hush.
The stream's low trill seemed loud. The tumbled
    brush
And rumpled tree-tops in the flat below,
Upon a fog that clung like spectral snow,
Lay motionless; nor any sound was there.
No frost had fallen, but the crystal air
Smacked of the autumn, and a heavy dew
Lay hoar upon the grass. There came on Hugh
A picture, vivid in the moment's thrill,
Of martialed corn-shocks marching up a hill
And spiked fields dotted with the pumpkin's
    gold.
It vanished; and, a-shiver with the cold,
He brooded on the mockeries of Chance,
The shrewd malignity of Circumstance
That either gave too little or too much.

Yet, with the fragment of a hope for crutch,
His spirit rallied, and he rose to go,
Though each stiff joint resisted as a foe
And that old hip-wound battled with his will.
So down along the channel of the rill
Unto the vale below he fought his way.
The frore fog, rifting in the risen day,

Revealed the havoc of the living flood —
The river shallows beaten into mud,
The slender saplings shattered in the crush,
All lower leafage stripped, the tousled brush
Despoiled of fruitage, winter-thin, aghast.
And where the avalanche of hoofs had passed
It seemed nor herb nor grass had ever been.
And this the hard-won paradise, wherein
A food-devouring plethora of food
Had come to make a starving solitude!

Yet hope and courage mounted with the sun.
Surely, Hugh thought, some ill-begotten one
Of all that striving mass had lost the strife
And perished in the headlong stream of life —
A feast to fill the bellies of the strong,
That still the weak might perish.   All day long
He struggled down the stricken vale, nor saw
What thing he sought.   But when the twilight
     awe
Was creeping in, beyond a bend arose
A din as though the kiotes and the crows
Fought there with shrill and raucous battle cries.

Small need had Hugh to ponder and surmise
What guerdon beak and fang contended for.
Within himself the oldest cause of war

Brought forth upon the instant fang and beak.
He too would fight! Nor had he far to seek
Amid the driftwood strewn about the sand
For weapons suited to a brawny hand
With such a purpose. Armed with club and
    stone
He forged ahead into the battle zone,
And from a screening thicket spied his foes.

He saw a bison carcass black with crows,
And over it a welter of black wings,
And round about, a press of tawny rings
That, like a muddy current churned to foam
Upon a snag, flashed whitely in the gloam
With naked teeth; while close about the prize
Red beaks and muzzles bloody to the eyes
Betrayed how worth a struggle was the feast.

Then came on Hugh the fury of the beast —
To eat or to be eaten! Better so
To die contending with a living foe,
Than fight the yielding distance and the lack.
Masked by the brush he opened the attack,
And ever where a stone or club fell true,
About the stricken one an uproar grew
And brute tore brute, forgetful of the prey,
Until the whole pack tumbled in the fray

With bleeding flanks and lacerated throats.
Then, as the leader of a host who notes
The cannon-wrought confusion of the foe,
Hugh seized the moment for a daring blow.

The wolf's a coward, who, in goodly packs,
May counterfeit the courage that he lacks
And with a craven's fury crush the bold.
But when the disunited mass that rolled
In suicidal strife, became aware
How some great beast that shambled like a bear
Bore down with roaring challenge, fell a hush
Upon the pack, some slinking to the brush
With tails a-droop; while some that whined in pain
Writhed off on reddened trails. With bristled
        mane
Before the flying stones a bolder few
Snarled menace at the foe as they withdrew
To fill the outer dusk with clamorings.
Aloft upon a moaning wind of wings
The crows with harsh, vituperative cries
Now saw a gray wolf of prodigious size
Devouring with the frenzy of the starved.
Thus fell to Hugh a bison killed and carved;
And so Fate's whims mysteriously trend —
Woe in the silken meshes of the friend,
Weal in the might and menace of the foe.

But with the fading of the afterglow
The routed wolves found courage to return:
Amid the brush Hugh saw their eye-balls burn;
And well he knew how futile stick and stone
Should prove by night to keep them from their
   own.
Better is less with safety, than enough
With ruin.   He retreated to a bluff,
And scarce had reached it when the pack swooped
    in
Upon the carcass.
                All night long, the din
Of wrangling wolves assailed the starry air,
While high above them in a brushy lair
Hugh dreamed of gnawing at the bloody feast.

Along about the blanching of the east,
When sleep is weirdest and a moment's flight,
Remembered coextensive with the night,
May teem with hapful years; as light in smoke
Upon the jumble of Hugh's dreaming broke
A buzz of human voices.   Once again
He rode the westward trail with Henry's men —
Hoof-smitten leagues consuming in a dust.
And now the nightmare of that broken trust
Was on him, and he lay beside the spring,
A corpse, yet heard the muffled parleying

Above him of the looters of the dead:
But when he might have riddled what they said,
The babble flattened to a blur of gray —
And lo, upon a bleak frontier of day,
The spent moon staring down! A little space
Hugh scrutinized the featureless white face,
As though 'twould speak.   But when again the
          sound
Grew up, and seemed to come from under ground,
He cast the drowse, and peering down the slope,
Beheld what set at grapple fear and hope —
Three Indian horsemen riding at a jog!
Their ponies, wading belly-deep in fog,
That clung along the valley, seemed to swim,
And through a thinner vapor moving dim,
The men were ghost-like.

                    Could they be the Sioux?
Almost the wish became belief in Hugh.
Or were they Rees?   As readily the doubt
Withheld him from the hazard of a shout.
And while he followed them with baffled gaze,
Grown large and vague, dissolving in the haze,
They vanished westward.

                    Knowing well the wont
Of Indians moving on the bison-hunt,
Forthwith Hugh guessed the early riders were
The outflung feelers of a tribe a-stir

Like some huge cat gone mousing. So he lay
Concealed, impatient with the sleepy day
That dawdled in the dawning. Would it bring
Good luck or ill? His eager questioning,
As crawling fog, took on a golden hue
From sunrise. He was waiting for the Sioux,
Their parfleche panniers fat with sun-dried
    maize
And wasna! From the mint of evil days
He would coin tales and be no begging guest
About the tribal feast-fires burning west,
But kinsman of the blood of daring men.
And when the crawler stood erect again —
O Friend-Betrayer at the Big Horn's mouth,
Beware of someone riding from the South
To do the deed that he had lived to do!

Now when the sun stood hour-high in the blue,
From where a cloud of startled blackbirds rose
Down stream, a panic tumult broke the doze
Of windless morning. What unwelcome news
Embroiled the parliament of feathered shrews?
A boiling cloud against the sun they lower,
Flackering strepent; now a sooty shower,
Big-flaked, squall-driven westward, down they
    flutter
To set a clump of cottonwoods a-sputter

With cold black fire! And once again, some
    shock
Of sight or sound flings panic in the flock —
Gray boughs exploding in a ruck of birds!

What augury in orniscopic words
Did yon swart sibyls on the morning scrawl?

Now broke abruptly through the clacking
    brawl
A camp-dog's barking and a pony's neigh;
Whereat a running nicker fled away,
Attenuating to a rearward hush;
And lo! in hailing distance 'round the brush
That fringed a jutting bluff's base like a beard
Upon a stubborn chin out-thrust, appeared
A band of mounted warriors! In their van
Aloof and lonely rode a gnarled old man
Upon a piebald stallion. Stooped was he
Beneath his heavy years, yet haughtily
He wore them like the purple of a king.
Keen for a goal, as from the driving string
A barbed and feathered arrow truly sped,
His face was like a flinty arrow-head,
And brooded westward in a steady stare.
There was a sift of winter in his hair,
The bleakness of brown winter in his look.

Hugh saw, and huddled closer in his nook.
Fled the bright dreams of safety, feast and rest
Before that keen, cold brooder on the West,
As gaudy leaves before the blizzard flee.
'Twas Elk Tongue, fighting chieftain of the Ree,
With all his people at his pony's tail —
Full two-score lodges emptied on the trail
Of hunger!
                    On they came in ravelled rank,
And many a haggard eye and hollow flank
Made plain how close and pitilessly pressed
The enemy that drove them to the West —
Such foeman as no warrior ever slew.
A tale of cornfields plundered by the Sioux
Their sagging panniers told.   Yet rich enough
They seemed to him who watched them from the
        bluff;
Yea, pampered nigh the limit of desire!
No friend had filched from them the boon of
        fire
And hurled them shivering back upon the beast.
Erect they went, full-armed to strive, at least;
And nightly in a cozy ember-glow
Hope fed them with a dream of buffalo
Soon to be overtaken.   After that,
Home with their Pawnee cousins on the Platte,
Much meat and merry-making till the Spring.

On dragged the rabble like a fraying string
Too tautly drawn.   The rich-in-ponies rode,
For much is light and little is a load
Among all heathen with no Christ to save!
Gray seekers for the yet begrudging grave,
Bent with the hoeing of forgotten maize,
Wood-hewers, water-bearers all their days,
Toiled 'neath the life-long hoarding of their packs.
And nursing squaws, their babies at their backs
Whining because the milk they got was thinned
In dugs of famine, strove as with a wind.
Invincibly equipped with their first bows
The striplings strutted, knowing, as youth knows,
How fair life is beyond the beckoning blue.
Cold-eyed the grandsires plodded, for they knew,
As frosted heads may know, how all trails merge
In what lone land.   Raw maidens on the verge
Of some half-guessed-at mystery of life,
In wistful emulation of the wife
Stooped to the fancied burden of the race;
Nor read upon the withered granddam's face
The scrawled tale of that burden and its woe.
Slant to the sagging poles of the travaux,
Numb to the squaw's harsh railing and the goad,
The lean cayuses toiled.   And children rode
A-top the household plunder, wonder-eyed
To see a world flow by on either side,

From blue air sprung to vanish in blue air,
A river of enchantments.
                              Here and there
The camp-curs loped upon a vexing quest
Where countless hoofs had left a palimpsest,
A taunting snarl of broken scents.   And now
They sniff the clean bones of the bison cow,
Howl to the skies; and now with manes a-rough
They nose the man-smell leading to the bluff;
Pause puzzled at the base and sweep the height
With questioning yelps.   Aloft, crouched low in
      fright,
Already Hugh can hear the braves' guffaws
At their scorned foeman yielded to the squaws'
Inverted mercy and a slow-won grave.
Since Earth's first mother scolded from a cave
And that dear riddle of her love began,
No man has wrought a weapon against man
To match the deadly venom brewed above
The lean, blue, blinding heart-fires of her love.
Well might the hunted hunter shrink aghast!
But thrice three seasons yet should swell the past,
So was it writ, ere Fate's keen harriers
Should run Hugh Glass to earth.
                              The hungry curs
Took up again the tangled scent of food.
Still flowed the rabble through the solitude —

A thinning stream now of the halt, the weak
And all who had not very far to seek
For that weird pass whereto the fleet are slow,
And out of it keen winds and numbing blow,
Shrill with the fleeing voices of the dead.
Slowly the scattered stragglers, making head
Against their weariness as up a steep,
Fled westward; and the morning lay asleep
Upon the valley fallen wondrous still.

Hugh kept his nook, nor ventured forth, until
The high day toppled to the blue descent,
When thirst became a master, and he went
With painful scrambling down the broken scarp,
Lured by the stream, that like a smitten harp
Rippled a muted music to the sun.

Scarce had he crossed the open flat, and won
The half-way fringe of willows, when he saw,
Slow plodding up the trail, a tottering squaw
Whose years made big the little pack she bore.
Crouched in the brush Hugh watched her.   More
      and more
The little burden tempted him.   Why not?
A thin cry throttled in that lonely spot
Could bring no succor.   None should ever know,
Save him, the feasted kiote and the crow,

Why one poor crone found not the midnight fire.
Nor would the vanguard, quick with young de-
    sire,
Devouring distance westward like a flame,
Regret this ash dropped rearward.
                                On she came,
Slow-footed, staring blankly on the sand —
So close now that it needed but a hand
Out-thrust to overthrow her; aye, to win
That priceless spoil, a little tent of skin,
A flint and steel, a kettle and a knife!
What did the dying with the means of life,
That thus the fit-to-live should suffer lack?

Poised for the lunge, what whimsy held him
    back?
Why did he gaze upon the passing prize,
Nor seize it? Did some gust of ghostly cries
Awaken round her — whisperings of Eld,
Wraith-voices of the babies she had held,
Guarding the milkless paps, the withered womb?
Far down a moment's cleavage in the gloom
Of backward years Hugh saw her now — nor saw
The little burden and the feeble squaw,
But someone sitting haloed like a saint
Beside a hearth long cold. The dream grew
    faint;

And when he looked again, the crone was gone
Beyond a clump of willow.
                                    Crawling on,
He reached the river.   Leaning to a pool
Calm in its cup of sand, he saw — a fool!
A wild, wry mask of mirth, a-grin, yet grim,
Rose there to claim identity with him
And ridicule his folly.   Pity?   Faugh!
Who pitied this, that it should spare a squaw
Spent in the spawning of a scorpion brood?

He drank and hastened down the solitude,
Fleeing that thing which fleered him, and was
     Hugh.
And as he went his self-accusing grew
And with it, anger; till it came to seem
That somehow some sly Jamie of a dream
Had plundered him again; and he was strong
With lust of vengeance and the sting of wrong,
So that he travelled faster than for days.

Now when the eve in many-shaded grays
Wove the day's shroud, and through the lower
     lands
Lean fog-arms groped with chilling spirit hands,
Hugh paused perplexed.   Elusive, haunting, dim,
As though some memory that stirred in him,

Invasive of the real, outgrew the dream,
There came upon the breeze that stole up stream
A whiff of woodsmoke.

              'Twixt a beat and beat
Of Hugh's deluded heart, it seemed the sweet
Allure of home. — A brief way, and one came
Upon the clearing where the sumach flame
Ran round the forest-fringe; and just beyond
One saw the slough grass nodding in the pond
Unto the sleepy troll the bullfrogs sung.
And then one saw the place where one was
     young —
The log-house sitting on a stumpy rise.
Hearth-lit within, its windows were as eyes
That love much and are faded with old tears.
It seemed regretful of a life's arrears,
Yet patient, with a self-denying poise,
Like some old mother for her bearded boys
Waiting sweet-hearted and a little sad. —
So briefly dreamed a recrudescent lad
Beneath gray hairs, and fled.

              Through chill and damp
Still groped the odor, hinting at a camp,
A two-tongued herald wooing hope and fear.
Was hospitality or danger near?
A Sioux war-party hot upon the trail,
Or laggard Rees? Hugh crawled across the vale,

Toiled up along a zigzag gully's bed
And reached a bluff's top. In a smudge of red
The West burned low.   Hill summits, yet alight,
And pools of gloom anticipating night
Mottled the landscape to the dull blue rim.
What freak of fancy had imposed on him?
Could one smell home-smoke fifty years away?
He saw no fire; no pluming spire of gray
Rose in the dimming air to woo or warn.

He lay upon the bare height, fagged, forlorn,
And old times came upon him with the creep
Of subtle drugs that put the will to sleep
And wreak doom to the soothing of a dream.
So listlessly he scanned the sombrous stream,
Scarce seeing what he scanned. The dark in-
        creased;
A chill wind wakened from the frowning east
And soughed along the vale.
                                    Then with a start
He saw what broke the torpor of his heart
And set the wild blood free.   From where he lay
An easy point-blank rifle-shot away,
Appeared a mystic germinating spark
That in some secret garden of the dark
Upreared a frail, blue, nodding stem, whereon
A ruddy lily flourished — and was gone!

What miracle was this? Again it grew,
The scarlet blossom on the stem of blue,
And withered back again into the night.

With pounding heart Hugh crawled along the
    height
And reached a point of vantage whence, below,
He saw capricious witch-lights dim and glow
Like far-spent embers quickened in a breeze.
'Twas surely not a camp of laggard Rees,
Nor yet of Siouan warriors hot in chase.
Dusk and a quiet bivouacked in that place.
A doddering vagrant with numb hands, the Wind
Fumbled the dying ashes there, and whined.
It was the day-old camp-ground of the foe!

Glad-hearted now, Hugh gained the vale below,
Keen to possess once more the ancient gift.
Nearing the glow, he saw vague shadows lift
Out of the painted gloom of smouldering logs —
Distorted bulks that bristled, and were dogs
Snarling at this invasion of their lair.
Hugh charged upon them, growling like a bear,
And sent them whining.
                Now again to view
The burgeoning of scarlet, gold and blue,
The immemorial miracle of fire!
From heaped-up twigs a tenuous smoky spire

Arose, and made an altar of the place.
The spark-glow, faint upon the grizzled face,
Transformed the kneeling outcast to a priest;
And, native of the light-begetting East,
The Wind became a chanting acolyte.
These two, entempled in the vaulted night,
Breathed conjuries of interwoven breath.
Then, hark! — the snapping of the chains of
     Death!
From dead wood, lo! — the epiphanic god!

Once more the freightage of the fennel rod
Dissolved the chilling pall of Jovian scorn.
The wonder of the resurrection morn,
The face apocalyptic and the sword,
The glory of the many-symboled Lord,
Hugh, lifting up his eyes about him, saw!
And something in him like a vernal thaw,
Voiced with the sound of many waters, ran
And quickened to the laughter of a man.

Light-heartedly he fed the singing flame
And took its blessing: till a soft sleep came
With dreaming that was like a pleasant tale.

The far white dawn was peering up the vale
When he awoke to indolent content.
A few shorn stars in pale astonishment

Were huddled westward; and the fire was low.
Three scrawny camp-curs, mustered in a row
Beyond the heap of embers, heads askew,
Ears pricked to question what the man might do,
Sat wistfully regardant. He arose;
And they, grown canny in a school of blows,
Skulked to a safer distance, there to raise
A dolorous chanting of the evil days,
Their gray breath like the body of a prayer.
Hugh nursed the sullen embers to a flare,
Then set about to view an empty camp
As once before; but now no smoky lamp
Of blear suspicion searched a gloom of fraud
Wherein a smirking Friendship, like a bawd,
Embraced a coward Safety; now no grief,
'Twixt hideous revelation and belief,
Made womanish the man; but glad to strive,
With hope to nerve him and a will to drive,
He knew that he could finish in the race.
The staring impassivity of space
No longer mocked; the dreadful skyward climb,
Where distance seemed identical with time,
Was past now; and that mystic something, luck,
Without which worth may flounder in the ruck,
Had turned to him again.
                              So flamelike soared
Rekindled hope in him as he explored

Among the ash-heaps; and the lean dogs ran
And barked about him, for the love of man
Wistful, yet fearing.   Surely he could find
Some trifle in the hurry left behind —
Or haply hidden in the trampled sand —
That to the cunning of a needy hand
Should prove the master-key of circumstance:
For 'tis the little gifts of grudging Chance,
Well husbanded, make victors.

                        Long he sought
Without avail; and, crawling back, he thought
Of how the dogs were growing less afraid,
And how one might be skinned without a blade.
A flake of flint might do it: he would try.
And then he saw — or did the servile eye
Trick out a mental image like the real?
He saw a glimmering of whetted steel
Beside a heap now washed with morning light!

Scarce more of marvel and the sense of might
Moved Arthur when he reached a hand to take
The fay-wrought brand emerging from the lake,
Whereby a kingdom should be lopped of strife,
Than Hugh now, pouncing on a trader's knife
Worn hollow in the use of bounteous days!

And now behold a rich man by the blaze
Of his own hearth — a lord of steel and fire!

Not having, but the measure of desire
Determines wealth. Who gaining more, seek
    most,
Are ever the pursuers of a ghost
And lend their fleetness to the fugitive.
For Hugh, long goaded by the wish to live,
What gage of mastery in fire and tool! —
That twain wherewith Time put the brute to
    school,
Evolving Man, the maker and the seer.

'Twixt urging hunger and restraining fear
The gaunt dogs hovered round the man; while
    he
Cajoled them in the language of the Ree
And simulated feeding them with sand,
Until the boldest dared to sniff his hand,
Bare-fanged and with conciliative whine.
Through bristled mane the quick blade bit the
    spine
Below the skull; and as a flame-struck thing
The body humped and shuddered, withering;
The lank limbs huddled, wilted.
                  Now to skin
The carcass, dig a hole, arrange therein
And fix the pelt with stakes, the flesh-side up.
This done, he shaped the bladder to a cup

On willow withes, and filled the rawhide pot
With water from the river — made it hot
With roasted stones, and set the meat a-boil.
Those days of famine and prodigious toil
Had wrought bulimic cravings in the man,
And scarce the cooking of the flesh outran
The eating of it.   As a fed flame towers
According to the fuel it devours,
His hunger with indulgence grew, nor ceased
Until the kettle, empty of the feast,
Went dim, the sky and valley, merging, swirled
In subtle smoke that smothered out the world.
Hugh slept.
            And then — as divers, mounting, sunder
A murmuring murk to blink in sudden wonder
Upon a dazzling upper deep of blue —
He rose again to consciousness, and knew
The low sun beating slantly on his face.

Now indolently gazing round the place,
He noted how the curs had revelled there —
The bones and entrails gone; some scattered
    hair
Alone remaining of the pot of hide.
How strange he had not heard them at his side!
And granting but one afternoon had passed,
What could have made the fire burn out so fast?

Had daylight waned, night fallen, morning crept,
Noon blazed, a new day dwindled while he
    slept?
And was the friendlike fire a Jamie too?
Across the twilit consciousness of Hugh
The old obsession like a wounded bird
Fluttered.
                He got upon his knees and stirred
The feathery ash; but not a spark was there.
Already with the failing sun the air
Went keen, betokening a frosty night.
Hugh winced with something like the clutch of
    fright.
How could he bear the torture, how sustain
The sting of that antiquity of pain
Rolled back upon him — face again the foe,
That yielding victor, fleet in being slow,
That huge, impersonal malevolence?

So readily the tentacles of sense
Root in the larger standard of desire,
That Hugh fell farther in the loss of fire
Than in the finding of it he arose.
And suddenly the place grew strange, as grows
A friend's house, when the friend is on his bier,
And all that was familiar there and dear
Puts on a blank, inhospitable look.

Hugh set his face against the east, and took
That dreariest of ways, the trail of flight.
He would outcrawl the shadow of the night
And have the day to blanket him in sleep.
But as he went to meet the gloom a-creep,
Bemused with life's irrational rebuffs,
A yelping of the dogs among the bluffs
Rose, hunger-whetted, stabbing; rent the pall
Of evening silence; blunted to a drawl
Amid the arid waterways, and died.
And as the echo to the sound replied,
So in the troubled mind of Hugh was wrought
A reminiscent cry of thought to thought
That, groping, found an unlocked door to life:
The dogs — keen flint to skin one — then the knife
Discovered. Why, that made a flint and steel!
No further with the subtle foe at heel
He fled; for all about him in the rock,
To waken when the needy hand might knock,
A savior slept! He found a flake of flint,
Scraped from his shirt a little wad of lint,
Spilled on it from the smitten stone a shower
Of ruddy seed; and saw the mystic flower
That genders its own summer, bloom anew!

And so capricious luck came back to Hugh;
And he was happier than he had been

Since Jamie to that unforgiven sin
Had yielded, ages back upon the Grand.
Now he would turn the cunning of his hand
To carving crutches, that he might arise,
Be manlike, lift more rapidly the skies
That crouched between his purpose and the mark.
The warm glow housed him from the frosty dark,
And there he wrought in very joyous mood
And sang by fits — whereat the solitude
Set laggard singers snatching at the tune.
The gaunter for their hunt, the dogs came soon
To haunt the shaken fringes of the glow,
And, pitching voices to the timeless woe,
Outwailed the lilting.   So the Chorus sings
Of terror, pity and the tears of things
When most the doomed protagonist is gay.
The stars swarmed over, and the front of day
Whitened above a white world, and the sun
Rose on a sleeper with a task well done,
Nor roused him till its burning topped the blue.

When Hugh awoke, there woke a younger Hugh,
Now half a stranger; and 'twas good to feel
With ebbing sleep the old green vigor steal,
Thrilling, along his muscles and his veins,
As in a lull of winter-cleansing rains
The gray bough quickens to the sap a-creep.

It chanced the dogs lay near him, sound asleep,
Curled nose to buttock in the noonday glow.
He killed the larger with a well-aimed blow,
Skinned, dressed and set it roasting on a spit;
And when 'twas cooked, ate sparingly of it,
For need might yet make little seem a feast.

Fording the river shallows, south by east
He hobbled now along a withered rill
That issued where old floods had gashed the hill —
A cyclopean portal yawning sheer.
No storm of countless hoofs had entered here:
It seemed a place where nothing ever comes
But change of season.　He could hear the plums
Plash in the frosted thicket, over-lush;
While, like a spirit lisping in the hush,
The crisp leaves whispered round him as they fell.
And ever now and then the autumn spell
Was broken by an ululating cry
From where far back with muzzle to the sky
The lone dog followed, mourning.　Darkness
    came;
And huddled up beside a cozy flame,
Hugh's sleep was but a momentary flight
Across a little shadow into light.

So day on day he toiled: and when, afloat
Above the sunset like a stygian boat,

The new moon bore the spectre of the old,
He saw — a dwindling strip of blue outrolled —
The valley of the tortuous Cheyenne.
And ere the half moon sailed the night again,
Those far lone leagues had sloughed their garb of
    blue,
And dwindled, dwindled, dwindled after Hugh,
Until he saw that Titan of the plains,
The sinewy Missouri.   Dearth of rains
Had made the Giant gaunt as he who saw.
This loud Chain-Smasher of a late March thaw
Seemed never to have bellowed at his banks;
And yet, with staring ribs and hollow flanks,
The urge of an indomitable will
Proclaimed him of the breed of giants still;
And where the current ran a boiling track,
'Twas like the muscles of a mighty back
Grown Atlantean in the wrestler's craft.

Hugh set to work and built a little raft
Of driftwood bound with grapevines.   So it fell
That one with an amazing tale to tell
Came drifting to the gates of Kiowa.

IV

THE RETURN OF THE GHOST

Not long Hugh let the lust of vengeance gnaw
Upon him idling; though the tale he told
And what report proclaimed him, were as gold
To buy a winter's comfort at the Post.
"I can not rest; for I am but the ghost
Of someone murdered by a friend," he said,
"So long as yonder traitor thinks me dead,
Aye, buried in the bellies of the crows
And kiotes!"
                    Whereupon said one of those
Who heard him, noting how the old man shook
As with a chill: "God fend that one should look
With such a blizzard of a face for me!"
For he went grayer like a poplar tree
That shivers, ruffling to the first faint breath
Of storm, while yet the world is still as death
Save where, far off, the kenneled thunders bay.

So brooding, he grew stronger day by day,
Until at last he laid the crutches by.
And then one evening came a rousing cry

From where the year's last keelboat hove in view
Around the bend, its swarthy, sweating crew
Slant to the shouldered line.
                                            Men sang that night
In Kiowa, and by the ruddy light
Of leaping fires amid the wooden walls
The cups went round; and there were merry
        brawls
Of bearded lads no older for the beard;
And laughing stories vied with tales of weird
By stream and prairie trail and mountain pass,
Until the tipsy Bourgeois bawled for Glass
To 'shame these with a man's tale fit to hear.'

The graybeard, sitting where the light was blear,
With little heart for revelry, began
His story, told as of another man
Who, loving late, loved much and was betrayed.
He spoke unwitting how his passion played
Upon them, how their eyes grew soft or hard
With what he told; yet something of the bard
He seemed, and his the purpose that is art's,
Whereby men make a vintage of their hearts
And with the wine of beauty deaden pain.
Low-toned, insistent as October rain,
His voice beat on; and now and then would flit
Across the melancholy gray of it

A glimmer of cold fire that, like the flare
Of soundless lightning, showed a world made bare,
Green Summer slain and all its leafage stripped.

And bronze jaws tightened, brawny hands were
        gripped,
As though each hearer had a fickle friend.
But when the old man might have made an end,
Rounding the story to a peaceful close
At Kiowa, songlike his voice arose,
The grinning gray mask lifted and the eyes
Burned as a bard's who sees and prophesies,
Conning the future as a time long gone.
Swaying to rhythm the dizzy tale plunged on
Even to the cutting of the traitor's throat,
And ceased — as though a bloody strangling smote
The voice of that gray chanter, drunk with
        doom.
And there was shuddering in the blue-smeared
        gloom
Of fallen fires.   It seemed the deed was done
Before their eyes who heard.
                                    The morrow's sun,
Low over leagues of frost-enchanted plain,
Saw Glass upon his pilgrimage again,
Northbound as hunter for the keelboat's crew.
And many times the wide autumnal blue

Burned out and darkened to a deep of stars;
And still they toiled among the snags and bars —
Those lean up-stream men, straining at the rope,
Lashed by the doubt and strengthened by the
    hope
Of backward winter — engines wrought of bone
And muscle, panting for the Yellowstone,
Bend after bend and yet more bends away.
Now was the river like a sandy bay
At ebb-tide, and the far-off cutbank's boom
Mocked them in shallows; now 'twas like a flume
With which the toilers, barely creeping, strove.
And bend by bend the selfsame poplar grove,
Set on the selfsame headland, so it seemed,
Confronted them, as though they merely dreamed
Of passing one drear point.
                  So on and up
Past where the tawny Titan gulps the cup
Of Cheyenne waters, past the Moreau's mouth;
And still wry league and stubborn league fell
    south,
Becoming haze and weary memory.
Then past the empty lodges of the Ree
That gaped at cornfields plundered by the Sioux;
And there old times came mightily on Hugh,
For much of him was born and buried there.
Some troubled glory of that wind-tossed hair

Was on the trampled corn; the lonely skies,
So haunted with the blue of Jamie's eyes,
Seemed taunting him; and through the frosted
    wood
Along the flat, where once their tent had stood,
A chill wind sorrowed, and the blackbirds' brawl
Amid the funeral torches of the Fall
Ran raucously, a desecrating din.

Past where the Cannon Ball and Heart come in
They labored.   Now the Northwest 'woke at last.
The gaunt bluffs bellowed back the trumpet blast
Of charging winds that made the sandbars smoke.
To breathe now was to gulp fine sand, and choke:
The stinging air was sibilant with whips.
Leaning the more and with the firmer grips,
Still northward the embattled toilers pressed
To where the river yaws into the west.
There stood the Mandan village.
                              Now began
The chaining of the Titan.   Drift-ice ran.
The wingéd hounds of Winter ceased to bay.
The stupor of a doom completed lay
Upon the world.   The biting darkness fell.
Out in the night, resounding as a well,
They heard the deckplanks popping in a vise
Of frost; all night the smithies of the ice

Reëchoed with the griding jar and clink
Of ghostly hammers welding link to link:
And morning found the world without a sound.
There lay the stubborn Prairie Titan bound,
To wait the far-off Heraclean thaw,
Though still in silent rage he strove to gnaw
The ragged shackles knitting at his breast.

And so the boatman won a winter's rest
Among the Mandan traders: but for Hugh
There yet remained a weary work to do.
Across the naked country west by south
His purpose called him at the Big Horn's mouth —
Three hundred miles of winging for the crow;
But by the river trail that he must go
'Twas seven hundred winding miles at least.

So now he turned his back upon the feast,
Snug ease, the pleasant tale, the merry mood,
And took the bare, foot-sounding solitude
Northwestward. Long they watched him from
    the Post,
Skied on a bluff-rim, fading like a ghost
At gray cock-crow; and hooded in his breath,
He seemed indeed a fugitive from Death
On whom some tatter of the shroud still clung.
Blank space engulfed him.
                Now the moon was young

When he set forth; and day by day he strode,
His scarce healed wounds upon him like a load;
And dusk by dusk his fire outflared the moon
That waxed until it wrought a spectral noon
At nightfall.   Then he came to where, awhirl
With Spring's wild rage, the snow-born Titan girl,
A skyey wonder on her virgin face,
Receives the virile Yellowstone's embrace
And bears the lusty Seeker for the Sea.
A bleak, horizon-wide serenity
Clung round the valley where the twain lay dead.
A winding sheet was on the marriage bed.

'Twas warmer now; the sky grew overcast;
And as Hugh strode southwestward, all the vast
Gray void seemed suddenly astir with wings
And multitudinary whisperings —
The muffled sibilance of tumbling snow.
It seemed no more might living waters flow,
Moon gleam, star glint, dawn smoulder through,
    bird sing,
Or ever any fair familiar thing
Be so again.   The outworn winds were furled.
Weird weavers of the twilight of a world
Wrought, thread on kissing thread, the web of
    doom.
Grown insubstantial in the knitted gloom,

The bluffs loomed eerie, and the scanty trees
Were dwindled to remote dream-traceries
That never might be green or shield a nest.

All day with swinging stride Hugh forged south-
        west
Along the Yellowstone's smooth-paven stream,
A dream-shape moving in a troubled dream;
And all day long the whispering weavers wove.
And close on dark he came to where a grove
Of cottonwoods rose tall and shadow-thin
Against the northern bluffs.   He camped therein
And with cut boughs made shelter as he might.

Close pressed the blackness of the snow-choked
        night
About him, and his fire of plum wood purred.
Athwart a soft penumbral drowse he heard
The tumbling snowflakes sighing all around,
Till sleep transformed it to a Summer sound
Of boyish memory — susurrant bees,
The Southwind in the tousled apple trees
And slumber flowing from their leafy gloom.

He wakened to the cottonwoods' deep boom.
Black fury was the world.   The northwest's roar,
As of a surf upon a shipwreck shore,

Plunged high above him from the sheer bluff's
    verge;
And, like the backward sucking of the surge,
Far fled the sobbing of the wild snow-spray.

Black blindness grew white blindness — and 'twas
    day.
All being now seemed narrowed to a span
That held a sputtering wood fire and a man;
Beyond was tumult and a whirling maze.
The trees were but a roaring in a haze;
The sheer bluff-wall that took the blizzard's
    charge
Was thunder flung along the hidden marge
Of chaos, stridden by the ghost of light.
White blindness grew black blindness — and 'twas
    night
Wherethrough nor moon nor any star might grope.

Two days since, Hugh had killed an antelope
And what remained sufficed the time of storm.
The snow, banked round his shelter, kept him warm
And there was wood to burn for many a day.

The third dawn, oozing through a smudge of gray,
Awoke him.   It was growing colder fast.
Still from the bluff high over boomed the blast,

But now it took the void with numbing wings.
By noon the woven mystery of things
Frayed raggedly, and through a sudden rift
At length Hugh saw the beetling bluff-wall lift
A sturdy shoulder to the flying rack.
Slowly the sense of distances came back
As with the waning day the great wind fell.
The pale sun set upon a frozen hell.
The wolves howled.

        Hugh had left the Mandan town
When, heifer-horned, the maiden moon lies down
Beside the sea of evening.   Now she rose
Scar-faced and staring blankly on the snows
While yet the twilight tarried in the west;
And more and more she came a tardy guest
As Hugh pushed onward through the frozen
    waste
Until she stole on midnight shadow-faced,
A haggard spectre; then no more appeared.

'Twas on that time the man of hoary beard
Paused in the early twilight, looming lone
Upon a bluff-rim of the Yellowstone,
And peered across the white stream to the south
Where in the flatland at the Big Horn's mouth
The new fort stood that Henry's men had built.

What perfect peace for such a nest of guilt ;
What satisfied immunity from woe!
Yon sprawling shadow, pied with candle-glow
And plumed with sparkling wood-smoke, might
        have been
A homestead with the children gathered in
To share its bounty through the holidays.
Hugh saw their faces round the gay hearth-blaze:
The hale old father in a mood for yarns
Or boastful of the plenty of his barns,
Fruitage of honest toil and grateful lands;
And, half a stranger to her folded hands,
The mother with October in her hair
And August in her face.   One moment there
Hugh saw it.   Then the monstrous brutal fact
Wiped out the dream and goaded him to act,
Though now to act seemed strangely like a dream.

Descending from the bluff, he crossed the stream;
The dry snow fifing to his eager stride.
Reaching the fort stockade, he paused to bide
The passing of a whimsy.   Was it true?
Or was this but the fretted wraith of Hugh
Whose flesh had fed the kiotes long ago?

Still through a chink he saw the candle-glow,
So like an eye that brazened out a wrong.
And now there came a flight of muffled song,

The rhythmic thudding of a booted heel
That timed a squeaking fiddle to a reel!
How swiftly men forget! The spawning Earth
Is fat with graves; and what is one man worth
That fiddles should be muted at his fall?
He should have died and did not — that was
    all.
Well, let the living jig it! He would turn
Back to the night, the spacious unconcern
Of wilderness that never played the friend.

Now came the song and fiddling to an end,
And someone laughed within. The old man
    winced,
Listened with bated breath, and was convinced
'Twas Jamie laughing! Once again he heard.
Joy filled a hush 'twixt heart-beats like a bird;
Then like a famished cat his lurking hate
Pounced crushingly.
                                He found the outer gate,
Beat on it with his shoulder, raised a cry.
No doubt 'twas deemed a fitful wind went by;
None stirred. But when he did not cease to
    shout,
A door creaked open and a man came out
Amid the spilling candle-glimmer, raised
The wicket in the outer gate and gazed

One moment on a face as white as death,
Because the beard was thick with frosted breath
Made mystic by the stars.   Then came a gasp,
The clatter of the falling wicket's hasp,
The crunch of panic feet along the snow;
And someone stammered huskily and low:
"My God! I saw the Old Man's ghost out
    there!"
'Twas spoken as one speaks who feels his hair
Prickle the scalp.   And then another said —
It seemed like Henry's voice — "The dead are
    dead:
What talk is this, Le Bon?   You saw him die!
Who's there?"
                Hugh strove to shout, to give the lie
To those within; but could not fetch a sound.
Just so he dreamed of lying under ground
Beside the Grand and hearing overhead
The talk of men.   Or was he really dead,
And all this but a maggot in the brain?

Then suddenly the clatter of a chain
Aroused him, and he saw the portal yawn
And saw a bright rectangled patch of dawn
As through a grave's mouth — no, 'twas candle-
    light
Poured through the open doorway on the night;

And those were men before him, bulking black
Against the glow.
                Reality flashed back;
He strode ahead and entered at the door.
A falling fiddle jangled on the floor
And left a deathly silence.   On his bench
The fiddler shrank.   A row of eyes, a-blench
With terror, ran about the naked hall.
And there was one who huddled by the wall
And hid his face and shivered.
                      For a spell
That silence clung;   and then the old man:
    "Well,
Is this the sort of welcome that I get?
'Twas not my time to feed the kiotes yet!
Put on the pot and stew a chunk of meat
And you shall see how much a ghost can eat!
I've journeyed far if what I hear be true!"

Now in that none might doubt the voice of
    Hugh,
Nor yet the face, however it might seem
A blurred reflection in a flowing stream,
A buzz of wonder broke the trance of dread.
"Good God!" the Major gasped; "We thought
    you dead!
Two men have testified they saw you die!"

"If they speak truth," Hugh answered, "then I lie
Both here and by the Grand.   If I be right,
Then two lie here and shall lie from this night.
Which are they?"
                    Henry answered: "Yon is one."

The old man set the trigger of his gun
And gazed on Jules who cowered by the wall.
Eyes blinked, expectant of the hammer's fall;
Ears strained, anticipative of the roar.
But Hugh walked leisurely across the floor
And kicked the croucher, saying: "Come, get up
And wag your tail!   I couldn't kill a pup!"
Then turning round: "I had a faithful friend;
No doubt he too was with me to the end!
Where's Jamie?"
                    "Started out before the snows
For Atkinson."

V

JAMIE

THE Country of the Crows,
Through which the Big Horn and the Rosebud
  run,
Sees over mountain peaks the setting sun;
And southward from the Yellowstone flung wide,
It broadens ever to the morning side
And has the Powder on its vague frontier.
About the subtle changing of the year,
Ere even favored valleys felt the stir
Of Spring, and yet expectancy of her
Was like a pleasant rumor all repeat
Yet none may prove, the sound of horses' feet
Went eastward through the silence of that land.
For then it was there rode a little band
Of trappers out of Henry's Post, to bear
Dispatches down to Atkinson, and there
To furnish out a keelboat for the Horn.
And four went lightly, but the fifth seemed worn
As with a heavy heart; for that was he
Who should have died but did not.

Silently
He heard the careless parley of his men,
And thought of how the Spring should come
   again,
That garish strumpet with her world-old lure,
To waken hope where nothing may endure,
To quicken love where loving is betrayed.
Yet now and then some dream of Jamie made
Slow music in him for a little while;
And they who rode beside him saw a smile
Glimmer upon that ruined face of gray,
As on a winter fog the groping day
Pours glory through a momentary rift.
Yet never did the gloom that bound him, lift;
He seemed as one who feeds upon his heart
And finds, despite the bitter and the smart,
A little sweetness and is glad for that.

Now up the Powder, striking for the Platte
Across the bleak divide the horsemen went;
Attained that river where its course is bent
From north to east: and spurring on apace
Along the wintry valley, reached the place
Where from the west flows in the Laramie.
Thence, fearing to encounter with the Ree,
They headed eastward through the barren land
To where, fleet-footed down a track of sand,

The Niobrara races for the morn —
A gaunt-loined runner.

                      Here at length was born
Upon the southern slopes the baby Spring,
A timid, fretful, ill-begotten thing,
A-suckle at the Winter's withered paps:
Not such as when announced by thunder-claps
And ringed with swords of lightning, she would
      ride,
The haughty victrix and the mystic bride,
Clad splendidly as never Sheba's Queen,
Before her marching multitudes of green
In many-bannered triumph! Grudging, slow,
Amid the fraying fringes of the snow
The bunch-grass sprouted; and the air was
      chill.
Along the northern slopes 'twas winter still,
And no root dreamed what Triumph-over-Death
Was nurtured now in some bleak Nazareth
Beyond the crest to sunward.
                     On they spurred
Through vacancies that waited for the bird,
And everywhere the Odic Presence dwelt.
The Southwest blew, the snow began to melt;
And when they reached the valley of the Snake,
The Niobrara's ice began to break,

And all night long and all day long it made
A sound as of a random cannonade
With rifles snarling down a skirmish line.

The geese went over.   Every tree and vine
Was dotted thick with leaf-buds when they saw
The little river of Keyapaha
Grown mighty for the moment.   Then they came,
One evening when all thickets were aflame
With pale green witch-fires and the windflowers
        blew,
To where the headlong Niobrara threw
His speed against the swoln Missouri's flank
And hurled him roaring to the further bank —
A giant staggered by a pigmy's sling.
Thence, plunging ever deeper into Spring,
Across the greening prairie east by south
They rode, and, just above the Platte's wide
        mouth,
Came, weary with the trail, to Atkinson.

There all the vernal wonder-work was done:
No care-free heart might find aught lacking there.
The dove's call wandered in the drowsy air;
A love-dream brooded in the lucent haze.
Priapic revellers, the shrieking jays
Held mystic worship in the secret shade.
Woodpeckers briskly plied their noisy trade

Along the tree-boles, and their scarlet hoods
Flashed flame-like in the smoky cottonwoods.
What lacked ? Not sweetness in the sun-lulled
        breeze;
The plum bloom murmurous with bumblebees
Was drifted deep in every draw and slough.
Not color; witcheries of gold and blue
The dandelion and the violet
Wove in the green. Might not the sad forget,
The happy here have nothing more to seek ?
Lo, yonder by that pleasant little creek,
How one might loll upon the grass and fish
And build the temple of one's wildest wish
'Twixt nibbles ! Surely there was quite enough
Of wizard-timber and of wonder-stuff
To rear it nobly to the blue-domed roof !

Yet there was one whose spirit stood aloof
From all this joyousness — a gray old man,
No nearer now than when the quest began
To what he sought on that long winter trail.

Aye, Jamie had been there; but when the tale
That roving trappers brought from Kiowa
Was told to him, he seemed as one who saw
A ghost, and could but stare on it, they said:
Until one day he mounted horse and fled

Into the North, a devil-ridden man.
"I've got to go and find him if I can,"
Was all he said for days before he left.

And what of Hugh? So long of love bereft,
So long sustained and driven by his hate,
A touch of ruth now made him desolate.
No longer eager to avenge the wrong,
With not enough of pity to be strong
And just enough of love to choke and sting,
A gray old hulk amid the surge of Spring
He floundered on a lee-shore of the heart.

But when the boat was ready for the start
Up the long watery stairway to the Horn,
Hugh joined the party. And the year was shorn
Of blooming girlhood as they forged amain
Into the North; the late green-mantled plain
Grew sallow; and the ruthless golden shower
Of Summer wrought in lust upon the flower
That withered in the endless martyrdom
To seed. The scarlet quickened on the plum
About the Heart's mouth when they came thereto;
Among the Mandans grapes were turning blue,
And they were purple at the Yellowstone.
A frosted scrub-oak, standing out alone
Upon a barren bluff top, gazing far
Above the crossing at the Powder's bar,

Was spattered with the blood of Summer slain.
So it was Autumn in the world again,
And all those months of toil had yielded nought
To Hugh.   (How often is the seeker sought
By what he seeks — a blind, heart-breaking
    game!)
For always had the answer been the same
From roving trapper and at trading post:
Aye, one who seemed to stare upon a ghost
And followed willy-nilly where it led,
Had gone that way in search of Hugh, they said —
A haggard, blue-eyed, yellow-headed chap.

And often had the old man thought, 'Mayhap
He'll be at Henry's Post and we shall meet;
And to forgive and to forget were sweet:
'Tis for its nurse that Vengeance whets the tooth!
And oh the golden time of Jamie's youth,
That it should darken for a graybeard's whim!'
So Hugh had brooded, till there came on him
The pity of a slow rain after drouth.

But at the crossing of the Rosebud's mouth
A shadow fell upon his growing dream.
A band of Henry's traders, bound down stream,
Who paused to traffic in the latest word —
Down-river news for matters seen and heard

In higher waters — had not met the lad,
Not yet encountered anyone who had.

Alas, the journey back to yesterwhiles!
How tangled are the trails! The stubborn miles,
How wearily they stretch! And if one win
The long way back in search of what has been,
Shall he find aught that is not strange and new?

Thus wrought the melancholy news in Hugh,
As he turned back with those who brought the
    news;
For more and more he dreaded now to lose
What doubtful seeking rendered doubly dear.
And in the time when keen winds stripped the
    year
He came with those to where the Poplar joins
The greater river. There Assinoboines,
Rich from the Summer's hunting, had come down
And flung along the flat their ragged town,
That traders might bring goods and winter there.

So leave the heartsick graybeard. Otherwhere
The final curtain rises on the play.
'Tis dead of Winter now. For day on day
The blizzard wind has thundered, sweeping wide
From Mississippi to the Great Divide

Out of the North beyond Saskatchewan.
Brief evening glimmers like an inverse dawn
After a long white night.   The tempest dies;
The snow-haze lifts.   Now let the curtain rise
Upon Milk River valley, and reveal
The stars like broken glass on frosted steel
Above the Piegan lodges, huddled deep
In snowdrifts, like a freezing flock of sheep.
A crystal weight the dread cold crushes down
And no one moves about the little town
That seems to grovel as a thing that fears.

But see! a lodge-flap swings; a squaw appears,
Hunched with the sudden cold.   Her footsteps
     creak
Shrill in the hush.   She stares upon the bleak,
White skyline for a moment, then goes in.
We follow her, push back the flap of skin,
Enter the lodge, inhale the smoke-tanged air
And blink upon the little faggot-flare
That blossoms in the center of the room.
Unsteady shadows haunt the outer gloom
Wherein the walls are guessed at.   Upward,
     far,
The smoke-vent now and then reveals a star
As in a well.   The ancient squaw, a-stoop,
Her face light-stricken, stirs a pot of soup

That simmers with a pleasant smell and sound.
A gnarled old man, cross-legged upon the ground,
Sits brooding near.   He feeds the flame with
    sticks;
It brightens.   Lo, a leaden crucifix
Upon the wall!   These heathen eyes, though dim,
Have seen the white man's God and cling to Him,
Lest on the sunset trail slow feet should err.

But look again.   From yonder bed of fur
Beside the wall a white man strives to rise.
He lifts his head, with yearning sightless eyes
Gropes for the light.   A mass of golden hair
Falls round the face that sickness and despair
Somehow make old, albeit he is young.
His weak voice, stumbling to the mongrel tongue
Of traders, flings a question to the squaw:
"You saw no Black Robe?   Tell me what you
    saw!"
And she, brief-spoken as her race, replies:
"Heaped snow — sharp stars — a kiote on the
    rise."

The blind youth huddles moaning in the furs.
The firewood spits and pops, the boiled pot purrs
And sputters.   On this little isle of sound
The sea of winter silence presses round —
One feels it like a menace.

                        Now the crone
Dips out a cup of soup, and having blown
Upon it, takes it to the sick man there
And bids him eat.   With wild, unseeing stare
He turns upon her: "Why are they so long?
I can not eat!   I've done a mighty wrong;
It chokes me!   Oh no, no, I must not die
Until the Black Robe comes!"   His feeble cry
Sinks to a whisper.   "Tell me, did they go —
Your kinsmen?"

                  "They went south before the snow."
"And will they tell the Black Robe?"

                              "They will tell."

The crackling of the faggots for a spell
Seems very loud.   Again the sick man moans
And, struggling with the weakness in his bones,
Would gain his feet, but can not.   "Go again,
And tell me that you see the bulks of men
Dim in the distance there."

                              The squaw obeys;
Returns anon to crouch beside the blaze,
Numb-fingered and a-shudder from the night.
The vacant eyes that hunger for the light
Are turned upon her: "Tell me what you saw!
Or maybe snowshoes sounded up the draw.
Quick, tell me what you saw and heard out there!"

"Heaped snow — sharp stars — big stillness every-
    where."

One clutching at thin ice with numbing grip
Cries while he hopes; but when his fingers slip,
He takes the final plunge without a sound.
So sinks the youth now, hopeless.   All around
The winter silence presses in; the walls
Grow vague and vanish in the gloom that crawls
Close to the failing fire.

                        The Piegans sleep.
Night hovers midway down the morning steep.
The sick man drowses.   Nervously he starts
And listens; hears no sound except his heart's
And that weird murmur brooding stillness makes.
But stealthily upon the quiet breaks —
Vague as the coursing of the hearer's blood —
A muffled, rhythmic beating, thud on thud,
That, growing nearer, deepens to a crunch.
So, hungry for the distance, snowshoes munch
The crusted leagues of Winter, stride by stride.
A camp-dog barks; the hollow world outside
Brims with the running howl of many curs.

Now wide-awake, half risen in the furs,
The youth can hear low voices and the creak
Of snowshoes near the lodge. His thin, **wild
    shriek**

Startles the old folk from their slumberings:
"He comes! The Black Robe!"
                              Now the door-flap swings,
And briefly one who splutters Piegan, bars
The way, then enters. Now the patch of stars
Is darkened with a greater bulk that bends
Beneath the lintel. "Peace be with you, friends!
And peace with him herein who suffers pain!"
So speaks the second comer of the twain —
A white man by his voice. And he who lies
Beside the wall, with empty, groping eyes
Turned to the speaker: "There can be no peace
For me, good Father, till this gnawing cease —
The gnawing of a great wrong I have done."

The big man leans above the youth: "My son —"
(Grown husky with the word, the deep voice
          breaks,
And for a little spell the whole man shakes
As with the clinging cold) "— have faith and
          hope!
'Tis often nearest dawn when most we grope.
Does not the Good Book say, Who seek shall
          find?"

"But, Father, I am broken now and blind,
And I have sought, and I have lost the way."
To which the stranger: "What would Jesus say?

Hark!   In the silence of the heart 'tis said —
By their own weakness are the feeble sped;
The humblest feet are surest for the goal;
The blind shall see the City of the Soul.
Lay down your burden at His feet to-night."

Now while the fire, replenished, bathes in light
The young face scrawled with suffering and care,
Flinging ironic glories on the hair
And glinting on dull eyes that once flashed blue,
The sick one tells the story of old Hugh
To him whose face, averted from the glow,
Still lurks in gloom.   The winds of battle blow
Once more along the steep.   Again one sees
The rescue from the fury of the Rees,
The graybeard's fondness for the gay lad; then
The westward march with Major Henry's men
With all that happened there upon the Grand.

"And so we hit the trail of Henry's band,"
The youth continues; "for we feared to die:
And dread of shame was ready with the lie
We carried to our comrades.   Hugh was dead
And buried there beside the Grand, we said.
Could any doubt that what we said was true?
They even praised our courage!   But I knew!
The nights were hell because I heard his cries
And saw the crows a-pecking at his eyes,

The kiotes tearing at him.   O my God!
I tried and tried to think him under sod;
But every time I slept it was the same.
And then one night — I lay awake — he came!
I say he came — I know I hadn't slept!
Amid a light like rainy dawn, he crept
Out of the dark upon his hands and knees.
The wound he got that day among the Rees
Was like red fire.   A snarl of bloody hair
Hung round the eyes that had a pleading stare,
And down the ruined face and gory beard
Big tear-drops rolled.   He went as he appeared,
Trailing a fog of light that died away.
And I grew old before I saw the day.
O Father, I had paid too much for breath!
The Devil traffics in the fear of death,
And may God pity anyone who buys
What I have bought with treachery and lies —
This rat-like gnawing in my breast!

                                    " I knew
I couldn't rest until I buried Hugh;
And so I told the Major I would go
To Atkinson with letters, ere the snow
Had choked the trails.   Jules wouldn't come
        along;
He didn't seem to realize the wrong;

He called me foolish, couldn't understand.
I rode alone — not south, but to the Grand.
Daylong my horse beat thunder from the sod,
Accusing me; and all my prayers to God
Seemed flung in vain at bolted gates of brass.
And in the night the wind among the grass
Hissed endlessly the story of my shame.

"I do not know how long I rode: I came
Upon the Grand at last, and found the place,
And it was empty.   Not a sign or trace
Was left to show what end had come to Hugh.
And oh that grave!   It gaped upon the blue,
A death-wound pleading dumbly for the slain.
I filled it up and fled across the plain,
And somehow came to Atkinson at last.
And there I heard the living Hugh had passed
Along the river northward in the Fall!
O Father, he had found the strength to crawl
That long, heart-breaking distance back to life,
Though Jules had taken blanket, steel and knife,
And I, his trusted comrade, had his gun!

"They said I'd better stay at Atkinson,
Because old Hugh was surely hunting me,
White-hot to kill.   I did not want to flee
Or hide from him.   I even wished to die,
If so this aching cancer of a lie

Might be torn out forever.   So I went,
As eager as the homesick homeward bent,
In search of him and peace.
                              But I was cursed.
For even when his stolen rifle burst
And spewed upon me this eternal night,
I might not die as any other might;
But God so willed that friendly Piegans came
To spare me yet a little unto shame.
O Father, is there any hope for me?"

"Great hope indeed, my son!" so huskily
The other answers.   "I recall a case
Like yours — no matter what the time and
      place —
'Twas somewhat like the story that you tell;
Each seeking and each sought, and both in hell;
But in the tale I mind, they met at last."

The youth sits up, white-faced and breathing
      fast:
"They met, you say?   What happened?   Quick!
      Oh quick!"

"The old man found the dear lad blind and sick
And both forgave — 'twas easy to forgive —
For oh we have so short a time to live —"

Whereat the youth: "Who's here? The Black
    Robe's gone!
Whose voice is this?"

                    The gray of winter dawn
Now creeping round the door-flap, lights the
    place
And shows thin fingers groping for a face
Deep-scarred and hoary with the frost of years
Whereover runs a new springtide of tears.

"O Jamie, Jamie, Jamie — I am Hugh!
There was no Black Robe yonder — Will I do?"

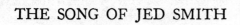

THE SONG OF JED SMITH

FOR SIGURD'S WIFE
MAXINE

I

The valley was beginning to forget
The dead June day, but southward clearly yet
The peaks remembered.

              Trappers by their gear,
With four trail-weary horses grazing near,
Two men were sitting, leaning on their packs.
Still as the shadows purpling at their backs,
They gazed upon the smoke that rose between,
Thin-fingered. From the canyon of the Green,
Low-toned but mighty in the solitude,
A never-never moaning voiced the mood
Some reminiscent waking dream had cast
Upon them. Henry's Fork that hurried past
Ran full of distant voices, muffled mirths.
A meadowlark, in gratitude for Earth's
Lush shielding, with a mounting bar that broke,
Enriched the quiet.

             And the elder spoke,
Stirring the embers into sudden fire:
"Well, that's a queer one! Was I nodding, Squire?
I swear I saw it!"

Lifted in surprise,
With thick, black beard belying boyish eyes,
A flame-bright face regarded him. "What's queer?
I wasn't looking, Art; just sitting here
And seeing things myself."

The failing flare,
Across the elder's grizzling beard and hair,
Revealed the mien of one whom many snows
Would leave green-hearted. "No, I didn't doze,"
He said; "and I was thinking nothing more
Than what to do about that saddle sore
The old mare's got; and it was only now,
All still and empty. Suddenly, somehow,
I tell you, it was eighteen twenty-five!
This valley came alive with fires, alive
With men and horses! Rings on glowing rings
Of old-time faces sang as liquor sings
After a drouth; and laughter shook the night
Where someone, full of meat and getting tight,
Spun lies the way Black Harris used to do.
Then it was now again, and only you
Were sitting yonder."

"Art, you make me dry,"
The other said, "you make me want to cry
Into my whiskers. Thirteen years away!
That's better than a million miles, I'd say,
Without a horse, and all the country strange!"

Now while they mused there came an eerie
    change
Upon the world. From where the day lay dead
The ghost thereof in streamered glory fled
Across the sky, transfiguring the scene.
Amazed amidst the other-worldly green
That glowed along the flat, as though a shout
Had startled them, they stood and stared about,
Searching the muted landscape of a dream.

There *was* a cry. The bluffs along the stream
Awoke to mock it. On a low rise there
To westward, vivid in the radiant air,
They saw a horseman coming at a jog,
A pack-mule plodding after, and a dog
That rushed ahead now, halted, muzzle high,
And howled.

                    The light-blown bubble of the sky,
As with a final strain of splendor, broke.
The peaks forgot; and like a purple smoke
Night settled in the valley.

                            Looming dim,
The rider neared the shadows greeting him
Beside the embers, while the outer gloam
Neighed welcome. "Hitch and make yourself at
    home,"
One bantered: "Hang your hat upon a star,

The house is yours. Whatever else you are,
It's not a horsethief by the nag you've got!"

The stranger laughed. "If supper's in the pot,
The nag has served me well enough," he said,
Dismounting. To the growling dog, "Down, Jed,
Old-timer! They've invited us to eat."

Now hand found hand. "Except for beaver meat,
And jerked at that, you'll find the cupboard bare,"
One said; "and, short of Taos, we'll have to share
Our drinking yonder with the bird and beast."

"I never make this valley but to feast,
And water won't keep ghosts away," replied
The stranger, fumbling at the horse's side
And stripping off the saddle. "Anyhow,
The hump and haunches of a yearling cow
Have fagged the old mule here. If that won't do
To make a good old-fashioned rendezvous,
I've come from Taos—the jug's full!"

                                    Bluffs to heights
Hurrahed with glee, and in the outer night's
Star-bearing silence troubled for a space
The somber summits.

                        "Come and show your face!"
The elder cried. "I'll swear, if I don't know
That voice—though he went wolfing years ago—

My name's not Black!" He seized the other's hand
And drew him to the embers. Stirred and fanned,
They reddened till the fed twigs took the spark,
And, cut upon the onyx of the dark,
A shaven face shone—sensitive and lean,
With eyes that narrowed less upon the seen
Than with some inward gazing. Leather-skinned,
It was, hard-bitten by the worldly wind;
But more the weather of a mind that seeks
In solitude had etched upon the cheeks
A cryptic story.

        "Holy smoke!" cried Black;
"Look, Squire! Unless it be a spook come back
To haunt us, old Bob Evans hasn't fed
The kiotes yet!"

        A joyful warwhoop fled
Along the valley. Eager voices, blent
In greeting, quickened into merriment.
The dog barked gaily and the horses neighed.
Impatiently the laden pack-mule brayed
Sardonic comment.

II

            Now the jug went round
The glowing circle, while the fat hump browned
And sputtered, dripping. Night, immense and still,
With stars keen-whetted by the mountain chill,
Dreamed deep around the trio, snugly housed
In living light. From where the horses browsed,
The blowing loudened in a lapse of speech.
A wolf howled, and the farthest empty reach
Of vastness mourned, as though God dreamed in
      vain
And 'wakened, filling with a wail of pain
The nightmare void of uncreated good.

The dog whined, bristling.

                Cozy in the wood,
The tongued flame purred content. Again the
      bright,
Brief moment vanquished the appalling night
Of timelessness.

          The youngest laughed, and said:
"Is this a wake? If one of us is dead,

[6]

Just count me in among the other two
And cut a chunk of meat!"

                    "A rendezvous,"
Mused Evans, with a far, unfocussed gaze
Upon the other. "Ghosts of better days,
With laughters never to be laughed again,
And singing from the lips of lusty men
Gone dust forever! Listen! Can you hear?
I ought to know. I've heard them year by year
With every June!"

                    "Well, let them drink with us!"
The youngest chuckled. "Bob, you loony cuss,
I like you; but you always lived too far
Above the belly where the doin's are
That make men happy. This child ought to know!"
With jug presented, "Spooks of long ago,"
He mocked, "here's looking at you! Bye and bye
We'll be as dead as you! But now, we're dry,
And men at that! Tough luck to be a ghost!
Old-timers, skoal! Here's how!"

                              He drank the toast

And snorted.

        "Squire," laughed Black, "as Milton wrote,
The place for education—mind, I quote!—
The place for education in your head

[7]

Ain't there at all! According to old Jed,
Bob's half a poet! Why, that look of his
Can see what never was and really is
Because it isn't—if you get the way
My stick floats! It was on the Snake one day.
Alone and far from home, we sat there glum,
Remembering how many friends had come
To crow meat since we crossed the Great Divide;
And, after long, he looked at me and sighed
And said: 'I wish I knew where Evans went.
The man's a scholar. Only accident
Has made him less than poet.' Who but he
Was like to know?"

                        The Squire laughed merrily.
"Be easy with me, Art, until I'm tight.
You'll be surprised, come later in the night,
And nothing in the jug, how clear and quick
I get the drift of any crazy stick
A man can float! Why, Boys, I used to grieve
And weep for men too sober to believe
Black Harris when he squared away to lie,
And me well educated! Hope to die,
I could believe him better when he lied!
You mind his forest that was putrified?
Him peeking through that underbrush of hair
And whiskers at the whole gang howling there,
Short-breatht with meat and three sheets in the
        wind,

Save only Jed, the man that never sinned,
Stone-sober, looking down his long, thin nose!
You mind? Old Harris and the 'Rapahoes
Hell-bent for hair—and plenty!—had a race.
The old man won, and came upon a place
Where trees soared taller than a tree can soar,
And then some taller! And the queerest roar
Ran high among them—pines in stormy weather—
And like a million castanets together,
The green leaves clicked, though not a zephyr
    stirred.
And in the branches, on his holy word,
Queer birds, like none this side of Jordan, sang.
'And would ye think,' says he, 'the whole
    shebang
Was putrified!' 'It must've made a smell
To kill a polecat!' someone says. 'Aw, hell!'
Says he, disgusted; 'How could such rock be?
The place was putrified, and every tree
Was agate and the birds was agate too!
That roar up yonder was a wind that blew
Before God's whiskers sprouted—yes, and man
Was only mud yet. When the place began
To putrify, the thing came on so strong
And fast, it caught that wind and every song
Them birds was singing at the time, you see!' "
The far-flung, many-echoed gaiety
Became a chuckle. "Harris never wed—
For long. 'The truth and me is hitched,' he said;

[9]

'I'll lick the man that tries to put asunder!'
Bob, who poured lightning in that jug, I wonder?
I half believe him! Pretty soon I will!
Let's have the meat now, Shakespeare!"

Silent still,
The other brooded with an empty stare.

"I mind," Black said. "We sat right over there
Beyond the horses. . . . What a bunch of men!
This valley will not see their like again
Until the evening and the dawn swap places
And days run backwards! I can see their faces
While Harris took his time to be exact
And dealt with each new whopper like a fact
That 'twould have been dishonest to forget!
Fitzpatrick, Ashley, Jackson, and Sublette!
Jim Bridger, newly bearded, half a boy
For all his doings! Hanna and McCoy,
La Plant, Reubasco, Harry Rogers, Ranne,
Luzano, Gobel, Gaither—man by man,
I see them laughing yonder, soon to die,
The men who followed Smith—and you and I
Return alone, Bob, out of thirty-two!
Jim Beckwourth, filled with tales of derring-do,
And hero of them all, to let him say,
Guffawing at the very sober way
That Harris had of flirting with his wife!
And old Jed Smith—!"

                    He drew his hunting knife,
And absently awhile he whetted it
Upon his boot. Then, having carved a spit
For each, he sliced the succulently rare
Fat meat and passed it.

                    "I can see him there—
The way his wide-set eyes turned slits of blue
When he was thinking; how his brown hair grew
In waves that broke like surf about his ears.
I knew him longest in his hardest years,
And seldom did he fail to keep it trim
And shave—as though he felt God's eye on him,
No matter what the hardship or the weather.
I see the way his straight brows grew together,
And knitted at a run of scurvy talk;
The nose that made you think about a hawk;
The lean six feet of man-stuff, shouldered wide,
Too busy with a dream that grew inside
For laughter. He was seeing all the white
Map westward as a page on which to write,
For men to read, the story of a land
Still lying empty as the Maker's hand
Before creation. From the Great Salt Lake,
Between the Colorado and the Snake,
From burning sand to high Sierra snow,
He wrote it. Some day men will read and know
The man he was. It does me good to boast
I knew him longest."

"But I loved him most,"
Said Evans, rousing with a weary air
Of slow return, his heart still otherwhere,
Remote and lonely; and the low voice took,
As from the gentle burning of his look,
A hint of smoke. "I loved him most; and yet
I failed him."

"Aw, drink hearty and forget!
You're far too sober, Bob!" the younger said,
Passing the jug. "Too bad about old Jed!
'Twas seven years ago we heard somewhere
A parcel of Comanches got his hair
Away down yonder on the Cimarrone."

"He died alone," the other said; "alone;
And where his bones are lying no one knows.
The fed wolves sang his dirge, and feasting crows
Were his ironic mourners."

"Let him rest
In peace," the younger bantered. "At the best,
Dying's a one-man job! Hurrah for now!
He must have gone to heaven anyhow;
I never saw him having any fun!
That's right, old-timer! Have another one,
And send the O-be-joyful 'round the ring!
We'll drink to good old Jed gone angeling—
But he won't like it if he's looking down!

He'll cock that one scarred brow of his, and frown
Without a word; the scar he got that day
He argued with the bear up Big Horn way
And came off best—a bit the worse for wear—
Some ribs caved in. But when you saw the bear,
Heart-stabbed and belly-slashed—well, you began
To know that Jedediah was a man
For all his Bible-reading, parson ways!
And so here's to you, 'Diah! Happy days!
Meat in the pot and sign in every stream!"

He drank, and passed the jug.

                  "And some great dream
To lead, and may the strange trail never end!"
The elder added.

                  "And no faithless friend,"
The other murmured, drinking.

III

Now the deep,
Tremendous silence of the night asleep
Possessed the little tent of light again.
A-haunch, head cocked, the dog surveyed the men.
One drooping ear for doubt and one pricked ear
For hope, he watched the red meat disappear
In alien mouths, commenting with a hurt,
Ingratiating whimper, and alert
To catch the morsels casually thrown.
The muted thunder of the canyon's moan,
The Fork's low murmur, the contented sound
Of grazing in the dark, made more profound
The sense of silence heavy on the world.

The feasting done, the dog lay down and curled
A tawny back against the ember light,
The slender, wolfish muzzle snuggled tight
Against a shaggy buttock. One eye slept,
And one, upon the verge of slumber, kept
Uneasy vigil lest the feast resume.

Now slowly shrank the circle of the gloom,
Chill-edged. Aroused from indolent content,

The Squire arose, yawned lazily, and went
Into the dark. An ax's *clink* and *chock*
Broke brittle on the everlasting rock
Of stillness, bluff and peak with flying shard
Resounding. Stooping low and breathing hard,
He reappeared at length; and having shed
His burden on the fire, sat down and said:
"That turn deserves another! Pass the juice!"

He took a swig, then made his girdle loose,
Sighed with eupeptic pleasure, being sated,
And chuckled: "Boys, I'm going educated,
The way you don't get cross-eyed with a book!
Just now out yonder when I stopped to look
Around and listen, all at once there came
A funny sort of feeling. 'Twas the same
Old 'Diah used to give me years ago:
A feel of something you could never know,
Except that it was big and still and dim
And had a secret. If you stuck with him,
Most any minute everything would change.
The mountains and the valleys would be strange,
And there'd be rivers like no common river—
A sort of evening-before-Christmas shiver
All up the backbone, like a youngster knows.

It was the time we wintered with the Crows
In 'twenty three and 'four, when I first felt
That way about him. Snow began to melt

Along Wind River. Winter wasn't done,
But in the soft late February sun
You heard the gulches roar. A big chinook
Was booming when we saddled up and took
The trail that led across the Great Divide.
And who had ever seen the other side
The Shining Mountains? Indians, and such
Assorted varmints, didn't matter much,
We being humans! It was waiting yet,
Since God A'mighty finished it, to get
The first real, honest seeing from our eyes!

We followed up Sweetwater. No surprise!
A frozen crick, and everything was old
About it. But we felt it getting cold
And colder as we rode along the flat,
Smooth valley westward, and we knew from that
How we were climbing. Mountains fell away—
Just sort of melted. Then the second day,
The word came down the line: 'We're in the Pass!'

But there was only common yellow grass
And sagebrush on a prairie, rolling wide
From common hills along the nearer side
To far peaks looking like a broken saw
Ahead and to the right across the draw
Along Sweetwater. Antelope were there
Beside the crick—like critters anywhere
In anybody's meadow. Empty skies

Were straight ahead above a little rise
Notched crooked like a hind-sight out of true.
There wasn't any shoutingful to-do
About it! But I galloped to the head
To have a look, and rode beside old Jed.
He didn't see me, didn't say a word
To anybody. Pretty soon he spurred
A ways ahead, reined suddenly, and stopped.
From where we sat and looked, the prairie
    dropped
Along the easy shoulder of a hill
Into a left-hand valley. Things got still
And kind of strange. The others, gathered
    round,
Quit talking, and there wasn't any sound
Except a bridle made it. Then it came—
That funny sort of feeling, just the same
I had out there a little while ago—
A feel of something you could never know,
But it was something big and still and dim
That wouldn't tell. It seemed to come from him
Just looking down the Sandy towards the Green
That had been waiting yonder to be seen
A million winters and a million springs
And summers! 'Twas the other side of things—
Another world!

        You gather I was wet
Behind the ears; a pea-green youngster yet,

Just turning seventeen, and wild as hell.
That river had been doing pretty well
Without us; and, as any beaver knows,
A river is a ditch where water flows,
And any side's the other where you ain't!
I mind I wondered was he going to faint,
Or was he praying, maybe, when he bent
His head. I caught him at it in his tent
That winter once! But even if he was,
It seemed the sort of thing a fellow does
With just that sort of feeling . . . Well, they say
We live to learn."

               "It's just the other way,"
Said Evans dryly. "Mostly we forget;
But 'Diah never did."

                "A few nips yet,
And you'll be even wiser than your 'teens,"
The elder chaffed. "I know what Evans means.
There's something sort of thrilling that you know
Until you learn so much that isn't so,
There's no room left inside for what you knew!
I felt a bit like that about him, too,
And me an oldster. He was hard and grim
And man a-plenty; but he had in him
What made you feel the world had just begun!
Queer how we call him old! Just thirty one—
Or maybe two—the year that he went under!"

"He had the humble wisdom that is wonder,"
Mused Evans.

          "Well, let's have another smile,"
The younger countered, laughing. "Afterwhile,
The way I'm getting wise and wiser still,
I'll bawl for milk! Where was I? Oh—the hill
Above the Promised Land—and 'Diah praying!
Leastwise, he didn't faint. Then he was saying
How that was where the water ran both ways,
And over there beyond the valley haze
The great Pacific rolled! I heard it roar—
Almost!

          It was a couple years before
That funny feeling left me. All the way
Down Little Sandy and the Big next day,
It grew and grew till it was everywhere,
And not a 'tarnal thing but sagebrush there,
And sage hens! Every time a covey broke
From cover—like a gun-shot lacking smoke—
It hit me like a signal something queer
Around us had been waiting for, to hear
And happen—if you gather what I mean!
And when we struck the valley of the Green,
'Twas beaver heaven!

          Listen to it moan
Out yonder, like a dog without a bone!

Lend me your bosom, Arthur, if I weep!
I'd give a leg to see the slow Spring creep
Among the willows by the stream once more
The way it did that year of 'twenty four
And everything brand new! Them days are dead,
And gone forever—followed after Jed
To heaven! Mind to quit and settle down,
And keep a cow and wife somewheres near town
And be a Christian!"

　　　　　　　　　"Well, why don't you quit?"
The elder chuckled.

　　　　　　　　　"Had a spell of it,"
The other answered. "Wasn't nothing there!
And even if it just ain't anywhere,
Out this way it's got room enough to be!
Get humpbacked looking for a living! Me?
What for? To have a funeral, and all
The neighbors happy for a chance to bawl
About how much they always thought of you—
And mostly didn't! Such a nice grave too,
With posies on it! When I rise to shine,
I'll take the belly of a wolf for mine,
The same as Jed!"

　　　　　　　　　Rejecting with disgust
This wrinkled desert of our mortal dust,
He tapped the fount of phantom youth again,

And raised a war-whoop. Blackfeet fighting men
Flung far defiance, then no longer prowled
The silence. And the dog leaped up and growled
Through bared teeth ready for the throat of harm;
Then, looking sheepish at the false alarm,
Lay down and grumbled. Hard to understand—
These men were!

              "Better raise this child by hand
On water, Bob?" Black anxiously inquired.
And, with the high disdain of the inspired,
Expansively the younger gestured. "Art,"
He said, "you old pig-eater [1] in your heart,
And hardly yet half wintered at the best,
You've got no tender feelings in your breast,
No tender feelings! Telling me to quit!
Been drinking, eh? And just can't carry it
The way a mountain man like me can do!

Well, to resume, as I was telling you
Before you up and started telling me,
If things could be the way they used to be
Them days with Jed, I'd give a leg or so
And run barefooted! Art, I'd even throw
Your mare in, and the sore upon her back,
If boot was needed!"

[1] *Mangeur de lard,* signifying a greenhorn in the mountains—
one who had not yet wintered in the country and lived on wild
game.

"Why the boot?" said Black;
"You've traded all your legs off."

                              Mournfully
The other shook his head. "And you and me
Old pardners, Arthur! Now, as like as not,
We'll never see them days. And all for what?
A bag of bones!"

                    He wiped away a tear
That wasn't there—but might have been, to
      hear
The timbre of a changing mood that came
Into his voice. " 'Twill never be the same
Till Jed comes riding that cayuse of his.
I wonder where in hell this Heaven is!
A long ways off, and nary blade of grass
Nor water hole beyond the narrow pass
Across the Shining Mountains; and the snow
Horse-deep and getting deeper, maybe! . . . No,
Not even Jed could make it back alive!

'Twas just the same the year of 'twenty five.
A summer and a winter and a spring—
And still the other side of everything
Was Christmas for the shaver that was me.
Who knew what might be hanging on the
      tree?
If God and 'Diah did, they wouldn't tell!

We had been trapping westward quite a spell,
With sign a-plenty. Beaver packs had put
The whole caboodle, mostly, flat a-foot,
And made the Crow cayuses cuss our luck,
If horses can. And then one day we struck
A river in the mountains flowing west
Among thick brush—so thick, we climbed a crest
To have a look at where the canyon led.

And, holy smoke! The way I thought of Jed
Had turned into a picture! Still and dim
And big with secrets! No horizon rim,
So far it was! You looked and looked, and then
From where you ended you began again
And looked a little farther. Bye and bye,
The country—just—got—thinner—and was sky,
Blue hazy, and the secrets hiding yet.
You fumbled round inside of you to get
A word, and drew a lungful fit to shout it;
But there was nothing you could do about it,
Except to look. Nohow, it couldn't be—
And there it was! You rubbed your eyes to see
Queer ranges to the southward, built of smoke,
As if you'd just been dreaming them, and 'woke
And couldn't quite remember. Pretty soon
You'd wake all over, and 'twould be the moon
That you were in, or anywhere not made
To pasture human critters. Half afraid,
You looked a little nearer there below;

And there was snow that couldn't have been snow
Around a sea of ice that wasn't ice,
Or was it? When you blinked and saw it twice,
'Twas more like water foaming at the lip,
And yet it didn't move. A crazy ship
That was an island had been sailing there
Forever—hadn't gotten anywhere,
And wouldn't. Wasn't any use in motion—
No place to go to!

     Could it be the ocean—
The Great Pacific? All at once, it could!
You held your breath—it *was*! From where we
   stood
And saw the sky and water mix, almost
You got a glimmer of the China coast,
Low-lying! Just look hard enough, you might!

Well, there was plenty arguing that night!
It was, it wasn't, and it was again
All over. But the was-ers won it when
We made the lake shore, even though it wasn't!
If lakes taste salty and the ocean doesn't,
Why 'twasn't ocean! Try it on your tongue!
The very sand was salt! The water stung,
Lead-heavy with it!

     Nothing seemed to care,
Excepting us and sea-gulls screaming there

Above us that it *was* the ocean too!
The rest just went on knowing what it knew
And being what it was, and didn't take
No interest in whether 'twas a lake
Or ocean, neither one! It sort of slept,
The way it had a million years, and kept
A secret you were half-way scared to know!
Seems funny! Only thirteen years ago,
And nary secret hiding anywhere!
You're only here again when you get there,
And then it's there again when you get here!
A bag of tricks!

    He went away the year
Of 'twenty six. We rendezvoused in June,
And then he left. Some river of the moon
That he went chasing after, seemed to me—
The wonderfulest river that could be,
Because there wasn't any where it flowed
Off westward there and made an easy road
To the Pacific—which we knew by then
The salt lake wasn't. Saw him once again,
On Bear Lake, when you three came back half dead
From California, Bob. And what a Jed!
A buzzard wouldn't eat him! Made me glad
He didn't take me!

    Now I wish he had—
I wish he had."

IV

"You're getting sober, Squire,"
Black said, and, sighing, stirred the dreamy fire
Until the dozing logs awoke in flame;
"Or else—which seems to figure out the same—
It's only getting human makes you sad.
You wish he'd taken you, and if he had
You'd know, with inside knowledge of the thing,
How buzzards soar, what makes the kiotes sing
Such mournful ditties, what the crows regret
With all their cawing. Maybe so—and yet,
Who ever saw a wolf with bowels of brass
Or bird with iron gizzard? Let it pass,—
Or, rather, let the jug!"

                              He rose and scanned
The stars awhile, eyes shaded with a hand
Against the groundling dazzle. "Night is new,"
He yawned; "and there's another nip or two
Left in the Dipper yonder, tipped to pour
Whatever angels drink. There's even more
Left in the jug. So here's regards to those
Bone-scattered where the Colorado flows

Among the damned Mojaves, and beside
The Umpqua where it bitters with the tide
Among the marshes—Jedediah's men!
And may they rise and follow him again
The other side of Jordan! Drink the toast,
Bob Evans!"

          "—Even to the cosmic coast,"
The other said, and drank, "where all stars cease,
And seas of silence answer with their peace
The petulant impertinence of life!"

"And here's to when I keep that cow and wife,"
The youngest bantered, "—just as like to be!"

"But when," said Black, "we started for the sea
That summer, Bob, not one of seventeen,
I'll warrant, cared to know what life might mean.
To ask that question is a kind of dying.
What matters to a bird a-wing is flying;
What matters to a proper thirst is drinking.
A tree would wither if it got to thinking
Of what the summers and the winters meant!
There was a place to go to, and we went,
High-hearted with a hunger for the new.
The fifty mules and horses felt so too
For all their heavy packs. The brutes are wise
Beyond us, Bob. They can't philosophize
And get the world all tangled in their skulls.

At Utah Lake the mourning of the gulls
Had seemed the last of what was known and
     dear;
And when we struck the bend of the Sevier
To follow eastward where it cuts the range,
The canyon seemed the doorway to a strange
New world. The ridden critters and the led,
Strung out along the river after Jed,
Pricked ears and listened. Nothing but the whine
Of saddle leather down the toiling line,
Until some cayuse at the canyon's mouth
Neighed; and the empty valley, rising south,
Was full of horses answering the din
Of horses where no horse had ever been
Forever. And the mules brayed, walking faster.
What need of any pasture, greener, vaster,
To pay them for the eager joy of striving?
If living is a matter of arriving,
Why not just start to rotting at the first,
And save the trouble? Thirty died of thirst
And hunger yonder in the desert hells.
Ask God why, when you see Him. If He tells,
You'll hardly be the wiser. Furthermore,
I'll gamble that He won't.

                              The valley bore
Southeastward, and there wasn't any game.
Our packs got lighter fast. So when we came
To where a small creek entered from the west,

We followed up along it to a crest,
And saw what fed our hunger for the new
But couldn't satisfy it; for it grew
Beyond the feeding. Where a high plateau
Stretched southwardly, a million years or so
Of rain had hewed a great unearthly town
With colored walls and towers that looked down
On winding streets not meant for men to tread.
You half believed an angel race, long dead,
Had built with airy, everlasting stuff
They quarried from the sunrise in the rough
And spent their lives in fashioning, and died
Before the world got old.

                              The other side
Of ranges west and south, a dim world ran
Uphill to where eternity began
And time died of monotony at last.
And when that rim of nothing had been passed,
Why surely 'twould be California then;
But would we all be long-gray-whiskered men
Before we got there? No one seemed to mind.
God only knew what wonders we might find,
And how He must be weary with His knowing!
No curiosity at all for going
And nothing new to look for anywhere!

Into the clutter of the foothills there
Below, we wound a weary way, and crossed

The valley of a stream we called the Lost—
And lost it was, if ever it had run!
The bare slopes focussed the September sun
Upon the blistering rubble. Round the few
And shallow holes that kept a brackish brew
The fifty critters pawed and fought and screamed,
Blaming each other; and the echoes seemed
To ape the clatter of the hoofs like laughter.

It wasn't any better soon thereafter
Among the tumbled hills gone bald with age
Millenniums ago. The scrubby sage
Was making out to live on memory yet,
But even it had started to forget
What rain was like. Our grub was getting low.
For days we hadn't even seen a crow
To shoot at; but we didn't seem to care,
For we were learning our first lesson there
In what thirst means; and we were walking
      now.
My roan was pulling like a stubborn cow
Not halter-broke, when, with a shivering slump,
He just sat down awhile upon his rump,
And then keeled over with a tired sigh.
So there was meat we couldn't stop to dry,
For need of water. Little we could eat!
It takes a proper tongue to relish meat,
And not some dead cow's crammed into your
      mouth!

The balance of the day we hurried south—
A creeping hurry; anyway, as fast
As we could snake the nags along. At last
'Twas night again, and not a blade of grass
Or drop of water. Seemed 'twould never pass.
You dozed, dog-weary, and the dreams you
    had
Of creeks and springs were just about as bad
As even waking was. A horse would dream—
Of wading, maybe, in a mountain stream—
And neigh himself and all the herd awake;
And there'd be panic neighing, and a break
That ended, in a flounder, with the ropes.
It surely didn't much revive our hopes,
When morning came, to find three others dead.

I thought 'twas kind of funny about Jed
That day. You see, I didn't know him then.
And there was peevish talk among the men
Of how he didn't seem to realize.
There'd be a freshness in his face and eyes
When he came striding from a spell of straying
Off trail somewhere. I know now he'd been
    praying.
You'd swear he knew a spring along the way,
And kept it for himself! He'd smile and say
We shouldn't doubt, but we should trust and
    know
There'd soon be water.

And, by God, 'twas so—
'Twas so that afternoon!

We struck a draw—
The toughest going mortal ever saw—
A dazzling oven, crooked as a snake
And full of boulders. But it seemed to make
Downhill and southward, so we shuffled in.
To think that such a flood had ever been
As rolled those boulders, almost drove you crazy!
I mind that everything was dizzy-hazy
When someone said that Louis Pombert's mare
Was down. What of it? No one seemed to care
Enough to save the saddle.

Bye and bye—
Hours later or the batting of an eye
Was all the same, for time just sort of stood
And wobbled like a drunk—a mule sawed wood
Down yonder. Then they all began to saw,
And horses whinnied up along the draw,
If they could manage better than a nicker.
The weakest of them whimpered, stepping
    quicker,
And when they stumbled, staggered up again
With bloody noses. Presently the men
Were hollering down yonder like a flock
Of addled crows. Another jut of rock,
And there it was—a world of running water!"

[32]

"Aw, Arthur, make it just a little hotter!"
The younger pleaded; "just a little drier,
So I can raise a thirst!"

                    "You grieve me, Squire,"
The elder said; "I thought you'd had enough
To be half human! Water's holy stuff,
Direct from heaven! When the grass gets green,
That's worship! Bob here gathers what I mean,
Eh Bob? You mind that day; you had the most
Tough water-scrapes with Jed!"

                    "The Holy Ghost,
The dove descending," Evans mused aloud.

The youngest laughed. "This go-to-meeting crowd
Should rise and let the kiotes lead a hymn!"

"We might be singing with the seraphim,"
Said Evans.

                    "Well, there was a church that night,"
Continued Black. "We circled in the light
Of one big fire; and when we had our fill
Of horse meat, which we didn't have to kill,
Because too much is deadly as the lack,
He got his Bible with the leather back
(That looked a worn-out boot-top, like as not,)
And fuzzy pages bulging with a lot

Of heavy reading. For a little while
He thumbed it, silent. No one cracked a smile
Or said a word, and there were godless cusses,
Whose on'ry fracases and rakehell musses
Had sent them where they were, among the others.
Like pious little boys who mind their mothers,
They sat there waiting, mannerly and prim.
And if they hadn't, there was that in him
To whale the devil out of any man.
I've seen him do it.

       Well, when he began
To read out loud, 'twas not as parsons do.
He said it just like anything that's true—
'The sun is shining,' maybe, or 'the birds
Are singing.' Something got into the words
That made them seem they couldn't be the same
That you remembered. For the Lord became
A gentle shepherd, real as Mr. Jones,
And he had made us rest our weary bones
In that green pasture by the waters there!
Laugh, Squire, and show your raising—I don't
    care;
I like to see you happy, bless your heart!"

"I didn't mean to spoil your story, Art,"
Explained the other. "Who am I to doubt it?
But what would those dead horses say about it,
Back yonder in the swelter?"

         "Well, you see,"
Black countered; "that was lack of piety.
I guess they hadn't gone to Sunday schools!"

"You reckon all of your Missouri mules
Were Holy Rollers? Not a one was dead!"
The younger chuckled.

        "Just the same," Black said,
"It wasn't funny and nobody snickered.
It scared me when a happy cayuse nickered,
The place had got so still when he was through.
And then he didn't preach, as parsons do;
He just sat silent, for the Book had said it.
What else was there to do when he had read it,
But let it soak like rain? And if he prayed,
You couldn't hear him do it.

        There we stayed
A couple days to let the critters eat,
And jerk the leavings of the pony meat
Against the chance there'd not be game enough.
For we were down to traps and trading stuff—
Red bolted goods and blankets, fufaraws,
Like beads and looking glasses, for the squaws,
And knives and arrow metal for the men,
So be it we should ever see again
A human face but ours.

And then we took
Down river—just a wider sort of brook,
But 'Diah named it for the President,
The Adams River. No fine compliment,
We came to think; but not so bad at first.
'Twas still a blessing to be shut of thirst
So long as you remembered how it felt;
But when you saw the packs of jerked horse melt
To nothing, and the red-walled canyon wound,
Until you only rambled round and round
From nowhere, nowhere—not a thing to eat,
But now and then a bite of rabbit meat—
You wondered was there treason in the name!

About to kill a pony when we came
At last to where a little creek broke through
And made a valley. There a garden grew
With tasseled corn and punkin vines between!
You stood and stared, misdoubting you had seen,
But there it flickered, sure as you were born—
The yellow-bellied crawlers and the corn
Late earing in the green!

We yelled hurrah
For good old garden sass. And then we saw
A little Indian woman running there,
All wibble-wobble and a mess of hair,
Hell-bent for cover—and she needed some,
Not having any more on than your thumb,

But one important patch of rabbit fur!
And, like the devils that she thought we were,
Young hellions cheered her, laughing: 'Go it,
  Gert!'
And 'Hump it, Maggie!' But the words of dirt
They flung at her stopped quick enough, when Jed
Came riding, looking like a thunder-head
With lightning in it just about to break.
'Respect a woman for your mothers' sake,'
He said, 'or take a licking!'

     Well, he took
Some knives and looking glasses, and the Book
For luck, no doubt, and vanished up the creek
Among the brush. It seemed a weary week
We held the herd till he appeared again,
About a dozen lousy-looking men
And women at his heels, with not a thing
Upon them but an apron and a string
Of rabbit hide. If that was human mud,
'Twas badly baked and furnished with the blood
Of rabbits. 'Diah treated them the same
As folks.

    And while we feasted, others came,
Like cringing cur-dogs that apologize
For being curs, to see with their own eyes
The four-legged spirit-critters and the gods
That rode them; for we made our thunder-rods

Spout cloud and lightning. Anyone would say
We celebrated Independence Day,
If there had been a barrel of lemonade!
For pretty soon nobody was afraid.
The women brought us cakes of pounded seeds
Messed up with cane, and strutted in the beads
They got from us. God-awful homely lasses
And scrawny grandmas peeped at looking glasses
And giggled. Men went running to their wives,
Like tickled boys, to show their shiny knives;
And wee, pot-bellied rascals dared to sneak
Just near enough to give our shirts a tweak
And show their little sisters who was scared!

It kind of looked as if the Lord prepared
A table for us!

              Well, the thought of it
Still fed us—anyway a little bit—
Down river. Anything might happen next,
The way it had, to fit the Bible text
He read that night. And, soon enough, it did!

The canyon narrowed, towering, and hid
The friendly day. A scary twilight fell.
As from the dusky bottom of a well,
We saw the blood-red rim-rock swimming high
Along the jaggéd knife-scar of a sky,
And dim stars mocked the middle afternoon!

We thought at first the place would broaden
    soon.
The few stars only brightened in the cut,
And, like a heavy snow of kettle-smut,
Night smothered down.

                    'Twas long before we slept.
Serenely in the diary he kept,
Jed scribbled by the fire without a word.
Unless a horse complained, you almost heard
Your thinker thinking. All the while the stream
Was like a sick man moaning in a dream
Of dying.

           We were plodding on our way
When first the rim-rock reddened with the day,
But up until the noon 'twas early morning.
It seemed that any minute, without warning,
The worst might happen. Maybe one more bend,
And there we'd come upon the canyon's end,
Some cave without a bottom, yawning black.

There was no hope of 'Diah turning back;
He wouldn't listen to the gloomy talk
Among the men. 'Yea, even though I walk
The valley of the shadow,' said the Book.
His face and eyes would have that freshened look,
When he'd been riding out of sight a spell,
As though he knew some good he wouldn't tell,

Just wanting to surprise us pretty soon.
The whole late evening that was afternoon
We plodded till the few trapped stars were bright.

The weakest of the horses went that night
To fill the pots. It didn't really matter
Which one we ate—unless the leather's fatter
In either of your boot-soles than the other.
The driftwood made a sickly sort of smother;
And while we watched the kettles in despair,
Jed asked old Rogers would he offer prayer;
And Harry would—but offer's not the word.
He took no chances that Jehovah heard,
Or interrupted with an old man's 'Eh?'—
The off ear cupped the hard-of-hearing way—
'Wha's that?' He bellered. 'Twas a fine oration!

Well, when we'd feasted on our transportation
And felt a little better, 'Diah read
Some verses from the Scripture where it said
The whole earth was the Lord's. A sneaking
        doubt
If that was anything to brag about
Grew big enough to dare you to deny it.
Then all at once the canyon got so quiet
The water didn't moan, the soggy wood
Quit wheezing. And the whole round earth was
        good,
The fulness of it—and it made you glad!

[40]

No, Squire, 'twas not the bellyful we had
Of leather soup. 'Twas far above the belt.
'Twas like old summers and the way you felt
A barefoot shaver—white clouds going over,
And apple trees and bumblebees and clover,
And warm dust feeling pleasant to your toes,
And wheat fields flowing and the corn in rows,
And stars to twinkle when the day was done,
While people rested, certain of the sun,
All safe and cozy!

               Words are mighty queer!
They try to tell you something, and you hear
Some old familiar rattle in your head
That isn't any nearer what they said
Than mules and mothers; but you think you know!
Then maybe, all at once, *they're simply so—*
And always were! They sprout like seeds and
      thrive!
If all the words men gargle came alive,
I wonder what would happen! 'Diah's sprouted.

And then he talked. Seemed foolish that we
      doubted,
So near the Spanish settlements might be.
And soon we ought to make the Siskadee
Old Ashley tried that spring to navigate,
But, getting nearer to St. Peter's gate
Than to the ocean, had to give it up.

And California! That was where the cup
Ran over!

        Well, we stumbled down that maze
And counted horses dying. —Also days
Since we had fed in yonder Indian heaven;
And number five was slow, but six and seven
Hung on so long they almost never quit.
The earth was needing axle grease a bit
Before we finished counting nine and ten!
Do you remember, Bob, what happened then,
And what we saw?"

           "The day broke overhead.
The endless canyon ended," Evans said;
And there was desert to the setting sun!"

"I guess we'd better have another one,"
Remarked the Squire, "before we undertake it!
Unless we do, I doubt if we can make it.
We've et an awful lot of harness leather!"

"The skin-rack horses nickered all together,"
The elder mused, as though he didn't hear;
"And up the haunted canyon in the rear
It seemed the dead ones answered. Starving mules
Heehawed, as if to jeer the two-legged fools
Who brought them there. We didn't make a sound;
Just looked across that country, hellward bound,

And filled our eyes with nothing, flabbergasted.
You made up stories while the canyon lasted,
But yonder was the story God had made.
It looked like even Harry hadn't prayed
Quite loud enough!

              Jed didn't seem to care.
Spoke quietly of California there,
And pointed to the white sun blazing down
Beyond that waste! There'd be an Indian town
Along the river we were coming to,
And there we'd rest. He spoke as if he knew,
And made hope certain as geography.
Why, come to think about it, you could see
The corn fields waving by the riverside!

Well, two more horses and a mule had died,
With others on the ragged edge of dying,
Before the Adams finally quit trying
To justify the wearing of the name.
And in the dragging afternoon we came
Upon the Colorado.

              Greasewood throve
Along the valley, and a stunted grove,
That huddled yonder by the river, made
The only promise of a little shade
In all that bowl of glare. Two yapping dogs
Came bristling; and we saw a house of logs

[43]

Squat-roofed with 'dobe in among the trees.
A nursing woman, hobbled at the knees
With frightened young ones, peeked at us and ran
Behind the cabin. Then an oldish man,
We took to be a Piute, filled the door.
If anything surprised him any more,
You didn't guess it by the look he had.
Was he amused or just a little sad
Or maybe both? The quiet, puckered way
He looked us over didn't seem to say
A thing for sure, except he didn't scare.
And when we sign-talked at him, asking where
The village was, he waved his hand around
The whole horizon, pointed to the ground,
Then tapped his chest and chuckled pleasantly.
'Twas Crusoe with the desert for a sea,
And he had built an island with his labors
Where there were only well-behaving neighbors—
The sun and moon and stars!

                We feasted there
On garden stuff, and Jed paid more than fair
With trading goods. The mules and horses had
Their fodder, and the little ones were glad
With bells to tinkle, while their mother chose,
With happy little noises in her nose,
The gaudiest of cloth. But all the while
Old Crusoe smiled a pleasant little smile,
Observing with that quiet squint of his,

As though he sort of knew what really is
And always was and shall be evermore,
So that he wasn't bothered looking for
What isn't, wasn't, and will never be."

"Another sort of turnip, seems to me,"
The younger said; "just dumb and half asleep."

"And maybe," Evans added, "rooted deep
In what I call the other side of things,
Where running feet are stilled and eager wings
Are folded, and all seeking is forsaken,
Because there's nothing to be overtaken
In such a peace of being."

                                    "Well," said Black,
"I've often kind of hankered to go back
And see if I could gather what he knew.
It must have worked on all the others too;
Nobody joked about him. All the way
Down river, when the going, day by day,
Grew harder, with the done-out critters dying,
I thought and thought of how you go on trying
And suffering to find, until you're dead,
When maybe all the while it's in your head
The way it was in his, if you could see.

But when we came to where the Siskadee
Broke out into a valley fat with tillage,

And saw the populous Mojave village
Among the trees, he didn't seem so wise;
For hadn't we arrived at Paradise,
However we had paid in Purgatory?
You're always wanting life to be a story
With some pat end to show what it's about.
Somebody's torn a lot of pages out,
If that's the case! You never quite arrive.

Well, it was mighty good to be alive
Among those gardens yellowing with plenty,
And see our critters, dwindled now to twenty,
Contented in the meadows, making fat.

Could we have read, just one year after that,
The bloody page that would be written, when
With eighteen more, Jed came that way again
From Bear Lake, fought with devils, met as friends,
And fled with eight! I guess the story ends
When anybody turns an empty page—
An ending without end. You'd swear old age
Had found them when they reached our camp beside
The Stanislaus, and told how ten had died
Bare-handed in the treacherous attack.

'Twas lucky, Bob, you didn't try it back
With Jed and Silas Gobel, your old friend

Of desert days. But what a rousing end
Old Silas made before his page went blank!
The eight had crossed, and from the western bank
They saw it happen on the further shore—
The whole tribe swarming inward, with the roar
A cloudburst makes, upon the helpless ten—
Men drowning quickly in a flood of men,
Save where old Silas, hardened at the forge,
And looming like a boulder in a gorge
Bankfull with freshet, labored with a limb
Of mesquite for a hammer at his grim
Last smithing job. If God has set the Right
To prove its mettle in the losing fight
Forever, 'twas another score for God!
Not all the horses Silas ever shod
Outweighed the burden of the spears that bowed
Those blacksmith shoulders; and the milling crowd
Rained arrows till the club no longer whirled
About him. When a howling eddy swirled
And slowly closed at last above his head,
The watchers yonder knew that he was dead
As any coward. Then the running fight—
Few rifles, many bows. And all that night
They fled until the desert blazed with day.

But that was still a good long year away,
And we were happy, being richly fed
With more than garden stuff. For Rumor said,
And 'twas the clearer being vague, somewhere

Far off beyond the jealous desert there
The ripened days of all the wide world went
To make a lazy country of content
Where it was always Spring—a dream of Spain,
Come true forever! Not a wish was vain
In yonder climate kind to all desires!
Hard-bitten youngsters, squatting 'round the fires,
Half tight already with imagined wine,
Discussed it, till you felt the soft sun shine
On drowsy vineyards; heard beneath the stars
The castanets, the strumming of guitars,
The singing senoritas! There it lay,
And only Boston clippers knew the way—
Ten thousand miles down under 'round the
    Horn!
To think that we, of all our breed, were born
To see it first by land!

                    Our luck was good.
You, Squire, would say Jehovah understood
We'd lack for horses, and provided some.
Well, anyway, some Indians had come
Across the desert with a stolen herd
Of Spanish Mission horses! Seemed absurd
Such scurvy rascals hailed from Paradise!
What scenes had filled their slinking, sleepy eyes
That didn't seem to care! Reubasco knew
Their Spanish lingo; and the wonder grew
The bigger for the little that they told.

'Twas late October, and the moon was old,
As we were, when we hit Mojave town.
'Twas young again, as we were, going down
The trail of sunset to the Promised Land,
Our first camp out. We scooped the seeping sand
Along a wash to make a little spring,
And didn't sleep much, for the whinnying
Of horses, waiting for the hole to fill
Again and yet again.

        The blue-black chill
Wore out and whitened to a withering blaze;
And after that we didn't count the days
Or nights of endless plodding, nor the sleeps
That ran to tangled dreams of water seeps
Clawed out in vain. We only counted drinks.
Dry washes running into empty sinks,
Bankfull with starlight, mocked us when we
      tramped
From sunset to the white of dawn, and camped,
Holed up in sand against the blistering light,
Until the purple chill came. Mind the night
We found the lake, Bob?"

           "I can see it yet,"
The other mused. "The moon about to set;
The ghostly yucca trees around us there,
Transfigured by some ultimate despair
That filled the stillness of the solitude;

[49]

The slimy cabbage cactus that I chewed;
The rasping, hollow sound of critters panting;
The sudden clearing, and the low moon slanting—
The low moon slanting on a lake! Dry salt!
A crazy notion 'twas the yuccas' fault
Seemed true, and yet I couldn't make it track!"

"Well, even though it wasn't wet," said Black,
"It made the going easy. Anyway,
You mind it ended with the break of day
And how that cool spring sparkled in the sun
There where the river that forgot to run
Spread wide to fill the lake that wasn't wet!
'Twas something queer you wouldn't soon forget—
The spooky yucca trees that seemed to know
The end of us and didn't care—the low
Half moon across the salt! But Oh, the night
We saw the full moon glitter on the white
Peaks yonder!"

"I remember," Evans said.
"The journey's end! And yet, the day when Jed
Went hunting water for us seems to glow
The brighter now. With burning sand for snow,
The blizzard booming down the empty river,
And 'Diah calmly praying to the Giver
Of all good things, before he left us there
Among the huddled horses! Could a prayer
Make headway yonder where the sun at noon

Ran through the howling smother like a moon
Gone mad with thirst? It seemed a cruel joke.
Yet there was something in the way he spoke
Of finding water—something in his face—"

"As if," Black said; "it might be any place
For anybody who could look that way!"

"And I believed the balance of the day,"
The other said. "But when the storm was through
At sundown, and the still cold moonlight grew
Around us, I forgot enough to doubt him.
The moon denied it knew a thing about him;
The silence said he wasn't coming back."

"It didn't know old 'Diah!" chuckled Black.
"Remember how he made us kneel to thank
The Giver of Good Things before we drank,
There where the river, hiding underground,
Came up as if to have a look around
And made a pool before it hid again?"

"The very horses kneeling with the men,
Eye-deep in joy! The moon near full and sinking,
And morning coming on while we were drinking,"
The other mused. "I like that picture better
Than yours, Art."

        "Well, that water did seem wetter
Somehow," Black said, "than any other brew

This side of where the Squire is going to,
Unless he mends his ways. He won't, alas!
But what about the day we topped the pass
And stopped to stare—with all of that behind us,
And only missing horses to remind us
Of what it cost? The Promised Land at last!
And when we climbed the mountain, saw the vast
Land lazing there with nothing left to seek
Forevermore—the high, thin silver streak
That must have been the ocean—scattered droves
In happy meadows—greenery of groves
And vineyards! Wasn't that a better sight?
And yonder, drowsing in the golden light,
The Mission of the Padres! Journey's end!"

He thought awhile in silence. "No, my friend,"
He said, "you win. The men and horses kneeling
Around the pool, the white of morning stealing—
It's better. Queer the way a man remembers!"

He gazed awhile upon the dreaming embers,
With silent laughter mounting to his eyes.
"And so," he chuckled, "there was Paradise,
And all us lanky, ragamuffin scamps
A-faunching! What does 'Diah do? He camps
To shave his whiskers!"

V

Chin to chest and nodding,
The younger, startled by the elder's prodding,
Jerked back to waking with a hostile glare
That softened to a silly grin. "We're there!
Wake up!" Black shouted.

Leaving with a leap
Some rabbit heaven of his broken sleep,
The dog lit snarling, shook himself to clear
The addled world, sat up and pricked an ear
To point the question of an injured whine.

"Where?" growled the Squire.

"The Land of Corn and Wine!"
Laughed Black; "and dark-eyed senoritas too!
But here you squat, you lazy loafer you,
And snooze!"

"Why, Arthur, I was only thinking
Of what's the use in talking about drinking,"
Explained the other. "Why not have a drink?
You just don't realize how hard I think

When I think hard. To prove I was awake,
I saw you all go swimming in that lake
To scrub yourselves. I'll bet you needed peeling!
And I know all about the fellow stealing
The horses at the come-to-glory meeting!
Well then, we're there! So how about some eating
And maybe just a gurgle? Woo! I'm froze!"

He shook himself, dog-fashion, as he 'rose,
And, yawning, vanished creekward. Snapping brush
Upon the treble of the harplike hush
Plucked desultory discord. He returned
Arm-laden; nursed the embers till they burned,
Blue-stemming into blossom round the logs;
Then moved the slashed hump nearer, with the
        dog's
High, whimpering approval. "There!" said he,
Now pass the moonshine, so as I can see
Your senoritas!"

                Edging nearer while
The trio drank, the fourth, with tongueful smile
Of ready gratitude, and both intense
Ears focussed on the simmering succulence,
Leaned hard as though his patience were a chain.
The humblest, prayerful whimpers proving vain,
He snapped the leash, and, with explosive barks,
Made pointed, if not impious, remarks
Upon the doings of Divinity.

Whereat the youngest of the Trinity
Gave heed at last and opened heaven's gate.

The Fork's returning chatter, as they ate,
Made bold against the canyon's phasic moaning—
Time troubling and Eternity intoning
The never and forever that are one.
It grew upon them when the feast was done;
And each sat silent, suddenly alone,
Negotiating, as the dog the bone,
Some all but meatless leaving of the past.

A warwhoop shattering the spell at last,
The lonely little worlds flowed back together.
"I sure do like this California weather,"
The Squire remarked, with hands before the flame.
"I'll need more educating, just the same,
Before I see your senoritas clear.
If yonder's any pleasanter than here,
I wonder why you beggars didn't stay."

"Well, take the donkey and his bait of hay."
Black stroked his whiskers sagely. "Round the mill
He chases fodder that is yonder still
Regardless of how far or fast he goes.
And why? Because a proper donkey knows
If he just chases hard enough, he'll beat it.
And maybe, when he's too done out to eat it,
He'll come to fodder heaven if he's pious!"

"Jed told me once God gave us goals to try us,"
Said Evans; "living was a kind of weaning.
We needed sugar-teats of worldly meaning
For some unworldly purpose of the soul.
It seemed the goal was learning that a goal
Is just the fleeing shadow that you cast,
Until pursuing teaches you at last
What mattered was the light upon your back."

"Just like old 'Diah," meditated Black,
Scarce breaking silence—"just the way he'd be
When there was no one left but him and me
And we'd be camping, maybe on the Snake.
All still, but for the sound the fire would make,
And then you'd notice he was looking through
    you,
That way he had. You wondered if he knew you.
You wondered if you knew him, even more.
And then he'd tell what he'd been groping for
Down deep inside of him; and while he told,
Like dreaming, something in him very old
And gentle made you happy to be sad.
For suddenly some precious thing you had
Or thought you had or would have, wasn't so;
And yet the very hurt of letting go
Was like a joy—till he turned young again.
Just thirty-eight now, counting nine from
    then!
You somehow just can't think of him as dead."

"I saw him very old once," Evans said,
"And gentle. Often when I sleep I see
Again, between a white-hot sky and me,
That look of glowing rain—like joy and tears.
I've lived upon it all these lonely years
From dream to dream. And when I see and
      wake,
It seems awhile that nothing is opaque
Or commonplace, but luminously new
With what it was that I saw coming through
His face that morning."

                    "Must have been the time,"
Said Black, "the whole caboodle tried to climb
The high Sierras for the shorter way
Back yonder to the Lake from San Jose,
The spring of 'twenty-seven. Peak on peak,
And not a pass! A snow-hell of a week,
With horses balking in the drifts to drowse
And stiffen, standing. Camped on Stanislaus
To wait and wonder how could he and you
And Silas ever live to make it through.
And then the desert yonder! Seemed to be
He never wanted much to talk to me
About it."

          "Yes," said Evans, "it was hell;
But there was heaven too. I want to tell
About the lives we lived, the deaths we died

Together. I've been telling it inside
These empty years alone.

                              You mind, no doubt,
'Twas late in May before we started out
With seven horses—one a little mare
Grown wise in leading packers; and a pair
Of rangy mules. 'Twas comical the way
Their long necks turtled under loads of hay
Lashed shell-wise! Seemed to know it, and
        revolted!
Remember how the camp cheered when they
        bolted,
Expressing what they thought of diamond hitch-
        ing—
All bray and flying hay and corkscrew pitching,
Until they had enough of it to follow?

They grazed that night along a flowery hollow
Beside a mountain brook where grass was growing
Lush green and tender. Next night it was
        snowing
Upon our camp between high canyon walls;
And like a momentary hush that falls
Before disaster, long drawn out with fear,
All night it snowed. The sky began to clear
At sunrise, and the dazzling heights ahead
Repeated what that falling silence said,
In cruel splendor.

[58]

Shallowing by noon,
With sloping walls, the canyon promised soon
To reach a pass. The tall pines crowding round
Appeared to know, and watched without a sound
Our sweating labor in the biting glare.
Loud in the knife-edge thinning of the air,
The panting of the horses only made
The muffled stillness deeper. And the grade
Grew steeper with the waning of the day.

The pack mules had no quarrel with the hay
That night.

      We scooped a clearing in the snow,
And, dozing with their muzzles to the glow
Of logs, the mules and horses made a wall
About us. 'Twasn't any time at all
Until the peaks were floating in the dawn;
And when they glittered, we were wading on,
Knee-deep.

     The stunted pines were getting scant,
And more and more the critters balked to pant
With straining nostrils, when we made a bend,
And there ahead we saw the canyon's end—
A sheer-walled pocket!

     Nothing else to do
But double back to where a gulch broke through

The southward wall. And 'twas a stubborn climb
Before we scrambled out by camping time
Upon a granite shoulder. In the last
Of day, we stared dumbfounded at a vast
White mountain maze beyond. The west went out,
And blue night came upon us like the doubt
That kept us silent. It was crystal cold.
A single squatting pine, that looked as old
And weathered as the granite, gave us fire.
God only knows what maniac desire
To live and flourish, packed into a cone,
Could bite into that rock and fight alone
For centuries! Gnarled, flattened like a flame
By ancient winds, it fought until we came
To burn it!"

       "Surely does sound queer enough,"
Remarked the elder, "for the sort of stuff
To make religion out of. 'Diah could,
I'll warrant!"

       "When you think of all it stood,"
Said Evans, "seems a crazy waste of trouble
For one warm night! He'd say we're seeing double,
The striving of the Spirit being one.
Well, howsoever, ours had just begun
Next morning; for the shoulder fell abrupt,
A swimmy distance, into valleys cupped
With crowding peaks that glittered blinding white.

[60]

We got the outfit down at fall of night
By angling back beneath the granite crest
To where the mountain steepened south and west
Into a canyon winding south and east.
Halfway to noon it seemed that neither beast
Nor man could make it to the canyon bed,
Unless a goat might. Bothered even Jed,
Until we came to where a rubble slide
Broke through the wall-rim. Looked like suicide
To try it; but the only chance was there.

It took some coaxing for the little mare
To lead the way. She pawed and shook her head,
All nervous like a woman—but she led,
Stiff-kneed and mincing, sliding on her tail.
A-slither in the wallow of her trail,
The horses followed; but the mules agreed
That horses were an idiotic breed,
And wouldn't budge without a lot of booting.
Well, finally they started out a-scooting
To get it over—and they did it brown!

Old 'Diah and the mare were half way down
And right side up, when, mortally insulted
And fighting mad, those critters catapulted
Against the rear. The rest of it was snow,
A little blizzard roaring there below
With heads and tails and hoofs and squealing in it!
It got to be a mighty long half minute

Before it ended, and the canyon thundered
Far off and dim.

         We held our breaths and wondered
How Jed was faring in the drift that churned
With scrambled horses."

          "That was where you learned
It's hard to kill a Christian, I'll allow,"
The younger bantered.

          "Didn't, anyhow,"
Said Evans. "Saw him crawling out as cool
As ever—maybe more so! Not a mule
Or horse had suffered in the cushioned tumble.
The mules appeared to be a bit more humble,
I noticed, when we skidded down the slope
And finished rolling.

         There's a lift of hope
In climbing, even though you want to drop,
Done out. A sort of something at the top,
That isn't there, is going to be good.
But yonder was the top, and there we stood
Spilled out along the bottom of a pit.
No way at all to climb back out of it,
If we'd a mind to. Had to go ahead;
And into what new trap that canyon led,
God knew; and He was keeping deathly still.

We mended cinches broken in the spill,
Re-set the packs, and waded on again.
The going wasn't very bad, and when
The pines had gathered round us, and the blue
Of twilight came, the canyon widened through
The cliffside of the valley we had seen
At sunrise.

        If you gather what I mean,
It sent a scary tickle up your spine
To feel that snow-hushed solitude of pine
Grow darker, darker, darker, listening.
And 'twasn't any sort of mortal thing,
That made you almost glad to be afraid.
It came on me that night, while 'Diah prayed,
That maybe 'twas the Everlasting Word—
That silence; maybe something really heard—
Not Sunday-like, but really!

                All the same,
We wakened just as there when morning came.
The forest listened on without a sound.
If God had heard, He hadn't got around
To doing anything about it yet!
But all day long you couldn't quite forget
That feeling, even when the snow had deepened.
And when the way grew rockier and steepened
Against the coming mountain, it was night.

There wasn't any blueing of the light;
It grayed and blackened: for the sky began
To cloud near evening. And a moaning ran
Across the forest-roof that dusted snow
Upon us in the quiet far below—
That waiting quiet.

              Wakened in the black
Of dying fires, we heard the timber crack
And groan above a steady ocean roar,
And spindrift scudded on the forest floor
In gusty whirls.

                Thank God it wasn't snowing,
With hell a-popping and a high wind blowing,
When finally the long night faded gray.
We couldn't wait. There wasn't any hay;
There wasn't anything a horse could eat,
Except the precious bags of Spanish wheat
They carried—not enough, for all we knew,
To see them to the Salt Lake rendezvous
Across a land no man had ever seen.

We struck an open where we had to lean
Against the howling suck along a draw
That led us upward. Straight ahead we saw,
By snatches in the blur of stinging sight,
The jumble of the mountains, height on height
At hide-and-seek behind the broken flurries.

But we were willing that tomorrow's worries
Should worry us tomorrow; for the hollow
Was drifting bad. The string began to wallow
Breast-deep by middle day, and we were walking,
If that is what you'd call it!

              No use talking,
We couldn't make it—and we couldn't camp.
And so we headed up a rocky ramp
Along the mountain's flank upon our right;
And if we had a stiffer wind to fight,
It swept the footing cleaner.

             Leaning low
And stopping often for the nags to blow,
We climbed. The hollow sagged away from under
And was a canyon flowing snow and thunder
A dizzy drop beneath a granite ledge
We snaked along. The precipice's edge
Was coming nearer. Pausing often, pinned
Between a wall of rock and wall of wind,
We fought to breathe.

           There was a jutting bend
To leftward, where the ledge appeared to end
In nothing. I can see old 'Diah there,
Lean inward, leading. I can see the mare
Step daintily and study with her nose
The doubtful trail; three horses after those,

And looming in the middle of the string
The bulk of Gobel. I was following
The willing mule and tugging at the other,
A balky brute.

            Above the howling smother
I heard old Silas, saw the stumbling critter
He guided, scramble in the pebble-skitter
To get its footing. Then it disappeared,
Hoofs up. The next two horses screamed and
      reared
Against the mule ahead of me. I guess
'Twas over in the telling time or less;
And there was Silas staring back at me,
Mouth open. There was nothing else to see
But empty ledge, between, and flying snow!

The steady thunder loudened there below
A rumbling moment. Then I heard Jed shout
My name, and saw him yonder, leaning out
Around the mare. He seemed about to fall.
And when he saw me huddled by the wall,
His frosted face went empty of the wild,
Scared look it had. It gentled, and he smiled—
By God, he smiled, and I can see him now!

We made it round the jutting point somehow,
And there the ledge swung rightward, and we saw
The rim-rock of a deep confluent draw

Slope up to where the mountain sagged away
To eastward. We were yonder when the day
Began to muddy; and the black night found us
Well down the ridge, a forest roaring round us,
The snow scooped back to make a cozy wall
About our fire.

       We hardly talked at all
Before we swooned into a heavy sleep.
I wakened when the cold began to creep
About the smouldering logs. The wind was
    dead.
I listened. Not a whisper overhead.
It seemed that something knew that nothing
    mattered.
I hurried with the fire until it chattered
About the logs. I didn't want to hear
A meaning in the stillness. 'Twasn't fear
Of storm and cold and hunger or of dying.
'Twas doubt if there was any use in trying:
And maybe if the Everlasting Word
Was silence, and its meaning could be heard,
'Twould be there was no meaning anywhere.
I watched the others sleeping soundly there
And wondered at the peace on 'Diah's face,
The look of nothing being out of place
In his world. Not a doubt what he would say!
And Gobel getting ready for the day
That was to come, with all that might of his

Unloosened; wise the way a good horse is
Without a thought of wisdom! So I slept.

The cold was not so bad when morning crept
Among the pines. The edge of it was round,
Or sort of cotton-muffled, like the sound
Of pot and skillet and the pawing feet
Of horses begging us for more to eat
Than we dared give them now.

                                   The sun seemed warm,
By midday, in a sky swept clean with storm;
And yet the ghostly summer that we felt
Upon our backs was not enough to melt
The crusted drifts we broke and sweated in.

A valley forest had begun to thin
Against a granite rise, and we could see,
Ahead and to the right, southeastwardly,
A maze of summits floating in the blue—
The same it seemed that we were coming to
Before we lost the critters. To the left,
Northeastward, where a barren hollow cleft
The rise ahead, there soared a single peak
Above a roll of shoulders.

                                   'Twas a week
That morning since the critters tasted grass,
And it was time we happened on a pass

Into a greener land. Their lightened packs
Grew heavier—ribs getting to be racks
To hang a skin. The water that they got
Had been the snow we melted in a pot
For days now. It was time to find a way.

We topped the drifted hollow when the day
Had faded out. With only brush to burn,
And scant at that, one kept the fire by turn,
And it was mine to wait the morning in,
That stretched-out moment when the wall is
    thin
Between two worlds, a brief forevermore
When time sleeps. Even Gobel didn't snore;
The mule and horses seemed to hold their
    breaths
While some hushed answer, more profound than
    death's,
Made starry splendor out of old despair.
Then suddenly the peaks were all a-stare
To southward, and the morning star was dim
Above the whitening horizon rim
Without a mountain! We had found a pass!

By noon the snow gave out, and there was grass
Along a canyon brook. Before the night
Came on us, we had made it from the height
Of January into blooming May
Among the foothills.

So we camped a day
Beside a brook. The critters grazed their fill,
And, groaning with pot bellies, greedy still,
Rolled in the lush green, hungry to the hide.
Deer stole upon us, gazing Eden-eyed
And wondering, to make a pleasant feast;
And we gave thanks that night.

A day northeast
We came upon a little river's mouth
And camped there by a lake. Then, riding south
And east by north, we kept the water's edge,
Where many a wild-fowl paradise of sedge,
All clack and chatter with another Spring's
Old promises, exploded into wings
That dimmed the sun.

A range of barren breaks
Loomed eastward in the twilight from the lake's
Far border. We could hardly wait to see
What sort of country it was going to be
The other side. Before the morning broke
We wakened when the ducks and geese awoke
To gossip drowsily along the shore;
And wingéd thunders, roar on dimming roar,
Fled in the starlight when I filled the pot.
The venison was fried, the coffee hot
Before the starry dusk began to pale;
And yonder at the summit of the trail

Across the breaks, we faced the level might
Of sunrise.

        Vaguer for the blast of light,
Appalling vastness lay before us there.
No echo answered when the little mare
Neighed nervously. We cupped our eyes to gaze.
Deep in the blear transparency of haze,
Yet strangely near, the saw-tooth silhouette
Of mountains, black with day behind them yet,
Began abruptly to the east and ran
To southward. Far beyond where they began
We made out others, patterned on the high
Horizon in the very stuff of sky,
Where earth and air were getting to be one.

We headed downward straight into the sun;
For yonder, if our reckoning was true,
A crow would fly to find the rendezvous
Beyond the world's end. Little likelihood,
You'd say, that any ever did or could,
To look across that country.

        All forenoon
It almost seemed we'd pass those mountains soon,
So near they blackened, featureless and flat
Against the dazzling sky. But after that,
They turned to light and shadow, floating there
As little solid as the oily air

[71]

They drifted on to keep the pace we made.
'Twas blazing hot, without a wisp of shade
To spell the horses in; and far ahead
As where it seemed the floating mountains fled,
It looked as if they'd had to wait for water.

But when it seemed the slanting day grew hotter,
Before the sudden coming of the cool,
We found a seeping spring that fed a pool
Sun-steeping in a gully, where the land
Of broken ridges gave away to sand
And sage-brush flats. We called it ' 'Diah's luck.'

And while the critters drank, blue shadow
    struck
The world, as though you saw the sudden chill.
It slowly climbed the mountains there, until
The tallest blued and deepened into black.
A thin new moon was floating on its back
Above the peaks behind us, gleaming white
With day yet, when already it was night
Upon the desert."

           Evans stirred the fire
And gazed upon it. "Bob," remarked the Squire,
"We'll need a better drink before we start
Across that country. How about it, Art?
Bob's gully stew ain't fit for man or beast!"
They passed the jug around.

         " 'Twas wet, at least,"
Said Evans. "And I doubt, if we had known
What that would mean when yonder moon had
     grown
And waned and darkened and was new again,
If even 'Diah would have ventured then
With all that lake and paradise of snow
Behind us. Now I'm glad we didn't know,
Because of what I saw when I had learned."

"It sounds like something Arthur's donkey
     earned,"
The younger chuckled.
                 "But he ground the grain,"
Laughed Black; "he turned the mill!"

                   "The mill of pain,"
Mused Evans, poring on the flame that curled
About the logs. As though a tortured world
Moaned in its sleep, the distant canyon took
The vast night silence from the nearby brook
And filled it.

        "Well, you'd swear that while we slept,"
Continued Evans, "yonder range had crept
Upon us to surprise us when we woke,
So sharply near it loomed when morning broke
Behind it. And before that day was done,

It towered in the slanting of the sun,
A bare black wall behind us to the right.

Jed thought we'd better travel on that night,
For straight ahead as far as we could see
To where the shimmering immensity
Dissolved in air and hazy mountains rose
From nothing, there was nothing short of those
That promised water. Was it even there?

We stopped to rest the horses when the air
Was chilling blue again, where they could eat
Their fill of greasewood, for it saved the wheat
And, being green, was wetter than the grain.

The black wall yonder loosened from the plain
And hovered with the growing of the gloom.
'Twas queer the way it seemed a trap of doom
About to close, just pausing to remind us
The water of the world was left behind us
Forever with the disappointed hope
When we had crossed that broken northern slope,
Searching the bone-dry gullies for a hole.
And when the day-old slice of moon, a bowl
Of phantom water, slowing sinking, slipped
Behind the range, it seemed the trap was tripped
In silence.

                We had walked a lot that day
To save the nags, and by the wheezing way

They breathed it wasn't time for riding then.
God only knew when they would drink again,
If ever; while we had a sup or two
Still hoarded in the horns—and that might do
Until we reached the mountains we had seen.

I told myself the country might be green
Beyond the range. How could you ever guess,
I argued with the dragging weariness
That wasn't me, about the lake and snow
Back yonder? But the very mule said no,
And balked by fits.

          —You didn't climb the range;
You sort of floated over with a strange
Convincingness, and there it was. You knew
The pasture that the creek went winding through
To where the big elm, leaning to the pond,
Made cool blue lace; the mumbling mill beyond
The shady quiet; cattle feeding, lazy—
The brindle cow that kicked, and good old Daisy
With speckled face and crumpled water-horn
With nothing in it; weary earing corn
Beyond the fence, nid-nodding; time for bed;
The new moon going down behind the shed
To fill itself back yonder at the lake;
And suddenly you stumbled broad awake
And walking yet. Or were you still asleep?
No, that was 'Diah wading shoulder-deep

In darkness yonder. What a killing stride!
Because the meadow on the other side
Was green, and sparkled dewy in the cool
Of morning!

     —Damn a hammer-headed mule
That wouldn't let you sleep!

       —The tripping sage,
The slipping sand, and every other age
A pause to spell the horses.

       —Getting cold.
You thought of frost. The night was turning old
And looked it. Tired stars that didn't care
At all if we were getting anywhere
Or if there'd ever be another dawn.

Then, all at once, you knew the night was gone,
And wondered vaguely when and where it went.
Somehow it should have been a big event
When finally the costly morning came.
The black range looming near us seemed the same
We left behind us when the moon was setting;
But, like some dream the desert was forgetting,
The other was a blur along the west
To southward, lying low.

       We stopped to rest
And have a bite; but when we spilled the wheat

Upon the blankets, not a nag would eat;
Just nuzzled it and wilted, standing propped
And dead asleep. The way the mule's ears flopped,
His long-drawn look of gloating in his plight,
Abandoned to the curse of being right
In all our quarrels, wakened, half and half,
A catch of fellow feeling and a laugh
Too weak for sound. Between a breath and breath,
It seemed I slept a sleep as deep as death
And long as weary time; for when Jed shook
The unchanged landscape back, it had the look
Of something that had happened lives away.
He spoke of water yonder where the day
Was like a wild beast crouching for the leap
Across the black wall. Wasn't time to sleep
Until the horses drank. And when I said
The rigmarole that grumbled in my head,
How I'd believe in water that I saw,
There came that flint-hard setting of the jaw,
That long-range hawk-gaze penetrating through
        you,
The way you said, Art,—wondered if he knew you
Or you knew him. And then his eyes went kind.
"That saying, Bob," he said, "is for the blind.
Believing is a better way to see."

It didn't make a bit more sense to me
Than to the mule I jerked and kicked awake.
The horns bone-dry and hell about to break

The black dam yonder, and the going tougher!
The plain wore out; the land was getting
     rougher—
Low ridges, crookéd, cactus-haunted draws
On fire with day, and no less dry because
You couldn't see a drink that wasn't there.

By noon you almost tried to touch the bare
Black walls and shoulders where a canyon yawned,
Moon-empty. Would they always stare beyond
That glass of distance there? We didn't talk—
Just moved. The very mule forgot to balk.
The ganted horses in a panting doze,
With hoofs too slow to overtake a nose,
Just kept on trying in a feeble way.

Now mind you, Squire, I don't pretend to say
It had a meaning. Who am I to know?
I'm only saying that it happened so,
And you can say no wonder that I wondered—
A bit heat-crazy, maybe.

                    But it thundered—
Right in the empty hell of afternoon!
I guess we'd all been sort of in a swoon
And busy with the stagger of the ground,
Or we'd have seen before. 'Twas less like sound
Than white-hot stillness throbbing, or the dull
Blood-mumble in the hollow of your skull,

[78]

Until a roar and tumbling rumble shook
The earth; and there was 'Diah shouting, 'Look!
Rain in the mountain, boys!'

                        You tried to doubt,
But sure enough a peak was blotted out
With cloud that poured, the way molasses does,
To where the canyon wasn't now, but was,
Moon-empty, just a look or two ago.
It sounded like stampeding buffalo
Where yonder patch of darkness boiled, and blazed
With slashers from the hidden height that raised
A thousand-bellied bawling in the herd.
We just stood gawking at it—not a word
For quite a spell—till Silas looked at Jed
As though a mule had kicked him. 'Well!' he said,
'By God!'

                        Now, Squire, I'm willing to confess
That when I heard old 'Diah mutter, 'Yes,
Who else, indeed?' it struck me he'd been praying
And 'twas the answer. Maybe what I'm saying
Sounds loony; but that empty glare of sky
And desert—all the nags about to die—
And then it thundered!—Was I loony, Art?"

"Well," chuckled Black, "not being very smart,
I wouldn't know, because I wonder too.
I mind a black old codger of the Sioux

Who seemed to make it rain. The Squire would say
He had a weather eye, and didn't pray
Until it had a mind to rain without him!
But I don't know.—Yes, 'Diah had about him
A way that made things wonderful and strange."

"Come on now, let's be getting to the range!"
The younger bantered. "Argufying whether
God did it, or the two of them together,
Won't make the water wetter, you'll allow!"

"But there was something in the thought, some-
        how,"
Continued Evans, "like a lift of wings;
As though the stubborn stuff of earthly things
Was thinner than you knew, or only seemed,
And suddenly the agony you dreamed
Evaporated in a waking wonder.

Arousing to the miracle of thunder
The little mare, with pricked ears, whinnied shrill
And set the horses nickering, until
The slow-believing mule awakened too
And, lifting up the only song he knew,
Mourned hopefully.

                        It met us on the run;
Against a broad arroyo's blast of sun
It rushed to meet us in a tumbling flood,

The tousled, rowdy water, full of mud
And sand and laughter. God! but it was good!
And then, as though the mountains understood
And said it for us, where the thunder-smoke
Trailed off along the range, a rainbow broke
And spanned the canyon with a gate of awe;
And you could hear the waters cry hurrah,
Beneath the glory of it far away.

We made the canyon in the slant of day
And fed the nags, but didn't eat a bite—
Just drank. And then—there wasn't any night.
The white sun blazing yonder never set;
You rubbed your eyes, and it was blazing yet—
But it was blazing on the other side
Above the mountain!

                              Seemed that you had died,
And found the way back, half a life the younger
And all a-tingle with a happy hunger,
Into a world that, after all, was kind.

I've often wondered what it is you find
Down yonder at the bottom of a sleep—
Not shoaling slumber, but the ocean-deep
And dreamless sort. There's something that you
        touch,
And what you call it needn't matter much
If you can reach it. Call it only rest,

And there is something else you haven't guessed—
The Everlasting, maybe. You can try
To live without it, but you have to die
Back into it a little now and then.
And maybe praying is a way for men
To reach it when they cannot sleep a wink
For trouble. Surely I was on the brink
Of knowing what I mean a blink or two
That morning there; and what I nearly knew
Gave everything a wonder-haunted look.

When we had eaten, 'Diah thumbed the Book
And read us snatches, letting silence speak
While he went on thumb-hunting others.—Seek
And you would find. You only had to knock,
And it would open. Water from the rock.
The hills of help. 'Twas what his silence said
Between the snatches, more than what he read—
As if some wise old-timer really meant
A plenty that he didn't just invent,
But something in the saying wasn't true
Until the words turned inside out for you,
And there it was, less meaning than a thrill
Upon the edge of meaning. In the still
Cool morning shadow of the canyon walls
It lingered; and the little waterfalls
Made singing of it when he prayed awhile,
His still lips saying with a happy smile
Whatever 'twas the reading hadn't told.

[82]

And then he shaved his whiskers, two-days old,
Discussing, while he slowly reappeared,
Boy-eager, from behind the mask of beard
And lather, certain stories rumor knew
About the country we were coming to—
About the Buenaventure, for the most.
We know that river was the kind of ghost
That likes to wander where a map is blank;
But there's no other river I can thank
As I can thank that happiest of streams.
It kept me going, singing in my dreams
By day and night out yonder in the waste,
And such bright water I will never taste
This side of Jordan. 'Diah made you feel
At least 'twas so deserving to be real
That we could hardly miss its upper reach.
I mind that even Silas made a speech
About it, catching 'Diah's eagerness.
He must have said a dozen words or less
That morning!

       When the sun was overhead
We started up the canyon, and it led,
Box-walled and boulder-cluttered, to a pass
That gashed the granite of the mountain mass,
A sheer and narrow gorge. We made it through
And saw, below, a canyon brimming blue
With swimming haze and shadow from the height;
And, farther on, the crawling edge of night

Upon some vast dead valley of a star
Where only emptiness and silence are
Forever and forever. Seeming steep
From where we stood, the desert, rising deep
Into the distance, faded to a line
Of mountains gleaming in the level shine
Of evening.

       Nothing like a river there.
It should have fetched a feeling of despair,
But somehow didn't, and I wondered why.
There wasn't any difference in the sky;
There wasn't any difference in the earth;
But something that had never suffered birth
And couldn't die, lived mighty in the scene
Of desolation; and I think I mean
The very same that trees appear to know.
You've seen the still, enchanted way they grow.
It wasn't in the desert we had crossed;
But now it seemed you never could be lost,
For always you were in it any place;
And by the look that came upon his face,
I knew what 'Diah called it, gazing there.

We scrambled down a gulch that led to where
The purple canyon deepened, and the change
Upon the desert and the distant range
Was like a revelation. Red as blood
Above the lavender, transparent flood

[84]

Of twilight, every summit was a rose,
And half the heavens quickened back of those
With ghostly colors. Maybe it was Jed
And how he felt; but 'twas as though it said,
'With this, and only this, to die into,
How can it matter what becomes of you
Or when, or where?' "

          He pored upon the flame
A little while and then, "When daylight came,
We heard the wind across the canyon rim;
And when we reached the mouth and saw the dim
Range yonder streaked against the dirty dawn,
It wasn't easy to go plodding on,
With quiet places and the pools of rain
Behind us there.

          By noon the sagebrush plain
Became a stinging smother in the dun
Sand-scurry and the swelter of the sun,
Moon-dim and hurrying.

          Our camp was dry
That night. There was no wonder in the sky.
We knew the sun was setting by the weird
And sickly half-light breaking in the bleared
Abruptly chilling air that darkened soon.
The wind gave out and died. The dusty moon
Hung dry above the rain pools far away.

It must have been the first or second day
Thereafter—no, I guess it was the first—
We lost another horse. It wasn't thirst—
We drank at noon. It happened after that.
A spring pool stewing in a sagebrush flat—
We stumbled on it in the stifling blow.
The roan went shoulder-lame and wouldn't go;
Gave up, done out with limping in the sand.
And Silas—well he never was a hand
For talking. Did his thinking dumb and hid it;
But when the time to do it came, he did it,
Stone-cold. I see that vise of hairy paw
Upon the horse's nose; the other draw
The hunting knife; the bubbling gush of red
Along a bulging forearm. Nothing said,
Excepting what the wind-pipe tried to say.

Against the strangled moaning of the day
We plodded, silent. Couldn't stop for meat;
And one nag yonder had a bag of wheat
He wouldn't need.

        As I remember now,
About the killing of the roan, somehow,
Or drinking at the puddle in the smother,
The changing of one life into another
Began for me. It may have been that luck
Forgot us there—three days before we struck
Another water hole—or was it two?

It must have been the stifling wind that blew
Three days on end. Another range to climb,
And, like a picture of forgotten time,
That emptiness beyond! The days of hope
And of despair begin to telescope
In there, as I remember. Dawns and noons
And sunsets tangle with the icy moons;
And ranges loom and vanish, yet remain
Forever rising from the rim of plain
Asleep with heavy heat. But in the mixed,
Unsteady flow are pictures strangely fixed
And sharp with vivid colors that are fast.
A moment, maybe, when you felt at last
The miracle of water singing through you,
And suddenly it seemed the desert knew you
And was a breast that pitied, and the blind,
Wide stare of heaven softened and was kind.

I mind the stillness, mightier than wind,
That dizzy noon we squatted there and skinned
The sorrel in the blister of the sun,
Because the days of hunger had begun,
And nights of phantom feasting. Couldn't eat
For swollen tongues. The scarlet strips of meat
Draped round us in the cactus patch to dry.
The heat-dim desert empty to the sky,
Blue-fretted with the everlasting range.
It's queer the way the picture doesn't change.
The strips don't blacken, and the sorrel's eyes

In everlasting, terrified surprise
Still look at me. The high sun doesn't set,
But I can see the way the moon looked yet,
Beyond the half that night. The purple air,
The glassy hush, the horses drooping there,
The ghostly cactuses and 'Diah praying;
And I can hear the mule's tongue-muffled braying
Like sorrow breaking into devil laughter.

I know it had to be the day thereafter
We drank—altho' I'm vague about the setting—
For how could I be sitting here forgetting,
By half, a story never to be told?
It must have been the day was getting old
Before we drank. I feel the driving sun
Upon my back. I see my shadow run
And reach ahead, unwearyingly swift,
Because it hadn't any feet to lift
Or any wooden tongue it couldn't swallow.
'Twas hard to follow, cruel hard to follow,
Because it had to keep the drunken road
That led to where the Buenaventure flowed
Bright waters in a heaven of a valley.
It didn't tally—something didn't tally
About the fleeing shadow that you cast,
Until pursuing teaches you at last
That nothing matters but the driving light
Behind you. I can feel the burly might
Of Gobel's arm, the hairy fingers close

[88]

About my shoulder—no, the sorrel's nose,
Or maybe it was roan. No matter whether.
Then three of us were dancing on together,
And they were saying that it wasn't far.

There was a drop of water like a star
That glowed back yonder where the sorrel bled
Along the sky-rim. Mountain overhead,
A burning mountain fading into sleep.
Of all the jumbled pictures that I keep,
That seems to be the one that fits the best.

Suns glaring in the east and in the west;
The swift nights turning into ghostly days
With growing moons; the same blue range to raise,
So often set behind us, yet the same.
And in that blurred eternity we came
To where a sharpened moment lingers still
And doesn't blur. There was a rocky hill
Beyond a soda flat. It seemed to float
Upon a bright white water. Creosote
And greasewood grew and gaudy cactus bloomed
All over it. Beyond, the mountains loomed
Not very far away. And when we neared
The gray-green hill, there suddenly appeared
A man and woman, standing to the waist
In brush. Clear-cut against the sky, they faced
The sloping day. A moment they were there
Above us, withered faces, tangled hair

And scrawny bodies blackened by the sun.
But while we gaped, there wasn't anyone
In all the world but us. We climbed to see
If there might be a village. Seemed to me
That we had dreamed those faces. Nothing stirred.
The broken land stared emptily. We heard
Our shortened breath. But, coming down, we
    found
A hollow rock they'd squatted by to pound
Grasshoppers! Made it easier to eat
The leather leavings of the sorrel meat
There in the haunted silence of a draw
That evening. Might have doubted what we saw
But for the footprints crowding in the sand
Below a spring. They made the lonely land
Seem lonelier and more remote from men.

It gets to be a troubled dream again
Beyond that range. The days of windy smother
And burning stillness overlap each other
And run together wearily the same.
But Oh! the valley where the deer were tame
And many, and the Buenaventure made
So cool a road of silver in the shade
Of leaning elm and rustling cottonwood!
No other meat can ever be so good
As that meat was, so tender and so fat!
Just one more range to cross, and, after that,
The tame deer feeding belly-deep in grass!

One night holds changeless—blown of purple
    glass
And haunted with a deathly hush of light.
I never saw the full moon burn so bright
Before or since. The cactus looked appalled;
And I can see the way our shadows crawled
Like living things. You sort of floated on,
A dream of torture, with a dream of dawn
And food and water floating on ahead
Forever. Maybe you were lying dead
Back yonder, staring sightless at the sky,
But what you died of couldn't ever die
And had to wander on forever so.
The ghostly desert's mockery of snow,
The cold moon's ghostly mockery of day,
The sound of feet forever on the way
To emptiness, the hollow-sounding breath
Of horses in the stillness that was death
And didn't hear! What was it that you knew—
With this and only this to die into?—
But that was far away before you died,
Past memory beyond the other side
Of mountains, many past remembering.

Now if you say it was a foolish thing
That happened there, I will not blame you, Squire.
There's half of me here sitting by the fire
Will share your laughter if you want to laugh,
Without denying that the other half

May somehow be the wiser, just the same.

Tall, out of purple emptiness it came
Serenely slow, and stopped to look at me.
It should have been a common yucca tree,
And was, except for something it was saying
Without a sound. That yucca tree was praying,
And had to pray forevermore in vain
With wide arms waiting wearily for rain—
A ghost that didn't know that it had died
Of thirst, and went on waiting, crucified
Forever!

        Then from very far away,
There was a voice remembered—'*Though He
     slay*'—
Why, it was 'Diah reading!

            Say it seemed
I came awake then, have it that I dreamed;
But still it's something that the dream was good;
And in a world so little understood,
There should be room for two to be mistaken.
Well, if I dreamed, the yucca seemed to waken,
And wasn't waiting any more in vain.
The lifted arms were drinking in a rain
Of living glory, like no earthly shower;
And now I saw the yucca was in flower—
Tall beauty pluming in a quiet light!

I don't know how much came to me that night,
And how much later when I mulled it o'er.
I know I wasn't weary any more
Till moondown faded in the morning.

Well,
I see it's like a dream you try to tell,
And wonder why it seemed to mean so much;
But if a dream can be a sort of crutch,
I leaned upon it often—till I 'woke
Again; or did I only dream it broke
And left three scarecrows limping in despair?—
No Buenaventure river anywhere,
No haunted yucca drinking in a rain
Of glory, making beauty out of pain
And ugly need!

But often, broad awake,
It seized me. Once it was a rattlesnake
That brought it back! The very devil's land
It was—all tumbled rock and shale and sand
Where squatty cactus starved and no sage grew.
It was the time the moon was starving too
And came up late and feeble, withering
Because there was a curse on everything
In all the world. There was a whirring sound
That made the land be still—and there he wound,
A deadly puddle stewing in the sun,
Head up to end what hunger had begun,

And weariness and thirst. A rage to kill
One foe at least just left me staring still
And wondering. Then suddenly it came!
It was the same, it was the very same
Still beauty saying what I couldn't hear,
So far away it was; with fangs of fear
Or thorns of bitter need to guard some good
Against a strange world neither understood
Nor understanding. Like a flower he grew,
Slow waving in a breeze that never blew
This side of heaven. Then he crawled away,
Still beautiful with what he couldn't say,
And scared because it never could be said.

It happened when the starved old moon was
    dead
And all our little talk was of the Lake,
There was a ridge ahead. Beyond would break
The sky-wide gleam of it; and there would be
Deer grazing by the rivers of that sea,
A little way beyond the ridge's brow.
The Buenaventure was behind us now;
And maybe if it really had been there,
The buzzards would have banqueted somewhere
This side of hope.

            There was a little spring
In yonder ridge, but not a living thing,
It seemed, had ever found that blessèd pool

Until three men, two horses and a mule
Came staggering—or ever would again.

We saw it from the ridge's summit when
The day began to brighten. Was it land
Or water there beyond the tumbled sand—
That still white sheet of nothing sloping high
Until it was the nothing of the sky
On fire again? One look at 'Diah told
The answer that I knew. It was an old,
Old man I saw a moment in his place,
The look of something broken in his face
That wasn't to be mended any more.
I see that I had never known before
How much I'd leaned upon him like a child,
Until he turned that face on me and smiled—
When nothing but the smile of it was Jed.
'You see, it's just beyond the salt,' he said,
'A little way.' And for a moment there,
Not anything but hearing Silas swear
Beneath his breath was left to fill the lack,
Until I saw that hawk-gaze coming back,
That long-range look of something that he saw
Beyond you; and the setting of the jaw
Was cruel in the face that it denied.
I didn't know how lean and hollow-eyed
It was until the light of it went dim,
That quicksand moment when I pitied him—
The leaner on his pity—even I!

Well, yonder looked as good a place to die
As any other then. But now I know
I went because he wanted me to go;
For more than pity happened in that bleak,
Forsaken moment when I saw him weak
Upon that ridge. I'd just begun to love him,
And something in the breaking manhood of him
Was stronger than his old unbroken might.

By noon the very hush was blinding white;
The world had shrunken to a tiny, round
White island, floating lost in a profound
White dazzle of a sea without a shore.
The more we toiled, the island moved the more,
To keep us toiling in the center still.
I think what drove me wasn't hope or will,
But just the stagger and the baffled stare
Of Silas, striving like a wounded bear
To crush a foe he couldn't overtake;
And 'Diah's haunted eyes upon a lake
He didn't see, those hollow, haunted eyes.

There's something happens when your last wish
        dies
I wish I could remember—something good;
But just about when it is understood
There isn't anything to tie it to
Of all the tangled wishes that were you;
But surely it is good.

I still can see
The mule, like something in a comedy
Beyond the mere indecency of mirth;
The horse's muzzle to the lifeless earth,
Negotiating where to leave a skin
Too big and heavy for the bones within
To carry long. I see the little mare.
That woman-patience in her eyes of care,
The drooping head, the placing of her feet
Just so—and so—brought back the chimney seat
At home, and me a boy, with Granny sitting
Forever there, her nose among her knitting
For fear the feeble fingers might forget.

It must have been the sun about to set
That conjured there ahead of us the ghost
Of breakers beating silent on a coast
Of silence. That was where the tumbled sand
Began again.

          We made the broken land
Beyond it, where the cold stars whirled away.
And there was nothing—there was dazzling day
On sandy, cedar-spotted hills that ran
To northward where the higher range began,
Patched black with cedar scrub.

                I wonder still,
Sometimes, what really happened on a hill,

Unsteady with the burden of the sun
That day; if truly there was anyone
Below us in the draw, and if we dreamed
That Indian woman and the way she screamed
As though we'd come upon her by surprise.
But in the mirror of her face and eyes
I still can see the horrors that she saw;
And surely there were youngsters in the draw,
With frightened faces peeping from the brush.
She offered weed seed messed into a mush,
And tried to tell us it was all she had,
While, plainly starving and as clearly mad,
Three nightmare creatures croaked a single
        word
The louder, hoping if she only heard
She'd give them water. Surely it was true,
For I can see the knowing look that grew
Upon her black face, terror-frozen still,
And how she pointed off across a hill,
Then took another look at us, and ran!
There must have been a tall tale for a man
To hear that night!

                        There was another side
To those hot hills, somehow; and by a wide
Sun-swimming flat, with cedar hills beyond,
The dizzy dazzle focussed in a pond
Of water—water—water! It was wet;
But I can see the whimpering critters fret

And slobber over it—the mule, with curled
Lip skyward, making faces at the world
To tell it what he hadn't breath to bray.

We weren't any better off next day,
Remembering that sickly tang of brine;
And if the horse's belly felt like mine,
'Twas little wonder he was satisfied,
At last, with any place to dump a hide,
And did it in the sand without a fuss.

I mind the antelope that stared at us
And vanished, floating. Didn't make you think
Of eating—only where they went to drink;
And so you floated after them, and came
Upon it, swooping giddily—the same
Sick pool back there.

              I know now we had turned
Northeastward, heading for a peak that burned
Away off yonder. When the twilight grew,
We stood upon a rise and saw a blue
Unending valley running north and south;
And 'Diah, talking of the valley's mouth
To northward and the lake that might be there,
Seemed far away—as far away as where
That snowy summit slowly lost the glow
And kept the secret that it seemed to know
In everlasting silence.

Down that slope,
'Twas gravity that moved us more than hope
Of water short of yonder paling height.
But deeper in the blueing of the light
Upon the still, cool sage-brush solitude,
We stopped to listen. Was it doves that cooed?
Doves in the desert? Water must be near
If there were doves about! But did we hear
Or dream the yearning homesick ache of it?
We stood there wondering what to make of it,
And gaped upon each other's faces. *There!*
Doves in the cool blue hush! The little mare
Heard too and whimpered; but the mule forgot
His burden of a head, and, doves or not,
Slept heavily.

We didn't find the spring,
For all our dragging search—not anything
But sage; and when it grew too dark to seek,
We headed up the valley where the peak
Had vanished with the secret that it knew.

Last year I found it, camped there in the blue
Of twilight when the doves began to moan—
For 'Diah yonder by the Cimarrone
And Silas by the Siskadee, asleep
With all their might unloosened. It was deep
And wide enough to swim us! By the cool
Sweet water, homesick for the very mule,

And thirsting just for thirst with Jed again,
1 marvelled, if we hadn't missed it then,
How much I would have missed!

                 The whole night through
We stumbled toward a vanished peak that knew
The reason why the doves kept mourning so—
Beyond the barn lot, dim and far ago
At twilight—just before the crickets wake—
The rusty pulley grieving at the lake,
The well, the lake, the well—the bucket sinking,
Blub—and the greedy gurgle of it drinking—
A dusty bucket in a well gone dry.

And all at once, the peak was gleaming high
Up yonder in a lake the sorrel bled—
The roan—the sorrel. 'Diah there ahead
And Silas in between the mule and mare—
All hunting with a microscopic care
For doves among the sage brush long ago.

But why was 'Diah talking like a crow
And pointing at the peak? Because it swam
And tossed so with the breaking of the dam,
The flood of fire.—

              I wakened in the shade
And quiet that a stunted cedar made.
I know it was a little cedar now;

But then I wasn't anywhere, somehow,
And it was chilly. Stooping there above,
An old, old man was looking for a dove,
And it was someone that I used to know;
But he had lost the dove so long ago,
I couldn't find the waste of bone and skin
His hunting, sunken eyes were burning in—
I couldn't find it in the sage at all.
But he was leaning from a canyon wall
And smiling, and a storm of doves moaned by;
And very far away I heard him cry
A name I knew—and every one of those
Dim mountains far away became a rose,
And he was blooming—like a yucca tree—
All gentle light. And leaning over me
Was 'Diah."
                    Evans brooded for a space,
Until the glow that came upon his face,
And wasn't from the embers, died away.
"I lived upon it waiting there that day,"
He said at length "—that look of joy and tears.
I've lived upon it all these lonely years
From dream to dream. And I have seen it break
Upon the drab world, even when awake,
As though the common hills and valleys knew
In some deep way. And when it seems they do,
I almost know what happens in a seed,
How cactuses can make of bitter need
Such beauty; and there's something in the look

Like hearing 'Diah with the dog-eared Book,
Still reading, on the further side of sound:
'Take off thy shoes. The place is holy ground
Whereon thou standest.'

                    Day was nearly done,
And I was troubled for a sinking sun
That couldn't rise again, it grew so weak.
Then there was 'Diah, back from yonder peak,
With water in a kettle!
                    Noon was pouring
White-hot on Silas when we found him snoring
Beside the spring, the mule and little mare
Drooped over him.

                    Another day from there—
Or was it more?—it seems like many more—
A lone butte rising from the valley floor
Was looking northward into empty sky.
I still can see Jed climbing, hear him cry
'The lake! the lake!'
                    That night the moon was new."

VI

The low intoning of the canyon grew,
Filling the silence of a story told
With something immemorially old,
Beyond all telling; till the Squire arose
And with a boot heel broke the glowing doze
Of gutted logs that startled into flame.
"I still can see the five of you that came
To Bear Lake camp," he said. "If you had died,
No buzzard would have thanked you for the hide
And rags you packed!—We'll need another log."
He melted into darkness; and the dog,
'Roused by the quiet of the brooding pair,
Sat up, limp-eared, and with a surly air
Flopped down again and snuggled into sleep.

The brittle mock of axes, biting deep
Into the crystal distances of night,
Died out. The Squire stooped back into the light,
Cast down his load upon the flame, and said:
"It's queer the way the night seems full of Jed
Out yonder—sort of hiding everywhere,
As though you'd maybe see him standing there
Behind you, if you just turned quick enough—

Taller than men and made of starry stuff
And stillness."

                    While they passed the jug aroun l
The silence deepened with the busy sound
The new wood made. "When he turned up again,"
Said Black at length, "with less than half his men,
Beside the Stanislaus, it seems to me
The graybeard that he wouldn't live to be
Had somehow come to haunt him like a ghost.
I felt it all the way along the coast
To Oregon. And when we camped beside
The Umpqua where it bitters with the tide,
You know what happened. We had gone that day,
Just he and I, to find a solid way
Among the marshes. Two escaped to tell,
Of all our comrades, how the Umpquas fell
Upon the camp—a scrambled tale and queer,
As though they'd had a nightmare; nothing clear
But Rogers towering and the axe he plied
Before he died the way old Silas died
Down yonder on the Colorado shore.

I felt the other 'Diah more and more
Until we met the others up the Snake
About the forks. Sometimes he'd seem to take
A trail I couldn't follow, all alone—
Who knows?—somewhere beyond the Cimarrone
As like as not. Beside a fire together,

Or maybe rubbing knees and saddle leather,
I'd know he'd gone exploring far away.
And then he'd get that long-range look and say
What made me feel 'twas good where he had been,
But 'twas no country I was ever in,
Or likely would be; something wise and old
As light and growing, but, in being told,
As new as morning or the first green grass.
'Twould be like seeing darkly in a glass,
Then face to face, the way he often read it;
And you would feel, the gentle way he said it,
A little shaver listening to his mother.
Between the common 'Diah and the other
There might have been a thousand years or two.
I often wonder if the other knew
That he was getting near to where he is.
Concerned, for all that might and youth of his,
About the vanity of worldly gain!
And making worldly trouble seem like rain
Upon the desert of our mortal stuff!
He used to tell me that he had enough
Of worldly goods to help his folks and others—
So no more beaver!"

        "Had a mess of brothers,"
Observed the Squire. "I hear 'twas on the way
To set them up in trade with Santa Fé
He got his hair raised."

          "Going to retire,"
Mused Black, "—and did."

      "I wonder," yawned the squire,
With lazy stretching. "Got a horse to bet
He's nowhere or there's blue horizon yet
He's chasing after with that hungry stride!"

"I should have been there with him," Evans
    sighed;
"I should have followed anywhere he went."
With grave and unintentional assent
The elder nodded, and the canyon's moan
Took up the old regret—*alone, alone,
Alone.* The younger, slumped upon his pack,
Blinked dreamily. "But when he started back
For California with another band—
And Silas—all the torture of that land
Came on me like a nightmare. I was gray
And old inside. And so he went away
Forever, maybe; but a thrilling doubt
Has grown upon me.

        Well, I knocked about
Among the mountains, hunting beaver streams,
Alone—no, not alone, for there were dreams
And memories that grew. And more and more
I knew, whatever I was hunting for,
It wasn't beaver. When the evening blued,
The listening stillness of the solitude
Would come alive with something he had read,
Or just a passing word or two he said,

[107]

Too trivial for memory till then.
And all our story would begin again
Self-spinning in the quiet—always new,
And more like longing livingly come true
Than memory. Or maybe on a rise
I'd see that look of breaking in his eyes
Far off; or suddenly a hill or draw
Would sadden with the vision that I saw
Beside the stunted cedar.

                Well, I spent
That winter down at Santa Fé, and went
Back to the mountains trapping in the Spring,
And all that Summer didn't hear a thing
Of 'Diah. I was hunting beaver sign
Along this way, the Fall of 'twenty-nine,
Before I heard about him from a pair
Of trappers—him and all the band somewhere
Up Teton way. But yonder up the Green
Beyond the Sandy, Indians had seen
The white men cross the Pass a moon ago
With many horses.

                   Wasn't time for snow,
Not heavy snow, although 'twas getting late
For proper mountain doings. It was fate
That I would never see him any more;
And so an early blizzard shut the door
Behind him, and I couldn't make it through.

I wintered at the Bear Lake rendezvous
With half a dozen men of Hudson Bay,
Who met the band up north and heard them say
He planned to winter at the Powder's mouth,
And calculated to be heading south
Back to the States for good, come early grass.

And winter getting deeper in the Pass,
And deeper! Hardest that I ever saw,
That winter! Didn't even fix to thaw
Till 'way along in March sometime, and then
It caught its breath and started in again
To snow and bluster. Seemed the hand of God
Was in it."

       Jerking backward from a nod,
The elder muttered: "Stayed until July—
Wind River—."

       "Hadn't heart enough to try
To overtake him when at last the snows
Were gone!" said Evans.

       Studying his nose,
The younger brooded owl-like, breathing deep.

"But there was one more rendezvous to keep,"
Continued Evans; "one more rendezvous.
It wasn't till July of 'thirty-two

I heard, and 'twas a year ago that May
It happened! I was down at Santa Fé—
A brawling mess of traders from the Plains
And mountain men and tangled wagon trains
From Independence. Just an idle word
Across the glasses, and it seemed absurd!
So many Smiths! It couldn't have been Jed!
For when I tried to think of him as dead,
It wouldn't fit the picture anyhow.
It isn't fitting better even now,
These lonely years away! But, bit by bit,
The tale grew bigger than the doubt of it,
And ended in the emptiness of air.
Killed southward of the wagon trail, some-
    where
Along the Cimarrone! And it was told
With half an air of being rather old
To matter in the brawling summertide
Of lusty, living men. But where he died
His brothers, even, didn't rightly know,
Recalling, with already seasoned woe,
How he went hunting water for the train,
And how they watched until the lonely plain
Went empty in the shimmer of the sun—
Forever. But they had his rifle gun
And silver-mounted pistols, dearly bought
From certain hangdog Mexicans who brought
The news to Santa Fé. And, word by word,
I bought their tale through, feeling, as I heard,

'Twas measured for the market or they knew
Too much by plenty.

                One more rendezvous—
And only silence waiting after all!

The nights were nippy with a tang of Fall
Along the lone road leading to the States—
The season when the dying Summer waits
To listen for the whisper of the snow
A long way off. Three horseback days below
The Arkansaw, and twelve from Santa Fé
I crossed the Cimarrone; another day
Beyond the waterholes, and that was where
He left the wagons.

                All around me there
Was empty desert, level as a sea,
And like a picture of eternity
Completed for the holding of regret.
But I could almost see the oxen yet
Droop, panting, in the circled wagon train;
The anxious eyes that followed on the plain
A solitary horseman growing dim;
And, riding south, I almost sighted him
Along the last horizon—many moons
Ahead of me.

           Beyond a strip of dunes
I came upon the Cimarrone once more,

A winding flat no wetter than the shore,
Excepting when you clawed a hole, it filled.
But hunting for the spot where he was killed
Was weary work. There had to be a ledge
Of sandstone jutting from the river's edge
Southwestwardly; and, balanced at the tip,
A bowlder, waiting for a flood, to slip
And tumble in the stream; and just below,
Not any farther than a good knife-throw,
A hiding place behind a point of clay.

But there was sand—and sand.

                              The second day,
When I was sure the Mexicans had sold
The buyer's wish, with twilight getting cold
And blue along a northward bend, I came
Upon it with a start—the very same,
Except the bowlder bedded in the stream!
And like one helpless in an evil dream,
I seemed to see it all. The burning glare,
The pawing horse, and 'Diah clawing there
Beneath the ledge, beyond the reach of sound
To warn him of the faces peering round
The point of clay behind; a sheath-knife thrown,
Bows twanging; 'Diah fighting all alone,
A-bristle with the arrows and the knife—
Alone, alone, and fighting for his life
With twenty yelling devils; left for dead,

The bloody, feathered huddle that was Jed,
Half buried in Comanches, coming to;
The slow red trail, the hard, last trail that grew
Behind him, crawling up the bank to seek
The frightened horse; too dizzy sick and weak
To make it past the sepulcher of shade
The sandstone ledge and balanced bowlder made
Against the swimming dazzle of the sun;
The band returning for the horse and gun
To find him there, still moaning, in his tomb
And roll the bowlder on him.

—Only gloom

And silence left!"

The voice of sorrow rose
And ceased. Assenting in a semi-doze,
The elder nodded sagely; and the Squire
Breathed deeper. Feeling by the fallen fire
The mystery of sorrow in the cry,
The dog sat up and, muzzle to the sky,
Mourned for the dear one mourning.